TREE FACE
AND
THE CRIPPLE

BY PAUL EBBS

The propeller made a grinding noise, and stuck fast at five to seven. Something gave up rotating behind the bulkhead and started to force its way into the cabin.

Thud. Thud. Thud.

Then the engine seized with a metallic squeal and there was silence. A thick arm of black smoke started to curl from the engine compartment.

My guts went cold.

Dad had just enough time to wake up before the Cherokee, now just a tin can of human beings, decided that aerodynamics was a thing it didn't want to be involved with anymore

In a rushing unstoppable collision of images, I remembered the Cherokee had crashed and Dad was dead. I opened my lids. The light was harsh white and hurt the balls of my eyes as if I was pressing my thumbs hard into them. After a few seconds of blinking, the world came back into focus. Some blue sky, and the river, hedged on the bank that I could see from where I was lying with thick groves of jungle.

I could feel water around my chest and managed to lift my head to look down the length of my body. I was half in, half out of the water. My useless legs tangled up in a branch. The branch that had knocked me out. I had beached against the bank by the side of the river, my head in a shallow puddle.

I raised myself up on my elbows, and winced at the pain in my shoulder. Looking at my shirt, I could see that there was no blood, but the material was ripped apart. I twisted my head to look at the Cherokee.

It wasn't there.

DEDICATION

This book is for Natasha Bee. She makes the difference.

Anyway, how do you start a story?
    Do I tell you everything? Even the embarrassing stuff?
Do I start at home? On the plane?
Or do I go straight to the bit where I killed my dad?
Yes. You did read that right.
Okay. Deep breath.
You see, what makes it difficult is that it's not just my story. There's my dad obviously, and there's Kik-Kik—it's her story as much as mine. It's also the story of the men who came to murder me.
    And it's Escobar's story. Oh yes, it's his story, big-style.

Anyway, before all that, there's stuff you need to know about me. I was in the car and with Dad and he was driving too fast. Somewhere between Birmingham and London, he lost control; the car flipped over and crashed into a ditch.
    He walked away without a scratch.
    I never walked again.
    You get used to the wheelchair after a while. Once you've learned that your legs will never move of their own accord again and that you would have to content yourself with talking to people's belly buttons for the rest of your life.

Anyway, I've started the story now, and it's going to be about me.
    So this is the story of how I, Sam Coker, became the God in the Tree.
    It's a true story about lies.

ONE

First off, I didn't mean to kill my dad.

It was an accident. I was flying the plane, and he was taking a snooze. He'd arranged for the Piper Cherokee to be adapted with a hand-rudder control for me at an airstrip on the edge of the jungle. It was expensive, but Dad teaching me to fly last year was his way of saying sorry for breaking my spine I suppose. Also, Dad was rich which meant the expense didn't concern him.

Anyway, I flew us up to Carlos' place in the mountains.

We were due to spend a week with Carlos, his wife Maria and their two sons Ramos and Escobar. Carlos was big in coffee or timber or something. Ramos and Escobar were big into football and wore canary yellow Brazil shirts every day. They were Brazilian, but we weren't in Brazil, because of something about tax, Dad said.

I don't know if Maria's servants washed the football shirts overnight—or if her sons are given fresh ones every morning. And as Carlos was probably a hundred times richer than my dad, and his son's rooms would put those on those trashy rich-kids TV programmes, to shame, I suppose it didn't really matter whether they were new or not.

Anyway, I watched them kicking their footballs about on their dry-brown pitch in the shadow of the house and generally hated every second of it. I'd not gotten over being jealous of seeing other kids having a kick-about. As I sat in the sweaty vinyl of the chair, if I could have still felt my thighs, I would have had more fun sticking drawing pins in them.

Dad and Carlos did deals in the massive dining room during the day. I wasn't allowed to spend time with Dad while he was doing "business", so I was stuck with the trick-shot twins.

There's only so much keepy-uppy you can watch in one week before you want to wheel yourself into the keepy-uppers' rooms in the night and leave poisonous spiders in their socks.

Especially Escobar.

Escobar, the older brother, didn't like me being around. Having to waste a week of his summer holiday babysitting a kid on wheels wasn't his idea of fun. He did what his dad expected of him, sure, but I could see that he wasn't enjoying it. Ramos, who was ten, was really into my wheelchair with its superfast bearings, and carbon fibre construction. "Like a Formula One car!"

Brazilians are as crazy about Formula One as they are about football.

Well, most Brazilians. Escobar rolled his eyes and asked me why I didn't get fat sitting down all day.

I showed him why I didn't get fat by challenging him to an arm-wrestling match. I twice forced his hands to the table top with ease. Then I gave him a full forty-five-degree head start and still beat him in two seconds. After that, I rolled up my sleeves and showed him the biceps I had grown pushing the wheelchair. "That's why I don't get fat."

Escobar, tight-lipped and shaking, left the table without a word, snatching up his football. He went out onto the pitch, ran up and down for an hour, dribbling between cones and striking the ball hard into the goal, the net billowing out behind with the force of the impact.

In the slow, humid evenings, we sat out on the veranda, Dad and Carlos drinking too much and smoking cigars as long as jumbo-sausages, watching Carlos's security guards patrol the perimeter fence with their snub-nosed machine guns. Dad said it was because of the rebels in the hills who were fighting the government in the capital. The rebels would take hostages for ransom, so rich people like Carlos needed protection.

Occasionally helicopters would fly over, and Dad and Carlos would point at them and giggle like girls. We never saw any rebels.

Once the week was up, Maria presented us both with Brazil kits (I was sick of the sight of them, to be honest), but I smiled and balanced the kit, wrapped in that crunchy cellophane, on my knees as I wheeled myself out to the plane on Carlos's airstrip.

His guards were stowing our luggage behind the seats and Dad was walking around the plane, kicking the tyres and checking the engine. Ramos was sitting in the pilot's seat looking intently at the dials and switches.

Escobar was not there to see us off.

Carlos sucked on an even huger cigar than usual and clapped me on the shoulder.

"Your papa says you'll be joining the family business when you leave school."

Well, what else could I do? Who'd give me a job, like this? But what I said was, "Yeah, Dad's teaching me about property and stuff."

What Dad'd actually said to me was that all I needed to know is that people would always need houses and flats, and the more he owned, the more he could rent out, and the more money he would make. As for starting my career in property, Dad said he'd put me in the office with Silly Sally. "She'll show you the ropes, no bother."

Anyway, I didn't say that to Carlos. Dad had obviously given him the impression that it'd be a bit more focussed than me just sitting with his office junior stuffing mail-shot envelopes and answering the phone. The idea didn't fill me with many positive thoughts either. Silly Sally always looked at me as if I was an injured puppy. Being stuck with her five days a week was going to be a nightmare.

"It's good to have sons," Carlos said. "A man lives on through his sons. Escobar is a year older than you, soon he will join me on a permanent basis."

"Not become a footballer?" I said half joking.

"No," Carlos said, with no humour in his voice.

I wheeled on in silence. Ramos jumped down from the Cherokee and went to study the propeller. Dad finished the checks and was ready to lift me into the pilot's seat. I could hear one of Carlos's engineers on the other side of the Cherokee, closing the engine casing and walking away on the compacted gravel of the airstrip.

Clang.

Crunch.

I looked back to the house—stunning white under a brilliant red-tiled roof. The mountains rose steeply behind, blue and craggy. Beyond them was the jungle—waiting in the baking summer sunshine, dark and huge.

I couldn't wait to fire up the Cherokee's engine and get away from there, get away from Escobar with his legs that worked. Legs that kicked footballs. Legs that could run.

If I knew then what I know now, as Dad scooped me easily from the chair and slid me into the plane, I would have punched and bit him and screamed until he agreed to leave me behind.

TWO

Thirty minutes after we cleared the mountains, the world was just two colours.

It was blue above and it was green below.

From horizon to horizon, the jungle spread out in a perfect blanket of emerald. The distance was hazy with the humidity coming off the trees as we flew at three thousand metres into the endless blue. Occasionally flocks of white birds moved below us, over the green, but other than that, nothing else moved except us as the rainforest sweated below. We were probably the only plane for a hundred klicks in any direction. There was not even a high vapour trail from a passenger jet above.

Technically, I shouldn't have let Dad sleep, but he was still hung-over from the night before, and I had enough confidence to follow the heading on our flight plan. It was that confidence that killed my dad. I hope I'll never be that confident again.

Dad had rolled up his jacket and was using it as a pillow. He was snoring but I couldn't hear it over the noise of the engine, I could make out his cheeks vibrating and his lips moving as the air escaped. I could also smell the stale alcohol on his breath and thought about waking him up to give him a mint.

I wish I had.

To tell the truth, I loved it. Flying was freedom. And it didn't matter that my legs were useless, and that I had to go to the toilet in a bag. It didn't matter at all. I thought about doing a few aerial manoeuvres, skimming the trees or a couple of edgy banks, but that would wake Dad up, and also I didn't know the plane that well. My Cherokee at home was solid and well maintained; this plane... well, best not to take any risks; I'd just point it in the right direction and in three hours, we'd be landing at the airport. This gave us more than enough time to catch our connecting shuttle to the capital and our flight back to the UK.

There's never silence in a light aircraft. You're too close to an engine that's a big powerful brute of a thing, hiding behind the bulkhead in front of you—heavy, hot and roaring. An angry metal animal, trapped and desperate to escape from its cage.

I felt like that sometimes. Just not when I was flying.

So when it came, the silence was more than a surprise.

The propeller made a grinding noise and stuck fast at five to seven. Something gave up rotating behind the bulkhead and started to force its way into the cabin.

Thud. Thud. Thud.

Then the engine seized with a metallic squeal and there was silence. A thick arm of black smoke started to curl from the engine compartment.

My guts went cold.

Dad had just enough time to wake up before the Cherokee, now just a tin can of human beings, decided that aerodynamics was a thing it didn't want to be involved with anymore.

THREE

Dad wasn't awake long. His last words were, "Sam! Pull back!" before the nose of the Cherokee dropped and he, not seat-belted, cracked his skull against the instrument panel and slumped unconscious into the foot-well.

I pulled back on the yoke as the Cherokee went into the steep dive. The windscreen was all trees rotating. I managed to correct the roll but the dive took all the strength of my arms. The bald truth was, with no power we were going down whatever I did. If we were going to have any chance of surviving the impact I was going to have to flatten our trajectory, open the flaps to slow us as much as possible and then try to belly-flop into the trees or...

A break in the canopy!

With a yell of triumph, I managed to control the dive and bring the too-heavy glider the Cherokee had become into something approaching level flight. A bright sparkle of water and the wide curve of a river came out of the jungle, churned red-brown with mud. It exited the trees, continuing ahead— straight as a runway and slightly wider than the Cherokee.

I had about three seconds decide where to ditch the plane before the top of the trees would make further thought a waste of time. So should I land in the trees or splash down in the river?

It had to be the trees. How would I get Dad from the plane and to the bank, assuming I survived?

And of course, it was this final decision that killed him.

I banked the Cherokee, so the uniformity of the trees gave the illusion of a flat grassy expanse beneath us. We flew parallel to the river, airborne now only through the power of magic and desperation. I applied full flaps and flared the wings of the Cherokee, presenting the underside of the plane to the canopy.

I let one hand come back off the yoke and searched for Dad's hand, and as my fingers clasped his, the Cherokee ploughed into the jungle.

I was thrown forward by the impact, the belt straps digging into my shoulders and belly and forcing me back. The Cherokee snagged on something behind and spun through ninety degrees so that we were now bursting sideways through branches of ever-increasing thickness. The Cherokee up-ended, juddering downwards as a series of shuddering impacts tore the wings from the fuselage. The right-hand windscreen was ripped away and the hot musky breath of the jungle rushed in.

That's when a broken branch ripped through the side of the Cherokee and speared Dad in the chest.

I didn't let go of his hand until we slithered to a stop, but I knew he was dead.

We stayed still for about five seconds. The air reverberating with sounds of tortured, creaking, splintering wood. Then the weight of the plane shifted and we tumbled backward. I watched the sky disappearing behind the canopy as my stomach tumble-dried and the Cherokee crashed and bounced down through the trees towards, as I thought, the ground.

The sudden rush of water as the Cherokee splashed down into the river was a terrifying shock, replacing the impact that I was expecting with a new and urgent fear. The world went from blinding bright to grim twilight as the Cherokee toppled over backward and landed upside down in the river. Something heavy and unforgiving crashed into my shoulder, winding me.

I knew Dad wouldn't be leaving the plane, so I hit the release on my straps and forced open the door in the rapidly filling cabin. Red water burst through, drenching me. I took one breath and struck out through the water, blindly making for the surface of the fast-moving river.

I broke surface to see that the Cherokee's tail-plane was snagged upside down on a bank beneath the trees, half in and half out of the water. I was about four metres from the bank and safety. I didn't feel anything was broken, my arms worked and my chest was fine. I took huge strength-giving gulps of jungle air.

That's when one of the branches, half-broken by the trajectory of the Cherokee, gave way from the canopy above. I had just a second to register that the thick bough was dropping on my head before it connected with my temple and the blackness engulfed me.

FOUR

Anyway, in the dream I could run and I could jump and the dream was warm and there was Dad and he was watching me as he ran the line with his flag and he was with Mum and she hadn't left and there was Escobar, and he had a big wide white impossible smile and a Piper Cherokee the size of a seven-four-seven was flying out of his mouth into the endless clouds and Mum cuddled me and Dad said he could taste chocolate and I didn't want to wake up.

I was cold and shivery and my head hurt. There was a ragged ache in my shoulder. I didn't want to open my eyes. Water was lapping at the side of my mouth. The water tasted gritty but fresh.

I was really, really cold. This didn't feel right when I thought about it for a moment. How could I feel cold in the jungle?

Jungle? How did I get here? I'd been in the Cherokee...

In a rushing unstoppable collision of images, I remembered that the Cherokee had crashed and that Dad was dead. I opened my lids. The light was harsh white and hurt the balls of my eyes as if I was pressing my thumbs hard into them. After a few seconds of blinking, the world came back into focus. Some blue sky, and the river, hedged on the bank that I could see from where I was lying with thick groves of jungle.

I could feel water around my chest and managed to lift my head to look down the length of my body. I was half in, half out of the water. My useless legs tangled up in a branch. The branch that had knocked me out. I had beached against the bank by the side of the river, my head in a shallow puddle.

I raised myself on my elbows and winced at the pain in my

shoulder. Looking at my shirt, I could see that there was no blood, but the material was ripped apart. I twisted my head to look at the Cherokee.

It wasn't there.

I didn't understand. Where was the plane? I looked in all directions, panicked and unable to comprehend. Looking at the branch again which tangled my legs, it became clear what had happened—the branch had floated me away from the crash site, taking me downstream at the mercy of the current.

How far?

I remembered my watch. We'd taken off at two pm and had crashed a little over half an hour flight time later. The face of my Rolex was caked with river mud. I wiped it off with my thumb, smearing the surface of the watch dark brown. It took a few more seconds of focussing to see the numbers.

Cold dread gripped me. Three hours.

It was possible that I was three hours downstream!

And then, the unbearable fact that Dad was dead and I'd killed him spiked back into my memory. Holding his hand, the branch bursting into the fuselage, the branch tearing—

Why hadn't I attempted the crash-landing on water?

The river had been wide enough! I'd have had an extra twenty metres of altitude to slow the Cherokee some more, I could have put it down on the surface of the river and as the plane sunk I could have found a way to drag Dad out of the Cherokee and somehow pulled him to the river bank... It was a stupid, stupid mistake. Dad had paid for my stupidity with his life. I dug my fingers into the soft squelchy red mud of the bank, squeezing and squeezing the muck between my fingers until my nails embedded in my palms and I gasped with pain and grief.

FIVE

I hadn't cried when I found out that I wouldn't walk again.

Dad told me the news in the spinal injuries unit. I know that he'd have had a meeting with the doctors and they would have discussed what and when I should have been told—I mean, I'd seen it acted out enough times on telly.

But I know Dad.

He would have held up his hands and told the doc that it was his responsibility to tell me, and tell me he would. I remember him and Mum coming into the room and Mum holding my hand with tears in her eyes, and Dad shaking, jamming his hands into his jeans pocket and forcing himself to look me in the eye. He knew what he'd done. He knew it was his fault. He told me that he was sorry, that the doctors reckon my spine was too damaged, and that I'd probably never walk again.

He begged me to forgive him, and then took my other hand, held it, and I watched him fighting the tears. I knew he wouldn't allow himself to cry, not like Mum. I knew then that I wouldn't cry either.

I didn't cry then either. And I've never really understood why.

But now on the riverbank, cold, wet, and alone, I allowed myself to cry. It started as a prickling in my eyes; it felt unusual, alien. Then there was a bubbling pin-prickly feeling in my nose, which spread to my lips as the first sob forced its way out of my mouth and out into the hot sticky air.

Then the sobs multiplied, blowing snot out of my nose in bubbles that became long strands, tears running down my cheek, sparkle dripping off my nose into the sand. Shoulders starting to shake and thud with the sobs, fighting their way past my need to breathe. My ears hummed. My eyes throbbed. My body flailed.

I must have cried for an hour. Crying out everything. Crying it all out, from that hospital room to this riverbank.

Eventually exhausted and out of tears, I saw that the sky was darkening, and that night was on the way. I couldn't stay lying here half in the water—for one thing, I hadn't checked my bags.

It's funny the ordinary stuff that suddenly brings you back to reality, isn't it? To you, the phrase "check my bags" probably means something you'd do at the airport or what you'd do when you get to the hotel. To me, with my snapped spine, it has a whole other meaning... So there I was, lying face down on a jungle riverbank, two hundred kilometres from the nearest town, with legs that didn't work and no hope of rescue tonight—not knowing how far I'd drifted from the Cherokee, and yet I was worrying about going to the loo.

But that's a fact of life for me I'm afraid. When your spine snaps and the connecting nerves die—all the bits below the waist stop working, not just your legs. However distasteful you might find thinking about the needs of the bowel and bladder— the reality for me is a hole cut in my side by a surgeon, which empties brown sludge waste into a plastic bag. Not for me the joy of hiding in the loo with a newspaper reading the football reports from Saturday, or taking a good book with me to the smallest room. Nope, all I had to do was unclip a plastic flange, chuck the bag away and then clip on a new one.

Gross or what?

I think that had taken more time to get used to than having to accept the wheelchair as my new mode of transport.

Peeing was a bit less complicated. Either I could press down hard on my bladder, forcing pee out through the dead muscles of my abdomen, or if I wanted, I'd been taught to pass a tube up inside me to release the pressure that way. Now that had been an odd teaching session to have to attend, I can tell you.

Embarrassment is not the word.

Anyway, what I'm trying to say is that matters of the toilet have to be attended to, whatever the situation, because if they're not, I can get ill. Seriously ill.

So I'll spare you the gory details, but for myself, I had to check how things were. I dragged myself free of the branch, and with my hands spading into the mud I made slow progress out of the water and up towards the tree line.

I rolled onto my side to check the bag, and to do a bit of pressing.

I'd be okay for a few hours yet.

The crying had left a hole, and that hollow feeling was, to be honest, a welcome distraction from the awful reality of the situation. Even with a working body, I would have still been up turd creek without a paddle, if you'll excuse the pun. There's no way even an able-bodied person could just walk out of the jungle. What chance did I have when my entire knowledge of surviving in the jungle consisted of watching one episode of those stupid survival reality shows, whilst waiting for the footy to start on Sky. I didn't really remember that much about the programmes anyway except for thinking who needs to fight to survive when there's a camera crew just over the next hill?

The feeling that I didn't want to overcome me in those minutes while I looked around was fear. It would have been easy to have given into it, and just lie there like a quivering jelly, but I knew I couldn't.

The branch, which had snagged me and then dragged my unconscious body away from the wreckage of the Cherokee, was turning and rolling in the current now that my weight had released it. Where once the branch had been beached on the bank, now it was lifting clear, bobbing and turning over.

That's when I saw the ruckkie.

Snagged on the other side of the twisty branch was my North Face Rucksack, which contained my spare you-don't-want-to-talk-about-it bags, my iPhone and MacBook, and my Beats. The bag was dipping into the water and the branch was slowly bobbing away from the bank. I watched it for a second before what I was looking at fully registered.

My iPhone!

Dragging my torso around and rolling down back into the water, I howled in desperation as my useless knees collided with the branch and pushed it further from the bank. I made a despairing lunge for the branch and my finger snagged in a rough curl of vine tangled around the bough... which then snapped off in my palm.

Swearing, I pushed myself headfirst into the water, launching myself with a huge splash that hurt my shoulder like crazy. With a desperate yell and flailing arms, I made solid contact with the branch. I rolled it towards me and made a grab for the ruckkie. My fingers closed around one of the shoulder straps, and trying hard to keep it clear of the water I flung it back to shore. The bag landed with a dull but heavy thud on the bank—which would have done no good for the expensive electronics contained within.

I twisted over in the river water, feeling the pull of the current that was drifting the branch downstream. Reaching down I found the riverbed and pulled myself back to the water's edge.

Pulling my body out of the water again, I flopped exhausted next to the ruckkie. Exhausted yes, but elated. I had my phone! Breathing hard, but oblivious to the aches in my ribs and shoulders, I undid the zips that met at the crest of the ruckkie. One phone call on the emergency number and I would be safe.

As the zips came apart, a sudden stream of cold muddy river water hit me full in the face. I pulled my hands moodily away, and the ruckkie toppled over like small black drowned animal—liquid pouring from its dead mouth.

SIX

Everything in the ruckkie was ruined, except the Ick Bags. They were in waterproof sachets, and I had enough to last me a week at a push.

A week here? Waiting for rescue?

Before all this happened to me the thought of twenty minutes alone without a fix of electronic input whether iPhone or game console or internet would have me moaning about being terminally bored. I wasn't a big reader and TV didn't hold my interest for long, unless it was footy, (Dad would try to get me to watch "classic" *yawn* movies, but I hated stuff in black-and-white).

Going into town with friends was great until they wanted to do something that involved anything fun. Having a wheelchair-bound mate kind of cramped their style. There would be that slow moment of silence when someone suggested a trip to somewhere not wheelchair friendly. This would be followed by an awkward, sweaty pause while everyone looked daggers at him, and then sadly at me. Then to top it off, there'd be an expectant silence while they all waited for me to deflate the situation by laughing it off or to look at my Rolex and say I needed to be home, so they should all go off without me.

Anyway, the idea of a day, or more, here on the side of a river, in the middle of a rainforest, without even a game of Super Mario Kart to occupy my thumbs, was a scary thought. Not as scary as my last view of Dad, but if I kept my thoughts squarely on trivia, my guts didn't clench, my eyes didn't fill with tears and I didn't want to just lie there wet and cold until I died.

So there, laid out in front of me were my drowned things. River water had blown their screens, their batteries were fzzzed and they were as much use to me as a pair of roller skates on a staircase.

The sky was much darker now, and the jungle beyond the tree line seemed to be getting restless. Rustles, hoots, calls, twitters, and groans began to leak out through the vegetation. I wish I'd paid more attention to the Discovery Channel instead of flicking through it on my boredom-inspired quest for footy or tunes. I could only guess at what animals were moving between the high trees in the darkness.

The uncomfortable idea that some of them might want to eat me shouldered its way into my thoughts as I squinted into the gloom. I could see the trunks of trees, low ferns and thick stripy-leaved plants around their base. The trees seemed to come in two types as far as I could make out—thin smoothish ones and thick roughish ones with triangular bases. I'm sure they had names, but I didn't know them. Everything I could see was a complete mystery to me.

I didn't even know the names of the trees in my garden back in London.

Give me a football kit, even one from those minnow teams in the Ryman League Division One South, and I'd give you the name of the team, the colours of their away kit, where they played, and who their top scorer was for the last three seasons.

When your mates are off having fun without you, you've got to do something to fill the time, haven't you?

I twisted around and looked behind me across the river; the shoreline on the other bank was perhaps twenty metres away and rose in a wall of unpromising jungle. As the sun faded above, the river washing by at just below wheeling pace became flat and dark. Vines, leaves, and twigs from submerged branches moved steadily by.

Alligators.

Were there alligators in the rainforest? I just didn't know. I'd seen alligators in Florida before the car accident—vicious, fast-moving predators that would love the easy meal of a cripple on a riverbank. I'd be like a packed lunch to it as it brought its huge prehistoric jaws down on my flesh.

Suddenly dry-mouthed, I pulled my body a little further from the water's edge, and towards the jungle wall. But was that the right choice? What was lurking in the trees? Lions? Leopards? Tigers? Was I going to be vulnerable to attackers from the water and the jungle?

You're probably sitting there laughing because I didn't know what was possibly in there waiting for me, aren't you?

Honestly mate, I didn't have a Scooby.

Yeah well, laugh it up. Go on.

With ignorance, comes quick terror, I learned that prickly truth fairly soon. And with that terror I started to breathe too fast—which made me all head-rushy and woozy on the panic. Suddenly every noise from the jungle, every ripple splash from the river was some half-starved creature with teeth the size of steak knives wanting to leap out of the gloom and rip me to shreds.

Trying to control myself before I went loopy-fruitcake, I rolled onto my front, put my hands over my ears, and began to count backward from a thousand.

It took until six hundred and twenty-six to get my breath back to normal. Once I controlled that, the panic subsided a little.

But I still needed something positive to concentrate on, so I laid the dead electronic devices in a line by my side, wondering, if and when they dried out, would they work again? Even if the iPhone could just pick up a signal, rescuers might be able to home in on it... I didn't even know if it was possible or if I'd seen it in an idiot film.

I was making this up as I went along.

Then a wave of chill realisation washed over me. Why did I assume there would be rescuers? The airstrip we'd left from to go to Carlos's place had been a minging place of tin roofs, spilled oil in the dirt, and a runway with more cracks than a dropped packet of digestives. There'd been no radio traffic between us and the control tower because the control tower was a man waving us off with a white flag whilst sitting in a canvas chair outside a hut.

Our flight plan, such as it was, wasn't taking us back to that airstrip; this flight had been to a larger facility, where we could pick up a shuttle back to the capital's international airport for our flight home. So until the bloke in his hut with the flag was told that the plane we'd rented hadn't arrived at the destination airport, no one would know we were missing.

This was just getting better and better.

And all I could see when I closed my eyes was Dad.

I'm not ashamed to say I had another little cry, forcibly stopping myself from making too much noise so as not to attract the attention of hungry sharks in the river or rabid dingoes in the jungle.

When I finally stopped my hiccoughy sobbing, it was dark.

That's when the jungle woke up.

SEVEN

I don't sleep with the light on. I don't wake up sweating thinking there are monsters under the bed. I never did even when it was okay to do things like that. My world is safe, warm, and electrically lit.

The jungle is none of those things.

All the things you take for granted, the things that make life bearable—from the comfortable click of the light switch to the rustle of your duvet as you snuggle under it to sleep are, on the surface, simple and easy to understand things. Here in the cooling humid darkness, where every sound was a threat and every unknown shape moving through the trees was a monster, I was rapidly learning there was nothing I could take for granted, that nothing was uncomplicated and everything could kill me.

Before today fear was something I felt when Chelsea went one down to Man U or when Dad asked to look through my internet favourites in Chrome before I'd had a chance to delete the naughty ones. Fear was an easy-to-control, understandable idea that I knew was not going to last forever.

Here, it's a whole other story.

There was absolutely no chance of me sleeping that first night. There was no moon to give even a hint of a shape to the surrounding darkness. A few unhelpful stars glittered between the thickening clouds but no light from them reached me.

Dad had once told me about a trip he'd made at school to the Brecon Beacons in Wales. They'd spent a couple of days potholing. When they'd reached the lowest depth, they had planned to get to the guide told them all to switch off their helmet lights so they could get a sense of "real darkness." The way Dad told it you'd think it was the most unnerving and horrible thing he'd ever done. He said he'd never before or since experienced darkness like it. He called it "a complete absence of light." He'd moved his hand right up in front of his face and could not see even a dim outline of it.

Thick blind darkness.

He said it had completely freaked him out and he'd been the first one to turn his helmet light back on. And yet, my darkness, the one I was experiencing now, was worse than that. If I couldn't see anything then at least I wouldn't be making up stuff to scare the shit out of me. If I'd been down the pothole at least there'd be no sabre-toothed jungle killers sharpening their claws and waiting for the right moment to investigate my guts. Most of all, if I'd been in the pothole, all I would have to do to stop the fear would be to reach up, flick that comfortably familiar switch and the lights would come back on.

However much I wanted that to happen now, it wasn't going to—and there was no comfortable switch to turn off the fear.

My clothes hadn't dried out much since I'd pulled myself from the river. The humidity in the rainforest didn't allow it. So now full dark was here and the temperature had dropped, I felt my body cooling and the clammy clothes made me feel uncomfortably chill. The jungle beyond the tree line might offer some protection from the breeze. I could hear it rustling the branches and leaves high up in the canopy.

My shoulder hurt like a bitch. I could feel a pulpy bruise forming in the flesh over the bone, which sang with piercing pain when I touched it. It didn't matter how I kept changing position to ease the pressure on it, within seconds it would be throbbing again with an insistent beat.

The air around me was filled with the twenty-six million insects who'd decided to buzz around in the night. Some sounded like mosquitoes and I batted them away as best as I could when I felt them land on my exposed skin—I wasn't always quick enough and soon I could feel hard bumps rising on my forearms and the back of my neck, followed by itching arriving with annoying intensity. Other insect sounds I did not recognise—clatters, chitters, buzzes, and shrill chirrups crowded the air around me. Occasionally fluttery wings would brush against my cheek or tickling legs would scuttle over my fingers causing me to snatch my hand away.

I cursed my useless legs long and hard for not allowing me the ability to get up and move around, to find shelter or at least to be able to stamp on the insects that were crawling about me.

However, it was the blackness that caused me the greatest discomfort. All around me was a solid wall of the stuff, with the only relief from a jagged slice of starry sky that was gradually filling with cloud. The blackness got into me, pulling my mood down further, and coupled with the noises coming from the forest, my imagination went into overdrive. If I could have reached into my head and given myself a swift imaginationectomy I would have done so without a moment's thought.

I created vast, hairy, poisonous spiders creeping up to me from the trees. Brittle bristled legs getting ready to grasp me, dagger fangs dripping with venom, anxious to sink themselves into my flesh—to paralyse me fully and finish the job my dad had started—spinning me in a thick web and dragging me back to their jungle larder...

I could hear huge bloodthirsty reptiles crunching through the rainforest on tree-trunk legs, pushing branches aside and sniffing me out with wet, lizard-snot-dribbling nostrils.

Hoots and growls became powerful apes with club-like hands poised to leap down from the trees, toy with me for a while, and then pull me apart limb by limb until all that would be left was my head rolling about on the riverbank, screaming, screaming, screaming...

... something rough and solid brushed against my face. I'd been so busy imagining things coming to eat me that I hadn't noticed that something had come out of the jungle to eat me!

The rough bristles raked down my face and I yelled out in terror. Hot breath, stinking like rotten meat washed over my face and the animal, no more than a hot lumbering ripple in the darkness, turned and growled at me. The stinking breath was joined by a sticky wash of spit, some of which landed in my mouth, tasting rancid and bitter. I gagged for a moment and then threw up. There wasn't much in my stomach so the bile burned my mouth and throat as it spewed out.

The beast squealed as I returned the compliment and struck out with my fists trying to hit it in a vulnerable place as well as push myself away from it. The rough-haired thing retreated as my fist connected fully with what I assumed was its vomit-splashed face. It howled, snarled, and kicked sand into my eyes as it spun around. I heard feet scrabbling in the dirt and a solid rustling thud as it ran back into the jungle.

I lay still for a moment, catching my breath, my ears filled now not with the animal and insect sounds around me but with the thumping of my heart, pushing up in my throat and thudding in my ears. I wiped at my mouth to get the taste of sick out. I found a puddle and scooped as much of its contents up to my lips as I could, spitting the resulting rank fluid out of my mouth.

I was alone again, apart from the insects. I knew then that I couldn't allow myself the luxury of wallowing in imagination and misery. The threats from the jungle were real and were dangerous right now. If I was going to defend myself with any success, then I must not be vulnerable to the animals of the rainforest. I knew that I'd been lucky that time, and the next one to find me might not be so easily frightened off. I needed to be awake, alert, and ready to defend myself.

I needed a weapon.

EIGHT

There was only one place to find a weapon—the jungle.

It took me a good while to find enough courage to start dragging myself towards the noisy darkness of the trees. I contemplated reaching blindly for the MacBook and snapping off the screen—somehow trying to find a way of breaking it in half and using the jagged aluminium as a kind of knife. But what if I could start it up and use its mobile internet card to get some sort of message out of the jungle?

It was the longest of long shots, but I had to wait for it to dry out at least.

There were plenty of small stones around me; flat and well-worn by the river that I could use as temporary weapons. They felt weighty and good in my hands as I dug them out of the sandy soil. But stones alone would be no good for close-up defence. I supposed I could have had a go at smashing them against each other to make a jagged edge, but I didn't want to draw attention to myself. I needed something that I could strike out with, something solid that I could thrust hard into the face of an attacking hyena or whatever.

I placed about a dozen stones into the ruckkie and dragged it along in the crook of my elbow as I moved towards the jungle. It was slow going; the bank was steep and I was hungry and exhausted by fear. After fifteen minutes or so, I reached the tree line. Ferny leaves and the stiff stems of plants brushed against my face as I crawled closer. The advantage an able-bodied person would have, of being able to step over obstacles, was of course not an advantage I had. At every lurch forward, I expected thorns to snag in my skin, or worse my eyes—or ground-based insects full of venom to bite me. For now, however, apart from the odd stinging whip of a fern flicking into my face as I moved on, the local insects didn't seem to be bothered with me.

I made progress, as the jungle thickened, by moving a metre, and then reaching out with my hands to feel for fallen branches. I was acutely aware that I was making sounds not usual in the jungle and that I was probably drawing as much attention to myself as I would have if I was breaking stones, but it was too late now, I was fully into the jungle and my course of action was set.

The forest floor was wet and mulchy. It smelt of compost, herbs, and animal shit.

Great. I was dragging myself through a toilet.

There was vegetation everywhere and lumpy roots erupted from the soil like gnarly elbows or deformed knees. They were tough and uncomfortable as I moved over them—I tried yanking a couple out of the ground but even with my wheelchair-pumped muscles I couldn't shift them from where they were clamped in the earth. If only I had something to cut them with?

I hadn't packed as so much as a penknife—I'm not exactly big on whittling.

My first smile.

I snorted a hissy laugh through my nose. Whittling is one of those really stupid words that you only have to say three times before it loses its meaning and just becomes funny. Dad and me would see who could come up with the stupidest word to make the other laugh on long boring flights, or just for the hell of it. "Whittling" always got me. He'd stare at me intently, serious-faced and without a flicker of a smile, (which would have meant he'd have lost that round), and he would have just said it, "whittling," and I'd have been in pieces, tears running down my cheeks and snot bubbling in my nostrils as I fought to catch my breath. The one that I always got Dad with was "gulch."

I sighed and felt the smile dying on my face, the moment suddenly gone. I guess thinking about Dad was always going to catch me like that from now on.

I was getting used to the things scuttling over my hands and upper body. Something thick and rubbery with a million legs curled around my wrist at one point and it took a few deep breaths and winces to untangle it, waiting as I was for it to bite, sting or tear at my skin, but it didn't. It moved off into the ferns, leaving a whispery feeling on my arm.

The noises around me seemed to fall into patterns, as if animals were taking their turns to call out—were they warning each other of the dangerous new animal crawling through their territory? Or maybe they were chatting each other up getting ready to mate. Who knew? Whatever they were up to, I made progress a fair way between the trees mostly unmolested. Something did crap on my head at one point—a sticky, smelly substance splatted right into my hair and as I wiped it away, it felt like uncooked egg white on my fingers and stank like something dead. I wiped my fingers as best I could on the surrounding leaves, but I would still catch rotten whiffs of it from my hand, or worse still from my hair. I think, if they're been anything in my stomach, I might have chucked up again, but there were only a few dry retches left.

My useless feet kept snagging on roots and plants, and my progress forward would be hampered by me having to roll around and push myself back to unhook them. It was at one such moment, that I found that one of my Nikes had come off.

I couldn't leave my dead foot to the mercy of insects and bacteria lurking in the soil. I wouldn't feel an injury or a cut, and an infection attacking me without my knowledge would kill me pretty soon—so I had to try and retrace my drag-crawl as best I could to find the shoe—which I did after about ten minutes of searching.

It was a struggle to put the shoe back on, lifting the leg under the knee and pulling the floppy limb up to my chest. But I was well practised in getting dressed in the morning. Both Mum, before she'd left, and Dad would offer to help me in the, but I always refused. Putting on my clothes was something that I wanted to do for myself. Obviously, I hadn't banked on needing to do it on the floor of the jungle in the pitch black, but the principle was the same. I got the trainer back on and I tied the laces of both shoes together, so that if one came off now, I would at least not have to go back to find it.

I was making fair progress now, but I still hadn't found anything useful to use as a weapon. There had been a couple of well-rotted crumbly branches that came apart in my hand, and a stiff twig, but it seemed that things on the forest floor rotted so quickly that until daylight, when my search could be more ordered, I wouldn't find anything.

The movement into the jungle had at least given me a sense of purpose, and a feeling that I was doing something positive to contribute to my survival—and gradually I felt the fear of attack lessening with every passing hour. I was drenched through from both sweat and the shallow puddles of water on the jungle floor, but I was calmer and warmer because of all the exertion.

I stopped my crawling and felt a convenient tree to roll myself around and rest against. There were thick vines or creepers hanging down and I was able, for the first time since I'd crash-landed, to pull myself up into something like a sitting position, I wedged my numb dead backside between two roots and this held me steady. I pulled one vine down either side of me and tied them across my chest to support me under the arm. It felt good to be up like this, it made my breathing easier, and I could scratch my mosquito-ravaged neck against the rough bark to get some relief from the itching. I could also tear up a few fern leaves from around the base of the tree and give my hair and hands a good rub, trying to shift the smell.

After that, I did a bag check, and a bit of pressing, made myself as empty as I could. The jungle seemed much less of a threat right now that I was inside it. I felt less exposed with the thick tree at my back and I definitely felt safer from attack. The noises from the animals were lessening too; I suppose they'd done most to their feeding, courting, and mating so were now too knackered to keep it up.

However, I knew I couldn't really relax my guard. I knew that my calmer feelings about the jungle were surfacing because I was getting used to it, not because I was in any less danger. I kept the ruckkie at my side and would every so often feel the stones within, imagining how fast I could reach in and pull one out to throw.

In fact, I was so busy readying the stones and feeling calmer that I completely failed to notice that night was turning into day.

I looked up to see the black turning to a dirty grey, and that there were different animal sounds drifting through the jungle. Birdcalls and various screeches echoed around me. I could see the smoky grey shapes of trees forming in front of me, and as I looked right up into the canopy, I could see that the sky was rapidly lightening.

I'd made it through the night.

The sense of elation rushed through my body in a shivering bolt of warm energy. The feeling was wonderful and I could imagine what the hot sun was going to feel like as it rose and filtered through the leaves and branches.

I looked about me. I was in a circular clearing of trees. I could clearly see the path I had flattened between them with my crawling. I could see my feet, with the laces of my Nikes tied together, and I could see the stains and dirt engrained into my jeans.

I took a deep breath, allowed myself a smile let out a contented sigh.

That's when I saw the face.

NINE

It's a jungle. It's full of murderous animals and killer plants. Poisonous mushrooms and spider assassins. I hadn't even considered people. Not once. Not even for a second. And yet, here, staring at me, silent and accusing, was a face.

It was carved and painted into the bark of a tree five metres from where I was wedged among the roots. The eyes were made from two sawn-off branches that had been removed close to the grey-brown bark. Black pupils had either been painted or burnt into the exposed white wood beneath. An oval face was carved around the eyes giving the face a shield-like shape. A rough triangle had been dug into the centre of the face for a nose and a wide-open mouth. Lips, bright with cherry red paint, enclosed a gaping hole of savage, daggery teeth. They seemed to have been carved deep into the wood, so that there was a hollow space behind them, like a splintery wooden mouth.

The face was perhaps two metres from the jungle floor and looked directly at me. I so hoped the red around those lips was paint, and not, as the cold thought washed through me, blood.

I jumped as a bright green bird fluttered out from behind the mouth with a harsh call and darted up into the canopy, confirming the presence of a hollow behind the teeth. I wiped my shaking hand across my dry lips and blinked the tears out of my eyes.

All the good work that the tree at my back had done in giving me a rest from the uneasiness and fear was now irrelevant. I could feel my heart beating like a war-drum in my chest as I searched the trees and vegetation around me for the savages who had carved the frightening face.

Again, my complete lack of knowledge, other than rubbish black-and-white jungle adventure films and stupid 60s and 70s cartoons my dad insisted on making me watch on Sky, widened the void of my ignorance into a messed up gulf of fear. The cartoons—his favourite were something called "Road Runner." In them, this stupid bird running along the road, was the main object of dinner-obsession by an idiot coyote with a stupid name. Only the Road Runner was smarter than the coyote, and every trap the dog laid for the bird backfired and the coyote was toasted, blown-up, thrown off a cliff, or squashed every single time. Sometimes all four at once. I had no idea what animals there were in the jungle here wanting me for dinner, and I totally didn't know if I was smarter than *any* of them. The jungle films were front and centre in my thinking though, with their dark-hearted cannibals and high priests tying white women to poles to await the monsters.

Were there still cannibals?

I mean real, honest to God, stick you in a pot and boil you up for soup cannibals? Was I going to end up roasting over an open fire while nut-brown savages drew straws to see who'd get first dibs on my liver? Was I going to be staked out on the ground, smeared with honey for the killer ants to come and feed on me, because I'd trespassed on the tribe's sacred burial site?

Or was that the Apaches from one of Dad's *mong* Westerns?

The face just looked at me. It didn't provide answers, just questions.

I tried to figure out what the face might mean—was it a warning? A "Trespassers will be Eaten!" sort of thing? Was it marking something sacred? Was it the start of their territory? Was it the end of their land? Did it signify danger—what did it tell me about the people who had made it? Who was living nearby in the jungle? What would they make of me if they found me?

Other than a pie?

I'd once seen a war movie with Dad set in a jungle somewhere during some war that I didn't care about. A bunch of dumb American soldiers had been stalked through the jungle for days by a tribe of savages. They were easily picked off one by one, because even though the soldiers were well equipped and well-armed, they were no match for the tribesmen with their deep jungle knowledge, arrows, and poison darts.

The last man had made it out alive, but not without a terrible cost paid by his comrades. I think he'd gone mad with the fear or something. He was blowing bubbles in his spit when they hauled him into the rescue helicopter anyway.

Stupid bloody film.

Not a single answer or tad of comfort was forthcoming from the carved Tree Face. He just went on staring at me. Like he could look right inside me. Like my skin was invisible.

I shuddered.

I felt exposed and vulnerable in a way that I hadn't felt yesterday on the riverbank. It was one thing going up against the local animals in the rainforest. They'd just be doing their thing, if they got me it'd probably be over with quick. But the cannibal tribe who'd carved that scary face on the tree. They might torture me for days—or worse—eat me bit by bit…

Stop.

It was the fear again. The fear that would kill me.

I took a deep breath.

It was just a face, that's all.

Tree Face

His lips could have been laughing or snarling. It wasn't clear. Depends how the light through the tree hits him, but he didn't look friendly. He didn't look like he was pleased to see me. He was more of a Stop sign than a Go sign.

He was properly scary.

What should I do about him? Okay, I needed to know if he was recent, or if he was old. Maybe he had been there for years and I was worrying over nothing. I mean there was at least one bird nesting inside the face—that didn't immediately suggest spear-carrying tribesmen were going to come out of the jungle and butcher me…

Maybe.

I hooked the ruckkie over my arm again and hauled myself out from between the roots. I rolled onto my front, and taking care not to get my Nikes hooked, I slithered back onto the mulchy ground and began pulling myself towards Tree Face.

Anyway, I reached the carved tree quickly; keen to fill in at least a couple of gaps in my knowledge.

I became very aware as I exerted myself for the first time in a good few hours how tired, achy, and thirsty I was. I hadn't drunk anything except to get the taste of sick out of my mouth since last night. The sleeves of my tee-shirt were soaked through with jungle humidity so as I reached Tree Face I paused for a moment to suck some of the moisture from the material. It had a hint of fabric conditioner and sweat, which wasn't the nicest of combinations, but at least it gave some relief to my dry mouth.

The dull thud of pain in my shoulder had also come back big-style, as I'd moved across the clearing. I'd had some relief from it while I'd been up against the tree, but now as I flexed my shoulders, the pain rose to the surface in hot clenches of agony. My vision swam with misery as the spasms moved through my shoulders. I couldn't hear grating from any bones that would tell me that I'd broken anything major. But the sense that something was in there, damaged and possibly fractured, made for uncomfortable thoughts.

I looked up at Tree Face.

Up close he was seriously ugly. The trick of eyes that follow you wherever you go was one that he could do with ease. Even though I was right below him, I could see his gaze nailing me with woody intensity. He looked ugly, sure, but he wasn't stupid—I could almost hear his splintery-brain behind the bark, working through growth-ring nerves and thinking that I was an ignorant, useless idiot, whose life expectancy was rapidly diminishing with every hour.

Tree Face's mouth took on a creepy leer from this angle, and his eyes were kind of narrowed. I could feel disapproval and contempt in that look.

Get. A. Grip.

The carving that made up the edges of his shield-shaped head looked old. It had been attacked by the elements—the wood below the bark, instead of being fresh white, had browned a little with age. Amber bubbles of tree sap—like that stuff they'd used to bring the Dinosaurs back in Jurassic Park, erupted from some of the wounds. They looked shiny and hard. Maybe Tree Face was ancient. He hadn't been cut yesterday, that was for sure.

Vines and creepers hung down around Tree Face like wrist-thick dreadlocks. His twisted mouth seemed to move as more green flashy birds fluttered in and out of it. This was more evidence at least that the carving was old. Birds had set up a nest within the gaping mouth. They must have been there a while at least. Wouldn't constant bothering by cannibals disturb them so much that they wouldn't stay?

I knew even less about the habits of birds than I did about cannibals, so it was pointless trying to work it out. I reached up for a dreadlock in my right hand and lifted the top half of my body a little off the ground. Taking another dreadlock in my left hand and testing them both to see if they would take my weight, I began to haul myself up to get a closer look at Tree Face.

I allowed myself a quick smile as I imagined Tree Face yelling and screaming as I pulled on his hair. His toothy mouth opened as the angles changed and I wanted to hear him yelling and screaming as I yanked myself higher.

My muscles protested, and my breathing became harsh and painful as I lugged my body up so I was face to face with the carving. Two birds, scared by my appearance at the mouth, flew out, one battering itself against my cheek. So startled was I that I almost let go of the vine and swung crazily for a moment, my bad shoulder thudding into the bark below Tree Face.

Now he looking like he was smiling at my misfortune.

Dad used to say that God Paid His Debts without money. I told Dad to shut up in my mind and got a real bad head-swim for my trouble.

Now that I was this close to Tree Face, I could see that there were hundreds of intricate tiny carvings across his face, and as many again surrounding the lines of the shield. Each one appeared to be the same, but as I looked closer, I could see they had subtle differences. They were of tiny stick-men, no more than a centimetre high, and each one running and leaping over the other. As my eyes teared up again with the pain of holding myself in this position, the stick-men seemed to run across the film of water covering my eyes.

I shook my head.

Tree Face's lips were bright red and dry. They looked as if they'd been painted yesterday. It was the only real suggestion that Tree Face was not abandoned and that he was being visited at regular intervals. I was hypnotised by that mouth, its harsh red circle of lips and rough carved pointed teeth. It loomed towards me—or was I looming towards it?

Everything was becoming dreamlike and warm. I groggily realised that the pain in my shoulder was receding and that the edges of my vision were darkening, as if the sun were dropping from the sky.

I tried to clear my head by shaking it again, but all I succeeded in doing was scraping my forehead against the bark. The stick-men were dashing about like mad things and I could swear I could hear Dad laughing...

Dad laughing...

I tightened my grip on the dreads. Tree Face was bending towards me, his big red-lipped mouth widening—I could hear the wooden muscles creaking as the tree craned its trunk up, I wouldn't let go of the dreads, because if I did, I would fall into his mile-wide mouth.

I was hanging above Tree Face the Cannibal.

And he was coming to eat me.

TEN

And it was all sky, and the clouds obscured the ground and Dad loved Mum and they held hands and walked along the shore of clouds and the seas of clouds washed their cloudy feet and on the cloud horizon boats made of clouds sailed the cloudy waves and I parachuted down through the cloud sky where everything was white and blue and safe and cloudy and all I wanted was here and the trees that were made of clouds held out their open-branch arms of cloud and in the puffy distance I could see the cloud-world turning and on the surface of the cloud-world, cloud cities burned in the cloud night and Escobar made of clouds waved up at me from the cloud jungle and I awoke at the foot of the tree, my mouth full of mud and my stomach grinding with hunger.

The sun was high overhead and the clouds were scarce in what I could see of the sky through the canopy. For a moment, I couldn't remember why I was lying in the mud at the bottom of a tree.

Then I saw Tree Face looking down at me and it all came back with a thunderclap that savaged my head like the worst migraine.

I hadn't drunk much or eaten for nearly twenty-four hours, I was injured, exhausted, and had forced myself to crawl into the jungle, and then had used creepers to pull myself up a tree.

It'd all been too much and I'd fainted. Fainted after getting seriously screwy in the head—hearing Dad and thinking that Tree Face was going to eat me.

I shivered. If I didn't find some food soon, then trips to the

mad places in my head were going to be a regular occurrence—
and that wouldn't help with defending myself again whatever
the jungle was going to throw at me, or the cannibals...

I was on my side, but it was clear that I'd been on my face in
the mud for at least some of the time I'd been unconscious—the
grit and dirt in my mouth told me as much. I wiped it away as
best I could and spat out the rest. I sucked some more moisture
from my tee-shirt but that only seemed to make the pangs of
hunger in my guts even worse.

My Rolex said that it was getting close to midday, which
meant I'd been out for about five hours. I pulled myself up
on the vines to lean sideways against the tree so that I could
see if anything had started eating my legs while I'd been out.
Thankfully, nothing had begun to make a meal of my shins or
knees. I did an Ick Bag change and some pressing, but to be
honest, there wasn't much to get rid of—clear evidence that I
needed food and drink soon.

I looked up at Tree Face and he looked right back at me, his
dreads moving a little as something black, furry, and monkey-
shaped moved in the branches high above. It called out once
and then it leaped to another tree and was out of sight in a
second. I didn't know if it had seen me or if I had scared it away.
I assumed the animals in the vicinity were probably used to
my scent now, if that indeed was how it worked, and weren't
bothered by me anymore.

As I shifted to look behind me, I saw the bowls.

There were three of them, roughly carved wood and two
of them had fruit in. The third held some liquid that was dark
purple, like blackcurrant. The fruits were fist-sized and yellow. I
didn't recognise them, but then that wasn't a surprise, I couldn't
always tell the names of the things Petra, Dad's girlfriend,
brought back from Waitrose, and so what chance did I have out
here?

The bowls were wedged between the roots of the tree to the
left of Tree Face.

Had they been there before I'd fainted?

I couldn't remember, and to be honest, I'd been so out of it,
I probably wouldn't have noticed them if I had. If they'd come

since I'd been out for the count, that raised more than a few worries.

I pulled myself fully onto my stomach and dragged myself over a knobbly root to examine the bowls more closely. The fruit didn't look that old, but it didn't look that fresh either. Bruises were starting to ripen on the fleshy surface, and an insect or something had nibbled at one of them. There were a couple of holes burrowed into the top near where a stem had been broken when picked. The bowl containing the liquid had a couple of dead insects floating in a scummy film that had developed across the surface of the juice.

As I got closer, I could smell the fruit, and it was suddenly the most delicious thing I had ever smelt in my life. It may have been attacked by insects, on the over-ripe side of rotting, but to my suddenly drooling mouth, it was the most inviting and alluring smell in the world.

I didn't know what the fruit was, but hunger was driving me now, not the need to be cautious. I picked up the least manky-looking fruit from the bowl and held it up to my mouth—for about a tenth of a second I hesitated, the flicker of a thought about poisonous plant life and me dying in agony crisscrossed my thinking, but that idea blinked out of existence as I bit into the fruit.

The skin was hard and waxy and was a little bitter; I pulled my mouth away and picked at the wound I had made in the side of the fruit. Inside the flesh was bright yellow and smelt of peach. I ripped the hole apart with my thumbs and brought the fruit back to my lips. It tasted amazing, juice ran down my chin and the peachy-pineapple-y flavour filled my mouth. I broke the fruit in half, and there were hundreds of black seeds in the centre, I suppose a bit like a melon. I scooped them out and wiped my hand down the tree bark to get the seeds off.

I finished the first fruit in about thirty seconds after that. Within two minutes all four fruit were gone and I was contemplating the dead insects floating in the bowl of dark juice. I fished the drowned flies out of the liquid and wiped them on the tree bark next to the black seeds. I dipped a finger back into the bowl and brought it cautiously to my mouth. At least the fruit was recognisable as fruit; the liquid could really be anything.

I considered that it might be sweet, because it had attracted the flies.

But then, it could also be poisonous, because it had killed them. Or had they just drowned happy, like that fat kid in the chocolate river in that stupid film about the chocolate factory...

Well, there was nothing to be gained from waiting, so I licked my finger.

Mistake.

The liquid was bitter and foul. It tasted of pepper and bleach. I spat it out and immediately wished there was more fruit available to rid my mouth of the taste. I looked accusingly at my finger. The end of it was stained bright red, just like Tree Face's mouth.

It was paint.

For a moment I regretted the taste of the paint a lot less than I regretted that I must be sitting here now, looking like I was trying out some of Petra's lipsticks.

Great.

The logic dominos started falling in my head. People were coming to Tree Face on a regular basis, leaving him fruit, and painting his mouth red. So, yes, just to make things worse, at any moment now I could be attacked by bloodthirsty cannibals who'd be more than a little put out that I'd eaten Tree Face's breakfast.

With a yell of frustration, I hefted the paint bowl up into the air and threw it against the tree.

Mistake number two.

As the bowl splintered in two, it spattered its contents over the tree and my face and chest. A good splash of it got in my eyes and made them sting sharply. I howled in pain and began rubbing them with the heels of my hands. If anything that made the stinging worse as I worked the paint further into my eyes and tear ducts.

There was a rushing burning in my nose as the foul liquid worked its way up my nostrils and I could taste it again in my mouth as in ran down the skin of my cheeks. I scrabbled about for something else to wipe my face on and caught hold of a ferny leaf. I ripped it from its parent plant and rubbed it over my eyes. It was cooling and soothing, wet from the humid air. The leaf soon disintegrated with the harsh treatment it was getting against my face, so I ripped up a couple of others and applied them to my eyes.

As the stinging began to subside, I blinked, snorted and spat, ridding myself of the sensations and flavours from the rank paint. My vision was blurry, but I could see enough to register that my hands, arms, and chest were so covered in blood-red paint that I must have looked like the victim of an axe-wielding maniac.

Anyway, I gave my eyes a last rub with the shredded fern leaves in my hand and flopped onto my side, with Tree Face's trunk at my back.

That's when the half-naked cannibal girl who had approached me silently from behind lifted up her spear to strike.

ELEVEN

My parents, well, Dad, had had the whole house changed and made wheelchair accessible for when I came out of the spinal injuries unit. Mum had tied a big pink bow over the front door, and when I went in, there were welcome home banners, a bunch of relatives cheering, and Silly Sally taking photographs.

It was as much as I could to put on a smile, when what I really wanted to do was get back in the private ambulance and tell them to drive me over the nearest cliff.

I locked myself in my en suite bathroom, with its wheelchair shower, wet-room flooring and air blower body dryer, and cried a lot. I put the taps on so they couldn't hear me crying through the door and I stayed there until everyone had gone.

I told Dad I wanted to go to bed. He wanted to help me, but to be honest I didn't want him near me. I know he hadn't meant to crash the car. I know he felt incredibly bad about it, but I still wasn't able to look him in the eye. There was a rotten clenching in my gut, even all those months after the accident when I thought about him.

Fast forward.

Thing is, right, I hadn't even wanted to go to Birmingham with him, but he'd insisted because Mum was away with her sister for something boring, and they didn't want to leave me alone in the house. It's not like I would have trashed the place with a party or anything, but might have had a few mates over at least—that's when I still had mates that is, not just boys who took pity on me by not chatting up girls in front of me.

That's when I was still trying to drum up the courage to speak to Jen...

No.

Not now. Maybe later.

So. Birmingham.

Dad had to do some business, or have a meeting or look over some documents or something, but he promised to take me to a football match when it was all done. West Bromwich Albion were playing Birmingham City in the FA cup. Proper grudge match local derby. That was the sweetener for me being in the hotel room all day while Dad did his stuff. I'd said to him that why did it matter where I was alone—at home or in Birmingham? But he wasn't having any of it.

I spent the day flicking through the movie channels and getting burgers and cokes sent up by room service. Dad has been smart and not left me a room key so that I wasn't able to leave. Which was a shame because the hotel was quite a cool one with a big gym and a swimming pool. I could have risked wedging the room door open I suppose and heading off for a bit of recreation, but in the end decided against it. I didn't want to jeopardise the trip to The Hawthorns for the footy. Even though neither teams were the one I supported, a match is a match.

So I stayed in the room.

The phone in the room rang loads of times during the day. Once was Mum just to check I was ok and that Dad hadn't abandoned me. I lied for him and said he was just in the shower and we were watching movies. I didn't want to cause a row as they both often fought over me—well it felt like they did anyway. Mum was cool and she rang off. But for the rest of the afternoon the phone went a bit crazy. Someone would ring, hear my voice, and ring off. That happened a few times, and then someone did ask if she could speak to John Coker. I must have been half-asleep and just grunted, and so she started to talk about the drop at 8pm tonight at the Newport Pagnell. When she realised she was speaking to me and not my dad, her voice froze in her throat. She apologised, said "Sorry wrong number." And the line went dead.

Funny I thought. She'd asked for Dad by name. How could it be a wrong number?

I thought about ringing Dad on the mobile, but knew he'd

get arsy if I interrupted him while he was on business.

The rest of the day, the phone stayed silent, and I just assumed that whoever was trying to get hold of him had managed it and that all was ok.

I spent a bit of time looking out the windows of the hotel room. We were high up and Birmingham could have been any city where we'd stayed, to be honest. If all the people had not spoken as if they had something wrong with their sinuses, it wouldn't have been any different from London.

The sky over the hotel was grey and fast-moving. The forecast was for filthy weather that evening and I was glad we'd thought to stuff our anoraks in the back of the car for the football tonight. Sitting in freezing rain does kinda make sitting in the stands uncomfortable—but it wasn't something we hadn't done a good few times before. It usually brought on our usual discussion about why the Premier League wasn't played during the summer months as it would be a lot warmer and we wouldn't have to eat so many sodding horrible pies to warm up.

I miss those conversations.

We didn't go to footy as much now. Wheelchair access is good at most grounds but since Mum and Dad split up and I stayed with Dad, he seemed to be busier, and we hardly ever made it.

I even missed the pies.

When Dad got back to the hotel, he was in a rotten mood.

He stomped back in with his ear glued to his mobile, threw his jacket on the bed, kicked off his shoes, and continued having the shouting match with my mum on the phone.

She'd obviously tracked him down during the day too. Perhaps it had been her who'd kept ringing off when she heard my voice, hoping to at least get Dad the once.

He was trying to defend his actions. "Look I didn't leave him at home did I? Would you have preferred that?"

I could make out Mum's voice on the line. It was shouty and abrasive. I couldn't make out the actual words, but I could guess at them. Dad listened, sighing and squeezing his own thigh hard with his hand. When he was able to get a word in, he almost screamed into the phone. "Well if you weren't swanning off with your bloody sister for retail therapy—on my bloody credit cards—maybe you could have been at home looking after him!"

Dad hung up the mobile, turned it off and threw it across the room. It skidded over the carpet and thumped into the wall, cracking the screen. Dad just said "Brilliant. Just brilliant," and stomped off to the shower.

When he came out, he was still tense and annoyed.

He picked up his broken phone and tried to turn it on, but it wasn't having any of it. He sighed again and threw it onto the dresser then started pulling on a tee-shirt and jumper for the cold night ahead.

Dad took some deep breaths. "So, how was your day?"

I shrugged. "Ok, I suppose. These were a lot of weird phone calls."

"Weird?"

I told him.

Dad agreed that it must have been Mum trying to trick him out, and that's why she'd finally given in and called him on his mobile while he was supposed to be working. That was always a no-no—which is why I hadn't done it. She probably did it to piss him off, he said. I shrugged again. I was fed up being piggy in the middle, but it was no good to tell them that. They were too busy tearing lumps out of themselves to hear me.

Then I told him about the woman who'd rang about the drop at Newport Pagnell services.

His whole body changed; suddenly he became very calm with a steely focus. I think he even put his hands on my shoulders. He looked straight at me and got me to repeat exactly what the woman had said.

"She said the drop at Newport Pagnell services was at 8pm."

Dad got up and went to his phone, hissing and grumbling under his breath. He took the back off his phone, and slid out the SIM. He snapped his fingers at me. "Your mobile. Now."

I handed him my mobile and he snapped the back off, removed the SIM, and replaced it with his. He didn't even bother to put the cover back before he was stabbing the display with his thumb and bring it up to his ear.

He walked into the bathroom and slammed the door so I couldn't hear who he was talking to or what he was saying.

When he came back, he handed me my de-SIMed phone and continued to get dressed.

"We can't go to the football. Sorry."

I looked up at him properly disappointed, "Why?"

"Because of bastards. Bastard snakes," he said.

TWELVE

The spear the cannibal girl threw sliced through the top of my shoulder.

Hot agony lanced through my skin, adding to, and then completely overwhelming the pain that had been there before. I felt rather than heard the spear thud into the tree behind me. The girl stood there, teenaged, brown-skinned, half-naked, face and eyes wild. I reckoned I had about a second to fight back or she'd grab the end of the spear, pull it out of the wood, and this time stick it through my face.

Before I thought about what I could do, I screamed at her.

I dragged that scream up from the very depth of my guts and yelled at the top of my voice. The sound reverberated through the trees but was deadened by the leaves. A bird squawked, another animal skittered off through the bush. I couldn't see its body but the sapling tops waved wildly as it moved.

The cannibal froze.

It gave me the time I need. I pulled the ruckkie towards me, reached into the open mouth, and pulled out a stone.

I chucked it as hard as I could at the cannibal.

She gasped as the rock hit her on the chin, splitting her lip. I pulled another from the ruckkie and held it up, my intension clear. The cannibal turned and ran. She crashed away into the jungle without a word.

Christ.

A cannibal.

A proper, real, brown as a corner shop owner cannibal.

A cannibal trying to spear me for her lunchtime kebab. If it weren't so scary, it would have been hilarious. Like something out of one of those stupid old movies Dad had always tried to show me. The jungle around me was suddenly alive with noise. My scream and the cannibal running away had spooked many animals. I could hear them flapping through the trees. That black monkey-ape thing swung from branch to branch until I could no longer see it. In the distance, from the direction of the river, animals I couldn't identify called to warn their mates that something was going down they might want to avoid.

My shoulder hurt like buggery.

I reached up to it, felt the torn material of my tee-shirt, and when my fingers came away, they were wet with blood. Gingerly I felt the wound. Sighing with relief, I could tell with my fingers that the wound was not wide and neither was it deep. It stung and would need to be covered up quickly if I was not to be infected, but it wasn't going to kill me.

The shaft of the spear had stopped vibrating and was now just oscillating slowly. I reached for it and tried to get a good enough grip to get it out of the tree behind me. I looked up. Tree Face was having a right laugh at my expense it seemed, his twisted mouth from this angle howled silently at my predicament, black stump eyes almost creased with mirth.

I couldn't get enough purchase on the spear to pull it out of the tree. It was stuck fast. Maybe if I moved away from the tree I might be able to pull it out, but I felt safer with the tree at my back looking out. At least the cannibal wouldn't be able to sneak up on me again.

Keeping my eyes on the surrounding trees as much as possible, I reached into my ruckkie, pulled out some antiseptic wipes (I used these for obvious reasons when changing my Ick Bag—don't make me go into details) and used one of the cool white, wet squares to clean the wound. It came away with pinkish blood, which showed the slice through the skin wasn't bleeding as much as it had to begin with.

I reached into the ruckkie again and pulled out the roll of Elastoplast. One of the rotten things about having to wear an Ick back in a hot climate is that the area around it could get well sweaty. The adhesive flange attached to my abdomen could sometimes peel up at the edges because of it, so I kept a roll of the pink fabric plaster for that purpose. I tore off a length and placed it directly on the wound on my shoulder. I didn't have any dressing materials and didn't want to waste an Ick Bag on it, so direct contact it would have to be. It would be an arse to take off, but at least the cut was covered. That was the main thing.

I had another go at pulling out the spear, but the cannibal girl had thrown it hard. I was lucky she was a rubbish shot.

The jungle was starting to settle again, and the noises I'd become used to, the everyday sounds I'd experienced through the morning into the afternoon recommenced. In the distance, something was whooping, but other than that, there didn't appear to be anything near for me to worry about.

I tried to think back to what I knew about tribes and stuff.

Not a lot.

I remember wheeling into the lounge where Dad was watching some long-hair documentary on a tribe that hadn't been contacted by civilisation yet, who chased away a cameraman or something. I didn't take a lot of notice. I'd only gone in there to watch the build-up for the Chelsea/Newcastle game, but Dad wanted to watch the stupid documentary until kick-off. So I went spun the wheels around and went back to my room and my PlayStation.

I don't think Dad was that interested in the documentary, to be honest; he was also typing feverishly on his laptop on Facebook to some guy with a Spanish sounding name. It might even have been Carlos. Dunno. But that was all I saw of the documentary.

Other than that and knowing there were Indians—or cannibals—out here in the rainforest I knew zip. Almost as much as I knew about the jungle and the animals therein. I might as well be an astronaut crash-landing on an alien planet with no computers or supplies. That's how far away I was from any useful knowledge.

That's me. Sam Coker. The Amazon Spacekid.

A bird clattered through the leaves and thumped down in front of me. My heart jumped and I picked up a stone ready to throw.

Only it wasn't a bird.

It was one of those fruits I'd found in a bowl.

I looked up, but it definitely hadn't fallen from the tree above me. Tree Face wasn't giving away fruit today. He was all about the leaves and the branches.

The thing that I'd thought was a green and orange bird was no such thing.

And neither was the second one that landed by it.

Or the third.

It was raining fruit.

I looked into the trees, trying to see between the trunks and foliage, but there was nothing.

The fourth fruit landed on my numb knee and rolled between my legs.

Whoever was throwing the fruits had found their range.

The fifth fruit plopped into the small gap between my dead legs like a basketball. Slam-dunk.

What was happening?

I picked up one of the fruit. Convinced there was something wrong with it, poisoned or drugged, or if I broke it open, a huge hairy spider with knitting needle fangs would climb out and try to eat my throat.

No more fruit came.

The jungle returned to tick-over.

I guessed the next move was with me.

I collected all five fruit and examined them carefully. The skins were smooth and unbroken, they were unblemished apart from a darkening bruise on a couple which might have happened when they thumped into the ground by my feet.

I took one more look around, saw nothing but the jungle, then began to peel the fruit.

It had the same fleshy body as the fruit I'd eaten before that the same black seeds in the middle. I bit into it.

It tasted like heaven.

It was much fresher and more succulent than the one I'd eaten before. I devoured it quickly, not even concerned that I swallowed some of the black seeds in my haste to wolf down the nourishment.

I looked up.

The cannibal girl was standing not a metre from me.

I thumped back against the tree, reaching for a stone, but she nimbly kicked the nearest stone from my reach.

Up close I could see she had a broad flat face, bright but dark eyes, black hair, ears which had lobes stretched with thick cylinders of wood. Her mouth was wide and her split lip and bruised chin hung limply. I could see she had a mouth like a half-demolished graveyard. Teeth going in all directions, some white, some brown and others black. It was like a disaster area in there.

She hooked her toe in one of the straps of the ruckkie and pulled it fully away from my ability to reach it. Then she put the spear end in her right armpit, and curled her right hand and elbow around it.

The cannibal girl began to pull at the spear, straining, digging her feet into the earth, leaning back to get purchase.

If I didn't find a way to stop her, she'd be free to finish the job she'd already started.

THIRTEEN

It was a battle I was never going to win.

The cannibal girl strained and growled like an animal, her feet digging deeper and deeper into the mud. She started to yank the spear shaft from side to side and up and down. My much stronger arms, muscles bellowing with pain, because of the wrong angle I in which I was using them, resisted as long as they could. My fingers, slick from sweat, the humidity, and the blood from my shoulder, began to slide down the wooden shaft of the spear. I felt splinters digging into my palms, the flesh pierced, promising more of my blood.

The girl's face was creased with anger and exertion. Her mouth stretched in a wide grimace, the place where I'd split her lip started to pull apart again and a large dot of blood began to grow. I concentrated more on that dot of blood. Using it as focus. Willing myself to hold on. If the spear came free, I was lunch.

But in the end, even using one arm...

One arm? What was she only using...

The spear came away from the tree with a splintering crack, the shaft slid through my fingers. The cannibal girl fell backward now the force holding her angled body let go. I released the spear before the sharpened stone head sliced my palms open. That's when the snake slithered across my neck, cheek, and chin.

"Bastard snakes! Snakes!" Dad said again in the Birmingham hotel room.

I brushed wildly at the whispery snakeskin as it coiled off my shoulder.

I tried to back away from the green-skinned, diamond-headed

reptile, but the tree was at my back, and up there Tree Face was killing himself with laughter. His viny dreads were shaking and I bet deep in the tree his wooden heart was creasing with joy at my predicament.

I tried to roll sideways away from the snake but there was a tree root hemming me in.

Then panic gripped me, I may even have let out a bit of a girlie scream. I pressed myself back into the bark, waiting to be bitten by poison fangs or speared through the heart by the girl. Either way, I was dead.

And that's when the snake began to fly.

With a curl of its body, it lifted out of my lap and seemed to hang in front of me. Its glazed eyes focused on mine. Its mouth gaping and the spear... the spear exiting a wound at the base of its jaw.

I looked past the dead snakes head. Along the shaft of the spear, to where the cannibal girl, sitting on her backside in the mud with a grin like an accident in a domino factory was holding the snake up for me to inspect its deadness.

She laughed.

She shook the spear.

The snake dangled all dead and harmless. Its tail slithered across my chest. I brushed it away.

The girl put her head back and roared with laughter.

A flock of birds lifted from the canopy and ascended to the heavens.

Tree Face stopped laughing. I don't think he was pleased.

The cannibal girl didn't try to eat me.

She stood up, took the snake out of my face, peeled it off the spear, and curled it expertly with one hand...

One hand...

... into a rope of snake and slung it over her shoulder like a handbag.

She sat cross-legged in front of me. Looking at me intently and pushed the fruits, which had rolled away in the struggle, back towards me. She pointed at the fruit and then at her mouth several times until I got the message.

I peeled a fruit and began to eat.

The cannibal had two arms, but while her right was strong, brown, and sturdy, the left was a shrivelled thing that dangled uselessly at her side like a flipper. The fingers were deformed, and seem to grow out of a knobbly, disfigured elbow. Occasionally the thumb—if it was a thumb—would twitch to a long-forgotten impulse and the palm would spasm but that was it. It was not a limb she could rely on to help her do anything.

Even peel one of the fruit.

So I peeled one and offered it to her.

Cannibal girl's smile disappeared and she shook her head. Pointed at the fruit and my mouth. It was all for me. She was adamant.

So I ate the fruit.

All the while, she watched me. Her face bright with fascination as if this was the first time she'd ever seen anyone eat fruit before. She rested her chin in her good hand and watched me unblinkingly until all the fruit was gone, and my belly felt fuller than it had done in a while.

"Thank you," I said.

She didn't reply. Just smiled.

I got the impression then that the withered arm wasn't her only disability. She looked at me like Lance did. Lance was a boy with learning difficulties at my school. He was always smiling, always happy, even when the other kids would bully him or call him names—not something I ever did but you know what schools are like. Actually, that's a lie. Of course, I'd joined in before the accident. Of course, I'd laughed at Lance's strangeness and awkwardness. The same way I laughed when the bigger boys picked on the immigrant kids from Syria and stuff. If you didn't laugh, they'd start on you, wouldn't they? I wasn't stupid. Rather them than me. So, yeah, I'd laughed at Lance. Things had changed after the accident when the boot that couldn't walk was suddenly on the foot that couldn't move... but yeah... anyway... It was like Lance didn't realise they were talking to him or about them. He would just laugh, smile at them, and go on his jolly way to his special class. It was probably more important to Lance to be in a normal school than to worry about a few cretinous creeps like us who would take the piss out of him.

I suppose I was the same with the wheelchair. I'd had the opportunity to change school if I'd wanted, but I was determined to stay. I wasn't going to let a set of wheels beat me—well that had been a long time ago and a lifetime away. Now I didn't even have my wheels. But the girl's expression had definitely made me think about Lance, with his easy smile and his lack of comprehension at what was going on. But like Lance on the football pitch, where his skills as a goalie were considerable, then the cannibal girl had learned how to use a spear.

She's made the most of what she had for sure.

The cannibal girl pointed to her chest and made two clicking noises.

Ok.

Yes.

I was distracted by her chest. I admit it, ok?

She was about my age and she was topless. I don't want to get all blokey about this because really, this is a story of survival and shit, but a pair of tits is a pair of tits, right?

So, I'll just acknowledge the distraction and move on. Fair enough.

So, yeah, she pointed at her chest and made two clicks in her mouth.

I suppose she was telling me her name. "Kik-Kik?" I said experimentally.

She smiled and pointed at her chest again, nodding.

Progress.

She knelt closer and pointed behind me at the tree. I looked up and saw her finger was pointing to the gash in the tree bark she'd made with the spear. It was still wet with snake blood. Then she pointed at me, and then the snake. She repeated the three stabs with her finger.

I nodded. She was telling me she'd killed the snake before it had the chance to bite me.

"Thank you," I said.

Her face was confused. Language was not going to be our primary method of communication—if I was going to use

Kik-Kik to help get me out of this hell hole, I was going to have to find another way. I pointed at the snake and frowned. Then I pointed at Kik-Kik and smiled.

She seemed to get the message.

Kik-Kik stood up and beckoned me to follow.

When I couldn't comply, she turned around, confused again. She beckoned again. More urgently this time.

I shook my head and pointed at my legs, frowning.

Kik-Kik squinted and thought for a few seconds, but I could see it wasn't really going in. I pointed at her withered arm and then pointed at my legs, trying to make the connection between the two.

This time some sort of realisation moved across her feature. Her eyes lit up, and she pointed above me. At Tree Face.

I looked up. Tree Face was impassive. The light in the jungle was fading towards twilight again and the shadows under his eyes gave him a distant faraway look, like he was ignoring us.

I shook my head at Kik-Kik.

She stamped her feet in frustration. Pointed at her withered arm, and then my legs and then at Tree Face.

I had no idea what she was getting at.

I thought I should give her a practical demonstration of the problems I had with just walking away from the clearing.

I grabbed two of Tree Face's dreads, one in each hand. Nourished by the fruit and feeling a lot better now that there was someone who would help me get away from here, I felt able to use in the strength in my arms fully. I began to pull myself up.

Kik-Kik watched with awe as I raised first my backside off the floor, and then my useless feet began to drag their heels along the ground as I brought myself higher. When my head reached the same level as Tree Face, that's when my feet lifted clear of the jungle floor. I moved my hips to show my useless legs dangling like her withered arm.

"I can't use my legs. I had an accident," I said uselessly.

It was all useless. All a waste of time.

Kik-Kik was looking at me in wonder. And then at Tree Face and then at me and then at Tree Face and then…

And then she started dancing and singing. Pointing at us both individually and then together.

And then she howled to the sky.

FOURTEEN

How do you explain a Piper Cherokee to someone who'd never seen an aeroplane?

Once the howling and the hissing and the dancing had settled down, and I'd lowered myself to ground level again, Kik-Kik sat with me again. She would occasionally point at me and then at Tree Face and it wasn't until I realised my lips were still covered in the same red paint as Tree Face's, that I realised she was probably laughing at the similarities between me and the carved monstrosity above us.

How wrong could I be?

Pretty bloody wrong actually.

That's when I started to make it worse by trying to explain how I got here.

I pointed at my chest, and then pointed at the sky.

You can see where this is going, can't you?

Yeah. But at the time I was still scared and desperate. I thought that trying to get Kik-Kik to understand that I'd flown here, crashed, and needed to be rescued was absolutely the right thing to do.

So I pointed at me, and then at the sky.

Kik-Kik pointed at the sky, her face full of wonder and awe.

I nodded. Smiled. Pointed at the sky and then at me. Pointed and smiled…

Kik-Kik nodded and smiled.

The sky pointing, nodding and pointing at me went on for a while until I was sure it had sunk in. Now we were getting somewhere.

Kik-Kik got up, and ran.

"Hey!" I shouted. "Wait! Come back! Where are you going?" But she was gone.

Perhaps she knew of the plane crash and knew that people were out looking for me. Hopefully she'd gone to get help.

I hoped that she'd be back soon. The night was falling fast.

I scrambled to my ruckkie, got out an Ick Bag and sorted myself out. The fruit was moving through me quickly, and so matters needed to be dealt with or well... unpleasantness. I didn't need there to still be light in the sky for me to change the bag—I'd done it more than enough times for it to be second nature now—but if darkness was falling, I didn't want to be buggering about with that if Kik-Kik didn't come back before the other snakes did. Or worse. The Lions. Or whatever.

As I changed the bag, I thought about Kik-Kik and her snaggled flipper. Couldn't have been easy for her to get by in the rainforest with an arm like that, and especially if she wasn't the full three-course meal in the upstairs department. She was bloody aces at the spear thing though.

That snake had been ready to paralyse the rest of me with its venom, and she'd thrown that spear from what... five or six metres? Hard enough to bury it in the wood like she had, without the accuracy on top. Like me and my legs, I guess, she'd had to compensate for her arm with other skills and strengths. It wasn't a walk in the park, or even a kick around in the car park out here. I was grateful that one of Kik-Kik's strengths was her accuracy and that she hadn't been robbed of her abilities to coordinate by the mental impairment I guessed she had. Otherwise, I would have been toast.

Darkness fell and the nightshift started in the jungle.

It became more and more convinced that Kik-Kik would not be coming back tonight.

I settled myself against the tree bark, looked up but couldn't see Tree Face—which cheered me up no end. I was getting more than a little annoyed at his constant sneering.

What was I saying?

Tree Face was a hole in a tree. Nothing more nothing less.

I hoped.

Another reason I was glad I couldn't see him.

I pulled my ruckkie close to my chest to use as a something to hug as much as something to shield me. But you won't catch me admitting to that.

And the sky was dark and light and dark and light and the clouds were mouths and the mouths were Kik-Kik's eyes and Kik-Kik was a plane and a cloud and a snake and the snakes in Kik-Kik's eyes moved down and out of the clouds of her mouths and Dad stood behind Kik-Kik in the clouds and everywhere was blue and green and everything was wet and clouds and trees and snakes and Kik-Kik and Escobar and Carlos and the cigars were making the clouds and I couldn't breathe in the clouds of cigar smoke and Dad was waving but there was a cloud shaped like a tree branch going through him and the clouds and Kik-Kik and the red river the red river of red river blood and the Cherokee was a real Indian shaped like a plane with feathers and a wigwam made of clouds in the sky and Kik-Kik was pointing at the sky and the clouds and Tree Face and the sky and me and the sky and pointing pointing pointing...

I made it through the night with just a million insect bites and all my limbs intact.

This was a plus even though it didn't sound like one.

I checked my Rolex as the sky started to fill with a hazy white light and shook my head free of the cloud dream.

It was 6.30am.

This was usually the time of the morning when I would roll over in bed, look at the clock and say a big fat "nope." I'm not a morning person, but then I'm not a lost-in-the-rainforest kind of person either so I guess the two things cancel each other out.

The morning heat from the sun was starting to cook the vegetation around me, steam and vapour was rising all around me as the light evaporated the dews and juices of the night. The jungle became indistinct and blurry. Although I couldn't see a great distance into the trees yesterday—wood for the trees and all that—now with the foggy air filled and deadened by the morning mist, like one of those black-and-white news thingies of pre-smokeless Britain. Chimneys rising into black skies, roofs belching smoke, causing killing fogs. I remember doing that in history at school—what did they call that old dense fog? Pea something, yeah Pea-Soupers. As the thickening mist wafted around me everything began to warm. I started to wish I was back in London. Even in that chilling, freezing choking fog. Anything would be better than this.

I ached from sleeping against the tree, my shoulders were stiff and my back creaked as I changed position, the throbby pain of the wound was still there, but the underlying injury from the crash seemed to be healing at least. My jeans were wet through from being on the jungle floor all night, but I figured my useless legs wouldn't mind. I glanced up at Tree Face. He was looking off into the distance, probably having as much trouble with the foggy vapours as I was. I suspected he was looking forward to Kik-Kik's return as much as me.

Obviously, when I got everything across to her about the plane crash and the predicament, she'd rushed off to her wigwam or whatever. She'd spoken to the village elders, and they'd sent a canoe or something upriver to the Missionaries from that film Dad made me watch. The Missionaries had radioed the town to tell the authorities that I was here and stranded, but alive and well. And now the rescue helicopters were already beating their blade through the sky, now that it was light. And the team of sweaty, bandana-wearing marines sent in to do jungle evac—like in that stupid film Dad had showed me—were even now checking their machine guns and chewing on the wet stubs of unlit cigars as they made their way to this position. I was convinced they—like in that stupid film Dad had shown me—were going to hover over the canopy and abseil down on ropes with a stretcher to lift me out of the jungle forever. And take me back to the city, where I'd be able to tell them where the plane had crashed and where Dad's body was, so we could take him back to London for a decent Christian burial and...

I blinked.

Yeah.

It wasn't going to be as easy as that, was it?

It doesn't matter how much my mind would run away from

me, fantasising about rescue, joining up all the dots to make a happy picture I could colour in with my thoughts, there was a creeping sense of dread seeping into my bones from the dank, wet fog.

What if Kik-Kik couldn't find me again?

What if a leopard or something had eaten her on the way back to her wigwam?

I shook my head. Don't be stupid, I told myself. That girl's a survivor. Look at the way she'd killed that snake. The truth is going to be in between those two extremes for sure, she'd not going to be rotting in a big cat's belly and neither is there a rescue helicopter on its way.

What happened was this: She'd gone back to her village. Told her dad or mum all about me, and they'd decided, because it was night, to come out and get me at first light. That's what had happened for sure. Any moment now Kik-Kik would appear with a few of her villagers and they were going to carry me back, feed me up and keep me safe until the authorities could be contacted.

All I had to do was wait, and Kik-Kik and the others would appear.

I was certain of it.

Ten minutes later, Kik-Kik emerged into the clearing.

She was alone.

FIFTEEN

It's not true that everything goes into slow motion when you're in a car accident. It's not true that your life flashes before your eyes either. There was no white light for me to walk towards and I didn't hear the calling of angels, or some of the other stupid shit some of the people who've asked me about it since. There was just Dad screaming, throwing his arm across my chest. Then the world spinning: first on one axis and we started to go sideways, then on another axis as the car began a sickening barrel-roll. Then the flip up into the air; the crash as we hit the central reservation; rolling along it for thirty metres, while the metal of the Armco barrier sawed the car in half and broke my spine. Then Dad thrown out of the car to end upside down in a bush and chuck the wreckage of the car, and me, broken forever, still strapped into the front of the car with an airbag in my face, saving my nose, but not my back, into a roadside ditch.

We hadn't even made it to the services at Newport Pagnell to pick up whatever it was that was being dropped off there for Dad.

We'd left the hotel in a hurry, and into a rotten storm. It lit the sky over the already dull-grey city with flashes of lightning that ripped across the sky in knife-sharp stabs of forked light.

The rain was hammering down and it seemed that everyone was on the roads trying to get out of the city that night. The slip roads were jammed with cars, and a jack-knifed lorry, spilling tons of waste paper out the back of its container held us up while the police set up a diversion, before finally waving us on. Dad kept looking at his watch, drumming his fingers on the steering wheel, his face flash lit by lightning, which seared my eyes.

I didn't mention the football match.

There was no point, even though I was properly gutted not to be going—it being the main reason Dad had sweetened the idea of the trip in the first place. I'd spent a night and whole day in a boring hotel room for nothing. But there was no point causing a row, there would be more than enough of those when we got home. Mum had been calling my mobile every hour on the hour. Dad had taken the phone off me in the end, throwing it onto the back seat.

"Let her stew," was all he said.

I could tell she was well past the stewing stage, she'd boiled over, the cooker was on fire and she wouldn't be calling the fire brigade. She would just be using Dad's backside to put out the fire.

I thought about bailing out of the car then and taking my chances in the rain.

Considering what happened, I wish I had.

Once out of the city and on the motorway, initially things didn't get any better, there were a series of accidents that although not spectacularly horrible, were enough to cause more massive jams. Dad stabbed at his sat-nav, trying to engineer a different route around the accidents, but we were between junctions now and locked into this section of the motorway.

Cars and lorries hemmed us in. The city moved past incredibly slowly through the rain-smeared windows.

At one point Dad made me lean over to the back seat, retrieve my mobile, (a generic Android, the one I had before the all-singing, all-dancing iPhone they got me for my last birthday) put his SIM back in to see if he could call ahead to whoever he was supposed to be meeting, but there was no answer. Mum had tried to call him too and the SIM was showing a number of missed calls from her when I snapped the back on and fired up the screen.

Before he called the number of his associates—from memory—he cleared the missed calls from Mum with a quick flick of his thumb and a bitter sigh.

"Watch out!" I shouted, and Dad slammed on the brakes. He'd been so intent on the phone and getting annoyed with

Mum he hadn't seen the huge articulated lorry in front of us had stopped.

We jarred to a halt just inches from the huge metal bars of its rear bumpers.

"Careful," I said.

Dad ignored me; he was already ringing the number he wanted.

As the car was stopped, and the rain was reduced to a slow but persistent hiss on the bodywork, I could hear the phone ringing on the other end of the line, in time with the blat-blat-blat of the wipers.

Someone behind started beeping their horn at us, because now Dad was on the phone, he hadn't noticed that the lorry had started moving off. Dad thrust the phone into my hands. It was still ringing. "If anyone answers," he said, "don't speak, just hand the phone back to me, yes?"

I nodded and put the phone to my ear. It rang continuously until the network cut us off with the "There is no answer" message.

The rain didn't let up, but the traffic did. Although there was still a huge number of cars and transporters on the motorway that night, at least we were starting to get somewhere. It didn't seem to help Dad's tension. He kept changing lanes, trying to move a little further up the road quicker than the other traffic around us. He undercut traffic in the fast lanes, and at one point took to the hard shoulder to get past a gaggle of cars that had slowed down too much. They beeped at us as we went past, but he didn't acknowledge them. I just saw his white knuckles gripping tighter to the wheel and his eyes, unblinking, on the road ahead.

The dashboard clock was ticking down the minutes of our lateness, the sat-nav told us that we were still thirty minutes from our destination, and it was ten minutes until Dad had to be where we were supposed to be.

I tried making conversation, "What are we picking up?"

"Not important." It was clear he did not want to talk to me. His foot pressed down harder on the accelerator and the car moved up past the speed limit, into a clear stretch of motorway.

Cars streamed behind us. He tailgated a BMW for a mile until it got out of our way. As we drove past it, the driver gave us the finger. Dad did nothing—just looked ahead.

The tension was thick and soupy. I couldn't tell if Dad was annoyed with me as well as being late for the drop-off. I hated these silences. They happened all the time at home. Dad and Mum could last hours. Days sometimes. It was bloody pathetic really. Adults acting like kids, but they were both so stubborn. Most of my mates' parents had split up, and I guessed it would only be a matter of time before mine did. It might actually be a good thing, I thought bitterly. At least those silences might not happen so often.

If Dad wasn't going to talk to me and the wrong SIM was sitting in my phone, the least he could do was let me listen to some music. I turned on the radio, looking forward to some tunes, which might at least change the mood in the car.

Without taking his eyes off the road, Dad lifted his hand from the wheel and turned off the radio three seconds after I put it on.

"Leave it off. They might call."

Great. No football. No conversation. No phone and no radio.

Sorry to be a bit disappointed, Dad, but this really is turning out to be the Worst. Journey .Ever.

Except it got worse.

A black stretch of road opened up in front of us, nothing on it, just us. The clouds even cleared a bit and the moonlight speared down from the sky illuminating the rain-slick road in silver.

Dad accelerated again.

Seventy-five.

Eighty.

Eighty-five.

I know it's wrong, but I love when Dad drove fast. Loved the sounds. The roaring of the engine, the rumble of the road beneath the tyres, the flashing trees, the curve of road, the flicking white lines, and the blinking cat's eyes. I steered with him in my mind. Pushed my foot down on the accelerator in my head, imagined the rush of the wind.

Ok, things were looking up.
The open road. Brilliant.

I think it was a stag or a deer or maybe a pony. I can't really remember and they never found out because Dad was too busy taking evasive action, travelling far too fast to ever have a chance of stopping in time. Slamming on the brakes and then turning the car into a skid. The police told him later, when he was getting charged with dangerous driving and losing his licence for year—which is why he went back to flying—that if he'd been below the speed limit, on a wet, badly lit road at night, his son may not have been so badly injured, and might still be walking.

I lay in the silence. Fully conscious as the broken car steamed, hissed and sparked around me. The engine ticked and I could hear liquid dipping onto the road. The moonlight was obscured by clouds and a soft rain began to fall through the torn open rear of the car.

I could feel the rain wetting my face and my hands.

I looked down and saw that one of my trainers and the sock beneath had been torn off. The foot was perfectly ok though, it looked pristine. There was no blood and no pain.

It wasn't until afterward, when I was in the ambulance, that it occurred to me that I had not felt the fresh, chill rain on my foot.

SIXTEEN

It wasn't until I stopped shouting that I noticed Kik-Kik's good hand was on fire.

She'd emerged from the fog alone but smiling. I'd leaned from side to side several times trying to look past and around her, to see the rescuers behind, but the leaves and vines returned to their previous stillness in the curling fog.

"Where are the others?"

I tried to keep calm, but had already forgotten that she couldn't understand a word I was saying.

Kik-Kik laughed.

That's when I lost it. Screaming at her, waving my arms around, pointing at the sky, at the trees at my legs, it was only when I picked up a stone and prepared to wang it at her stupid, subnormal, stunted-flippered body that I saw the smoke rising up from her arm.

I hadn't seen it initially because of all the morning mist, but now she was closer I could see and smell the smoke. She was holding a closely packed ball of dry moss and twigs above which curls of smoke were drifting up from soot-blackened areas surrounded by glowing embers. Her palm was protected by a flat piece of bark, which stopped the transmission of heat to her flesh.

Kik-Kik had brought me fire.

I dropped the stone, exhausted from shouting. My throat burned on the screaming and the smoke from her fire. Kik-Kik didn't drop her smile once as she shrugged a creeper-woven ruckkie off her left shoulder and let it drop to the ground with a squelchy thud.

Then she put the burning bark on my dead legs. I made to push it away, but she shielded it with her good hand. Bent over, and blew gently on the dark heart of the ball of twiggy-moss. The orange embers glowed and more smoke came off into the air. It irritated my nostrils and I was forced into a massive sneezing fit. Kik-Kik thought this was hilarious. She mimed that I should bend forward and blow gently on the smouldering vegetation.

I blew and it glowed orange with heat.

Kik-Kik gave her stupid grin, got up and went to collect wood for a fire.

I could not understand why she hadn't brought anyone back with her. Not even one of her parents? Surely she wasn't alone out here in the wilderness like I was? No. She just couldn't have told anyone.

Why??????

Maybe she was a cannibal after all and was keeping me all to herself, and was laughing inside at the idea I was keeping the fire going she was going to roast me over later.

I pushed the unpleasant thought from my mind and tried again to wonder why she hadn't told anyone.

That glimpse of a documentary I'd seen Dad watching that time came flickering back in my memory. Maybe if she told her people about me they'd want to kill me like they did with all white strangers. Maybe they were scared of white strangers. Maybe they might think I was going to cut down their rainforest or drill for oil or something. Maybe her not telling them had saved my life.

I dunno.

Why wasn't Kik-Kik scared of me?

I looked up at Tree Face. A shadow from low hanging branches was covering his eyes so I couldn't really tell what he was thinking right now, or use his expression to give me any more ideas. Maybe like me, he didn't like being woken so early.

The smoke was starting to fade from the ball of embers so I blew on them again. The slow-burning materials glowed once more and a fresh column of choking smoke rose. I had to admit to it was a cool method to make fire portable. Hardly any twigs or dried mosses had burnt through in the few minutes Kik-Kik had been away. I reckon you could go many miles, even a couple of days with a set-up like this. I'd seen on those idiot survival programmes people tiring themselves out rubbing sticks or whizzing a whittled piece of doweling in another piece of wood, trying to make fire—they always looked properly knackered when they'd finished—this way, you only had to go through the rigmarole of rubbing sticks once every few days. Clever stuff.

I looked up from the fireball, and then quickly looked down again. Kik-Kik was squatted on the other side of the clearing having a long and protracted wazz. It wasn't so much the peeing that made me look away, but it was her smiling and waving as I made eye contact.

This really was another world.

I knew I'd have to attend to my own bladder and bowel functions at some point, but I wouldn't be doing it in front of Kik-Kik. You have to draw the line somewhere, don't you?

Kik-Kik went off again, adding to the pile of dry wood she was building.

I had to work out how I was going to get her to talk to someone about me. And then for them to not want to kill me.

I looked at my Rolex. It was just coming up to 7.15am.

Rolex...

The Rolex was worth a couple of grand. It was a serious watch. I'd seen James Bond wearing one in a film—I didn't mind those ones that Dad had showed me. At least they were in colour and there were modern ones to watch as well as the ones from the 18th century. I liked James Bond, and he'd been given this watch by Q (the guy who made all the gadgets) and it had been a computer and well as a bomb or something—the details didn't matter, what did matter it was a cool watch. Dad got it for me for my birthday. It wasn't a computer or a bomb but it was still a very cool thing. Waterproof, shockproof, self-winding, a heavy piece of gold on my wrist.

The thought occurred to me that I might be able to buy my way out of the jungle with it. Maybe if I got Kik-Kik to take it back to her village with the promise of a lot more money if they'd only send word to the outside world about me...?

The beginnings of a plan began to form in my mind—but

it would all depend on me communicating the idea to Kik-Kik.

Kik-Kik returned with her pile of wood, dumped it down, and began to build a fire.

Soon I could feel the warmth of it on my skin. Although the early-morning mist was clearing, the smoke from the fire was replacing it, hanging in the trees around us. There was no wind to blow it away, and for the first time in a long while, I was starting to feel dry. The heat from the fire was a welcoming warmth; perhaps it would spread its nourishing flingers through my brain and unlock some ideas about how I might be able to tell Kik-Kik to take the watch back to her village.

Maybe I could draw pictures.

With what?

On what?

In the earth with a twig or something? Maybe. The only thing I'd ever drawn in my life was a complete set of football kits for the teams in the top four English leagues. And most of that had just been colouring in a template. Would I be able to scrawl a cartoon in the dirt for a girl whose lift didn't go right to the top of the building in the first place?

Kik-Kik had the fire going nicely now and had a good high pile of sticks next to it for further fuel. I wondered if the fire would serve also to keep the most dangerous animals away, and maybe keep the mozzies off me too. I scratched at the back of my neck as Kik-Kik reached into her creeper-woven ruckkie, bringing out two pieces of fruit and the dead snake.

Oh great.

The snake's head had already been cut off and the belly gutted. The skin flapped where the head had been, and holding the tail of the snake between her feet and the neck in her mouth, Kik-Kik unzipped the flesh from the skin with one fluid movement. She spat the ick out of her mouth and then chucked the snake on the fire.

Her huge grin was back in an instant. She pointed at the snake, then at her mouth, then at me and then... weirdly at Tree Face.

I looked up at Tree Face. He didn't seem overly keen on the idea of eating snake either.

I smiled weakly.

I couldn't survive on fruit alone, and I'd heard that snake tasted like chicken, so I reckoned until I got back to civilisation, this beggar couldn't be a chooser.

The white meat singed and blackened at the edges in the fire. I could hear the fat in it sizzling and the smell that rose up, even though I knew it was snake, didn't really bother me that much. In fact, it was making my stomach rumble as it reached my nose.

Ok, I thought. I can do this. It's just meat. Only meat. I can do this.

Kik-Kik pulled the cooked snake off the fire and placed it on a large clutch of leaves she'd plucked from one of the low-lying bushes. She pulled the meat into three sections, picked up one piece, and held it in the flat of her hand.

She started saying something that was below even a whisper. There's no way I'd have a chance of making any of it out over the crackling of the fire, but it seemed to have a rhythm to it. As if it were a poem or... yeah... a prayer. It was like something she'd learned off by heart but didn't really care or understand the meaning of... like when they made us say the Lord's Prayer in school before assembly.

Kik-Kik stopped, got up, and went to Tree Face, she closed her eyes, said another two lines of whatever she was intoning then popped the warm, succulent meat into Tree Face's mouth.

Lucky sod I thought. I'm starving here.

It kind of made sense though. Tree Face might have been a god of her tribe or something, and this was an offering for a good harvest, or for rains (yeah, like the needed rain around here) or to heal the sick or fix her flipper arm. Whatever. I hoped it would be my turn next.

It was.

Kik-Kik came back to the leaf, picked up the next bit of cooked snakes in the palm of her hand, held it out towards me, and began to pray.

Kik-Kik finished praying and tried to pop some cooked snake in my mouth as she had with Tree Face. I was so stunned that I just let her do it. I didn't however begin to chew on the succulent meat for a few seconds while I tried to get my head around what had just happened.

Was Kik-Kik praying to me?

SEVENTEEN

A rush of thoughts filled my head straightaway. I imagined her going back to her village (I saw wigwams and half-naked people with feathers in their hair, like from some dumb black-and-white Western) and not telling anyone about me because of how special she thought I was. I saw her sneaking around, acting normal—well, normal for her—and preparing the snake while no one was looking, waiting until everyone was engaged in the other business of the tribe, grabbing the fruit, the bagged snake, and the portable-fire and coming back to me.

To pray to Tree Face and me.

Then the jumble of images became yesterday, and I felt swimmingly out of my body, as if I was watching what had happened from up above, and sometimes from Kik-Kik's eyes. There I was, sitting under Tree Face, with my lips red like his, face spattered with paint, then hauling myself up so she could compare our faces rather than her seeing that my legs didn't work. And then me being quite adamant that I'd come from the sky to land here.

I'd come from the sky.

Here.

To her.

With a face just like Tree Face.

Kik-Kik knelt in front of me again, bowed her head and said a prayer.

Kik-Kik thought I was a god. The God in the Tree.

Kik-Kik threw some more sticks on the fire and sat watching me for a good half an hour.

What could I say to her? What could I communicate to her that would get her simple savage brain to understand I wasn't a god? Is this going to be my life now?—sat here waiting to die while some idiot mong-wog brings me fruit and dead snake to eat?

I felt tiny. I felt like the life had been sucked out of me. I could feel Tree Face's gleeful eyes burning into the top of my head from above. I imagined his mouth in a joyous leer, loving it.

Kik-Kik reached into the bag, brought out some red berries, waved her hand over them, I guess telling me not to eat them, and then, taking up the two bowls I hadn't broken in my silly rage, that had last held paint and fruit. She got up and ran into the jungle.

Was that it?

Was I alone until morning?

I looked at my Rolex. It wasn't even mid-morning yet. The sun was still going up and up; the sky above was azure and cloudless. Through the canopy, the air was starting to hum with warmth and insects.

I took the chance to sort out my Ick Bag and void my bladder. I squeezed the waste out of the bag into a bush at the extremity of my reach, used a wet wipe to clean the mouth of it as best I could, and then reattached it to the flange. If I could do this a couple of times with each bag, maybe three times, then I might last eighteen or more days. After that, the bags would be lethally full of bacteria that I wouldn't be able to reattach to my side, and would kill me as sure as leaving the flange open to the elements. I didn't fancy dying in a slurry of my own waste, but until I could find a way to get out of this, that was exactly how my future looked.

I thumped my useless legs with frustration. If only one of them had worked, I might be able to crawl out of here. If only my dad hadn't been such an idiot driving so fast to get to somewhere he didn't want to go!

If only...

My world had reduced to a series of if onlys.

My world was like a clock running down. My world wasn't

like my watch, self-winding, my world was shrinking... like me.

I had another little cry, but wiped my eyes as I heard something moving through the trees.

It was Kik-Kik returning from the river, carrying one bowl in her good hand, and the other awkwardly in her flipper hand, using the wonky fingers to press it into her side. She seemed to be able to apply some pressure on the arm with her shoulder, and somehow lock it into place with a muscle in the top of her arm, but the look of concentration on her face was telling me it wasn't at all easy for her and some of the water had slopped down her belly and thigh.

One bowl she gave to me to drink—my first drink since yesterday! And the other she set about using to grind up the berries to make more paint.

There were a couple of dead flies floating on the surface of the water, and I picked them out like someone picking a fly out of a soup in a swanky restaurant. The water didn't taste like an expensive soup, it was sandy and tasted a bit like dirt. Bits got stuck in my teeth but it was the best I was going to get so I drank half of it down in a few gulps.

Kik-Kik seemed pleased. She held out her hand, bowed and prayed again to me.

Whether she was asking for something for herself or just wishing me well, I couldn't tell. I can tell you this though, I was getting totally weirded out by the idea of being the object of prayer.

I mean I never went to church or nothing, Dad and Mum didn't either. When they'd filled in forms for me for various things to do with my spinal injury applications for funding or whatever, I saw that they put my religion, such as it was as CofE. For all the notice I took of it, if you'd told me CofE stood for Chelsea of English (Premier League) I'd have believed you, as football was the closest thing I had to a religion, and I prayed at the altar of the game whenever I got the chance.

But God and stuff?

Nah, not my thing at all.

I suppose out here in the middle of nowhere, without education or running water gods and stuff were the common thing. That Kik-Kik had her own private tree god and now her own private living god shouldn't really have surprised me. She's out there where the buses don't run—of course she's going to believe in all that rubbish.

But it didn't matter how superior I felt to her right now, she had legs that worked, people in her village and a god to pray to who she believed might give her a non-flippity-flappity flipper arm.

That's when an idea so awesome popped into my head; I almost snorted snot out of my nose laughing at it.

Brilliant.

Kik-Kik looked up at me laughing. I wiped my nose as she smiled.

I beckoned Kik-Kik off her knees and motioned to her to come over. She sat down in front of me.

I pointed at her flipper.

Her eyes narrowed.

I reached out to it and stroked it.

Kik-Kik flinched it away from me. Perhaps out of the unfamiliar feeling of someone touching the twisted limb, or maybe out of shame. I knew exactly how she felt on that count, it was bad enough when people talked over my head as if I wasn't there, but it was even worse when they knelt, rubbed my still-as-stone knees, and looked at me with the cow-eyes of pity. I hated that.

I smiled.

Reached out and touched the flipper again.

This time Kik-Kik didn't flinch and tolerated my touch. The flipper was cold and stiff to the touch. The fingers gnarled and twisty coming out of the weirdly lumpy elbow. I looked at her to reassure her and I could see the distaste in her eyes. She wasn't enjoying this at all. I stroked the arm and then took my hand away and stroked my perfect arm. Then I repeated the process. Twice.

Kik-Kik's face calmed down and her eyes softened. Then I pointed at my arm, and then at hers.

Repeat.

She touched my arm, then hers, and nodded. Making the

connection. I pointed at the flipper, and then at her other arm and then at mine. Hoping that she understood that I, as her God, was promising her an arm just like mine.

Yes, I know that makes me a sleaze-bag for exploiting her beliefs, but what the hell was I going to do? If I didn't do something—I was going to be stuck here until I died.

She touched the flipper, her good arm, and my arm.

I smiled.

Then I took off my Rolex and gave it to her. She certainly didn't understand that.

I picked a stick from the kindling pile, cleared a space in the dirt, and drew a wigwam. I then took hold of her hand with the Rolex and moved it to the dirty drawing. I pointed at her, at the wigwam, at Kik-Kik and back.

Then I pointed at me, and the sky.

Her eyes narrowed.

I pointed at the wigwam, at the Rolex, me, the sky and finally her flipper and then my arm.

It looked like it was sinking in.

It looked like a smile of understanding was playing across her lips.

Kik-Kik nodded and leaped to her feet holding the Rolex.

I clapped with joy.

Yes! Yes! Bloody YESSSSSSSSSSSSSSSSSSSSSSSSSS!!!!!!!!!!!!!!!!!!!

She'd got it! Kik-Kik understood!

Kik-Kik went to Tree Face and posted the Rolex into his mouth.

The last I heard of the two grand watch was it clattering down inside Tree Face's hollow wooden stomach and Kik-Kik beginning to happily dance about rubbing her flipper, waiting for the magic to work.

EIGHTEEN

"You bloody bloody stinking effing bloody effing flipper-armed stupid NIGGER MONG!"

I'm not proud of the things I called Kik-Kik in those minutes after she fed the Rolex to Tree Face. When I calmed down, a lot later, after the battle on the river bank, the irony that I was just as disabled and in the context of the rainforest, just as stupid as Kik-Kik would appear if I dropped her at Tottenham Court Tube and told her to find her way to Stamford Bridge without a Scooby—but man. My watch!

I yanked myself up on the vines, my feet being flicked in all directions on the end of my useless legs. Once up to the level of Tree Face's mouth I knew I could easily hold my body weight on one hand, so gripped hard to the thick dreadlock with my right arm, and stuffed my left arm into Tree Face's wide-open leering gob.

My hand moved easily past the teeth. Inside the tree it was cool and damp as if the trunk of the tree was open to the elements someway further up and the rain and moisture from the jungle was managing to get inside. On a ledge was the back of the throat was something that felt like a bird's nest to my desperate searching hand. I pulled it out, hoping against hope that the Rolex was sitting in it—but I knew it wasn't to be. I'd heard the watch rattling down into the tree, but it didn't stop me pulling out the messily constructed nest, looking in it, and then flinging it and the three delicate eggs it contained behind me.

I reached down.

It seemed like the whole tree was hollow. I could get down way past the elbow but Tree Face's wooden teeth were jagging into the flesh of my arm, and my grip on the dreadlock, although still firm, was starting to show signs of weakening.

I was lucky I chose that moment to pull my arm out of the mouth to change position to see if I could reach any lower, because that's when the dreadlock broke and I slammed to the ground face first. If my arm had still been in Tree Face's mouth his teeth would have stripped the meat from my arm bones with the weight of my body.

I screamed my frustration and punched the tree hard, splitting the skin across two knuckles but I didn't care. I didn't care about my hand and I didn't care about Kik-Kik.

I began to drag myself away from the tree. Hand over hand. Pulling at vegetation, ripping up plants and bushes, twisting my shoulders like a swimmer in the water, dragging my useless legs behind me.

I went on and on, following, I hoped, the path through the jungle that I had made to get me here. I couldn't hear Kik-Kik following and that was fine by me; if I didn't see the idiot disabled prat ever again it would be too soon.

The ground was easier to move over in this direction than the one I'd taken getting here. It was slightly downhill, back (as I hoped it was) to the river. I figured if I was going to be rescued it would be better if I was down by the river; at least I could be seen from there, maybe make a sign in the sand that could be seen from the air.

I DIDN'T CARE

I just wanted to get away from the girl and her stupid bloody GOD.

I swam on and on like this through the jungle. Ignoring the encroaching exhaustion and the cramps that were starting to fire off in my muscles. I was getting away. That was the only thought in my mind. I was getting away from her and I was getting away from Tree Face.

Tree Face might have still been laughing. There were calls and noises in the jungle from the animals I was disturbing. Some of the calls sounded like snickering laughs, or their movements away from my desperate scramble sometimes sounded like a hissing snigger.

Some bushes exploded next to my face as I obviously disturbed something big and hairy sleeping in the middle of them. I only caught sight of the flank of the animal as it scarpered and I didn't even care if it had leaped out from the bush the other way and bitten my throat out.

I DIDN'T CARE

The jungle was thinning now and the ground was becoming waterlogged. Up ahead I could see the red waters of the river through the leaves. White waves that caught the sunlight, flashed through the trees. I redoubled my shuffling, yanking pulling trajectory. Using tree roots and creepers to pull me even faster down the slope.

The ground slithered beneath me, my breathing grew ragged and I could feel my heart beating louder and louder in my chest. It sounded like a road drill smashing through the concrete of my ribs. My eyes were blurry with tears and my brain sang with hate and frustration and misery and fear. I burst from the tree line and began hurtling down a much steeper part of the beach than I was expecting towards the river. I was about twenty metres upriver from the floating platform of branches that had dragged me all the way here. As I lost control of my momentum and began accelerating towards the water it was no consolation to realise that if I'd come ashore here at this spot, I probably wouldn't have made it into the jungle anyway, would never have met Tree Face, the idiot, or lost my Rolex.

In fact, this is exactly where I STARTED TO CARE!

I thrust my hands out in front of me, trying to slow my tumbling body down. On the steepening incline, all that did to my on-rushing momentum was jack-knife my useless legs over my head like pipe cleaners in a hurricane, flipping my body completely over.

I grabbed at anything I could on the bank, but it was completely smooth mud and sand, and even digging my hands into the surface of it did nothing to slow me. All that I could do was wait for me to slide all the way into this fast-flowing stretch of river and wait for the water to rise up over my head and drown me.

It would be a better end, I thought, than a lingering death in the jungle.

In the end, my useless legs saved me.

Because there was no tension in them, and they were flying loose, they rucked up underneath me like folds in a mat on a shiny floor. Under normal circumstance that manoeuvre would throw you off your feet and into a head cracking fall to the polished floor.

But here, the rucking and painless folding up under my backside, knees splaying out and trainered feet digging in, proved to be a much better brake than either of my hands.

I slithered to a halt half a metre from the water's edge.

The sun was fully up now, bright and killingly hot. I felt it burning my face and drying the moisture of the jungle off my clothes and exposed skin. The river was noisy and flowing faster than it had been when I'd been deposited here; if I'd gone in the waves at the speed I'd started falling towards them, I would have been dragged away from the beach quite easily. I know I'm a pretty strong swimmer, but the current right now looked treacherous.

I breathed hard, rubbed my eyes.

I would have to turn myself back over if I was going to get back up the bank. That shouldn't be too hard, I reckoned, but craning my neck back up the way I came, I realised that I was now in a hollow. A little cove with steep banks on three sides. I might be able to make it back up to the tree line, but it was going to be a struggle.

I looked at the water, and downstream to the rough platform of boughs and branches stuck in the bend in the river. It looked stuck fast in the bank and wasn't going anywhere at all.

Crazy idea…

What if I slipped into the river water, and let the current carry me down to the collection of branches? It would only take a few seconds, I was a strong enough swimmer to at least give my body a good chance of staying on the right course because I wouldn't be fighting the current. It would bring me back to a flatter, less precarious section of riverbank.

A better place to create some kind of message in the sand that might be seen from the air.

Ok.

Worth a shot. Nothing was going to happen to get me out of here unless I did it myself.

I reached down, unfolded my slightly less-useless legs from underneath me, and pushed myself into the water.

NINETEEN

Cold and wet. Rain falling on my face. Going into my eyes. Not having the coordination to wipe it away. Lights in the distance. Screeching brakes. The moon through the clouds.

Dad.

"Sam! Sam! Oh Christ! Sam!"

It was a good job other cars had stopped and someone sensible got out to persuade Dad that pulling me from the wreckage of the car might not be a good idea. Someone removed the keys from the ignition because the smell of petrol, mixed in with wet mud and heated metal, was getting stronger. Someone else held a coat above me so that the rain was at least off my face.

I couldn't see Dad, but he knelt next to me holding my hand telling me he was sorry and he was gutted and he wanted me to be all right.

I didn't feel injured. That was the weird thing. The car was completely destroyed. I suppose that was the point; they're designed to crumble and break up to dissipate the energy of the crash before it has a chance to jellify the occupants. But I really would have expected to feel the pain associated with doing a full nine-hundred-and-eighty-degree barrel-roll along the Armco, surrounded by bursting airbags and exploding glass, but weirdly I felt ok.

Trapped by okay.

I squeezed Dad's hand to reassure him

Dad moved into my field of vision. He on the other hand was a mess. The tumble from the car at high speed had ripped his clothes and his hair was all over the place. There was a small trickle of blood from his nose, and his knuckles on one hand had been scraped raw. There was a cut on Dad's shoulder bleeding hard onto what was left of his tee-shirt. I couldn't see the rest of him, but at least he'd run or walked here under his own steam and he wasn't unconscious, upside down in a ditch.

I could hear people in the background talking on phones. I think even at one point there was a flash of a camera phone until someone angrily told someone else in no uncertain terms to sod the eff off.

Dad stayed with me as the sirens approached. I saw blue lights flashing in the rain, high above where the wreckage of the car had landed.

I held Dad's hand as long as I could to keep him calm, until the firefighters and the paramedics slithered down the side of the steep bank of the ditch to reach me. Dad was taken off to be checked over, but really, I think just to get him out of the way while the white-helmeted lead firefighter discussed with the paramedics the best way to stabilise me before they could cut me out of the car.

The paramedic was called Judy, and she was calm and kind and smelled of coffee and garlic. She apologised for her breath—she'd just had pizza on her break or something. I smiled. "It's cool," I said. "I love pizza."

Judy promised me some when we got back to the hospital.

"But I feel okay," I said. "I just can't get out. I think my legs are trapped. But I don't feel injured."

Judy just smiled and carried on putting lines for fluid and whatever into my arm and the back of my hand. "Better to be safe than sorry," she said. "And besides. The pizza there is stupendous."

I didn't find out she was lying to me until much later. The pizza at the hospital was horrible.

The firefighters and Judy carried on their work, calmly and professionally, until I was freed from the wreckage. I felt a bit woozy and dislocated. Perhaps Judy had given me a sedative or a painkiller. I felt warm and snug and as they strapped me into a stretcher to lift me back up the bank to the waiting ambulance, I could have easily dropped off to sleep.

I was still in no pain and just assumed, like when you haven't exercised for a while, the pain would come tomorrow. I remember the first time I used the rowing machine in Dad's gym back at the house. I felt fine while I was doing it; fine, but exhausted after it; but it wasn't until the next morning that I began to suffer for it. My muscles all stiff and my legs quick to cramp.

Blimey, I missed those days sometimes. The days that my legs could cramp.

But back then, I figured I was probably in shock—not that I really knew what in shock meant—it was just something actors said on TV when someone had been in a traumatic situation— and that tomorrow, the pain would be all over my body and I'd be experiencing delayed suffering or something.

Didn't know how wrong I could be, did I? I never felt pain in my legs again.

Dad met us as the firefighters brought me in stretcher, stumbling and climbing, back onto the road. The ditch had been much deeper than I thought and they'd had a struggle to get me back up. Their heavy boots caked in mud, hands thick with dirt.

I smiled at Dad in my drowsiness and Judy was there too, putting her cool dry, pizza-smelling hand on my forehead, smiling. "Let's get you that pizza. Four seasons or meat-feast?"

The night in A&E was a blur of lights, faces, CT scans, MRI scans, drugs, being prodded and pulled about. Doctors who didn't introduce themselves who were stifling yawns like they'd been awake all their lives, and stumpy HCAs in grey uniforms being bossed around by Staff Nurses in blue.

I was taken to a room stuffed with equipment and everyone had a go at finding out what was going on inside me.

Sometimes they talked in whispers I couldn't hear, and other times they would lead each other away to look at charts and readouts and X-rays.

I saw them talking to Dad at one point and Dad looking like he'd had all the breath sucked out of him.

Mum arrived like a blast of chill air from a freshly opened freezer.

She was just in her trackie, with her hair clawed back into a simple ponytail. This was clearly a woman who had travelled here in a rush. She hadn't even touched up her makeup. This was serious.

Mum ignored Dad, and after squeezing my hand and kissing my forehead, she started complaining loudly about the bloody NHS and how she wanted me moved to a private hospital, where I could be looked after by professionals.

The lead doctor, a grey-haired bloke with a red stethoscope and bug-eyed glasses everyone called "Daniel" or "Doc" explained to Mum that they were professionals. He told her he wouldn't be releasing me from here until he was certain of the extent of my injuries, and that after that she'd be welcome to transfer me to Caracas General if that's what she wanted. But if she didn't stop insulting the staff of this fine teaching hospital he'd have her thrown out into the car park.

I think I heard one of the HCAs start to applaud before she was side-eyed by a staff nurse and Mum shut up.

Dad hung back and Mum stood at the end of the bed while the staff did their monitoring and testing.

Something came back to me from what Doc Daniel had said. "Extent of his injuries." That was the weird thing. I still didn't feel injured. I could see. I could hear. I could feel my shoulders and my chest moving as I breathed. If I concentrated hard enough I could hear my heart beating, and I was sure my stomach was rumbling because I was so hungry and had been specifically promised pizza by Judy.

My elbows moved and I tested each one of my fingers on both hands against my thumb, digging the nail into the soft pad just to make sure.

What craziness was this?

Extent of my injuries.

I finished my exam of myself by clicking my heels together like Dorothy in that idiotic wizard-and-dwarf movie with the Tin Man and whatever. There's no place like...

Except.

My heels didn't click together.

I tried again. Harder.

Nothing.

I lifted my knee. My knee didn't lift.

Tried the other knee.

Same.

A cold feeling washed into my guts. I felt again the rain falling on my face and hands, but making no impression on my feet. I remembered the firefighter removing me from the wreckage of the car, but not having to cut me free.

If they didn't need to cut me free, why hadn't I got out of the wreckage myself? Why had I just laid there? Why did I assume I was trapped?

"I said Sam, did you feel that?"

I snapped back to the hospital room. Mum had been moved back and there was a new doctor. An Indian woman, whose badge I could clearly see said "Dr. Shah, Spinal Injuries SHO."

"What?" I said.

"Can you feel this?"

I looked down my body. Dr. Shah was sticking a thin pointy piece of metal into my thigh. I could see the skin depressing. I could see the look of expectation in Dr. Shah's face.

And no.

I couldn't feel it.

TWENTY

The current took my useless legs and easily dragged the rest of my body out of the shallows and into the flow. Taking a deep breath to provide extra buoyancy I used my arms to twist me around and started to travel headfirst towards the tangle of branches dug into the bank up ahead.

I'd calmed down mostly now I had something to concentrate on. With focus and purpose my mind didn't need to wander, or to waste time hating on Kik-Kik or Tree Face—the Rolex could be rescued later with a chain saw. I had to deal with getting myself rescued first.

It was good to be off the jungle floor too, to be floating. Swimming was the greatest feeling next to flying that I'd known since the accident. When you're stuck to the floor, or to a wheelchair, just spending a few minutes in the swimming pool felt like coming alive after being dead—and as my arm muscles grew in strength so did my ability in the water. I might not be any good on the football pitch any more but I could hold my own in muck about swimming races with friends.

Even Jen came to cheer me on…

Anyway, back to the matter in hand. I was building up speed in the swirling wave broken red water of the river. It tasted fresh enough even though it was coloured like rusty blood by the earth in this part of the Amazon. It was gritty in my mouth, but the mad scramble away from Tree Face and the blinding sunlight now I was free of the jungle were adding to the sense of exhaustion and thirst.

The platform of branches reached its gnarled limbs up a good two metres out of the water. The bark near the surface of the river was black and slick with moisture, but higher up the wood was drying to a dusty grey and the leaves, which had been green and fresh a couple of days ago were browning and shrivelling. If you weren't brilliantly good at being alive in the rainforest, you were very easily dead.

I held out my hands and let the current take me. The platform was rushing closer and I was going to hit it at some speed. I didn't really want a twig spearing me in the eye as I washed into the tangles. I'd lost enough crashing in the jungle; I could seriously do without any more injuries.

The branches were springy and giving as I rammed into them on the fast-flowing current. I was embedded in the raft of trees a metre or so, and the water built up a hissing vortex of white-headed turbulence around me now that I was going with the flow.

I'd travelled in a hot air balloon once with Dad before the accident, and when you're up at a thousand feet, even on a windy day, being in the basket below a balloon is the most serene feeling of movement you can ever imagine. When you're moving with the wind, at the same speed as it moves, you can hardly feel a breath of the breeze on your skin. Thudding into the branches just then was exactly like the thump of a hot air balloon coming into land—the sudden stop and the realisation that the world was moving much faster around you than you're expected.

I was about three metres from the bank, and there were a tangle of branches in the way that I'd have to pull myself through or around. If I'd left it longer before holding up my hands for impact, I might have been able to steer myself closer to the bank, but it was what it was.

First part of the mission was accomplished.

Not that I had that much of a plan. Especially as it occurred to me that I hadn't brought my ruckkie or Ick Bags with me, so at some point I was going to have to go back to Tree Face and possibly Kik-Kik to retrieve them. I really did feel like being on the beach made me more findable by the rescue services—once anyone noticed that the Cherokee hadn't returned to its base.

I parted the wet branches in front of me and tried to see if there was a route through. It didn't look too bad. There may have been once branch that I would have to pull my useless legs over, but it seemed clear of surface snags.

I thought about having a look under the water to see what barriers there were to my progress but it would have been a total waste. The water was cloudier than tomato soup, so I'd just have to travel hopefully I guess.

That was one of Dad's old sayings. "It's better to travel hopefully than arrive." I didn't really understand what it meant until I crashed a plane in the jungle and made the last-second decision that had killed him, but now I reckoned I'd got a handle on it, because I totally felt it had been better travelling here than arriving.

I began to pull my body forward, dragging thin twigs and thicker branches out of the way and shrugging off the power of the current as it bit into my side.

I travelled about a metre before my foot snagged on a branch below the surface embedded in the riverbed. I tried to yank it free just by twisting my shoulders and pulling with my arms, but I was going to have to reach down.

Holding onto a branch over my head thick enough for me to encircle with my hand, I slipped down the length of it to where it elbow-dipped into the water. However wet my palm became I wouldn't easily be dislodged.

I reached down into the water, running my hand down the leg that felt snagged. It was well stretched out behind me and my leg was stuck solid.

Great.

I reached down further, my hand holding the branch slipping nearer to the water, my face getting closer to the waves.

I thought about calling out for help. Maybe Kik-Kik had followed my mad slide from the jungle. I scanned the blazing-hot shore, baking in the relentless sun. I couldn't see her through the branches. Maybe she'd stayed with her other God, or buggered off back to her bloody wigwams. Whatever, she wasn't in sight, and calling out would probably just alert something hungry to my distress.

Something rough and cold slid along the length of my hand.

I flinched it out of the water and pulled myself up as high as I could go with the snagged leg.

Had it been an animal?

A fish?

Did they have piranha in South America? In the Amazon?

I'd seen a movie about them once. It wasn't a bad one really. Dad had showed me on late night telly. A horror movie. I remember them saying that a flock (I think they said flock) of piranha could strip a fully-grown cow down to its bones in ten minutes or something. If there were piranhas feeding on my dead legs I wouldn't feel them until they had eaten their way up past my pelvis.

I shuddered.

More than likely it had been a stick or some vegetation tumbling down the river and crashing into my hand.

I swallowed.

I couldn't stay here. I was too vulnerable. I had to free my leg, so I started reaching back down my body again.

I got past my knee, and then halfway down my shin before finding what it was that was snagging my foot. My other hand was again at the surface of the water on the branch and I was going to have to stick my head under the waves if I was going to go any lower.

There was nothing for it. I took a huge breath, dipped my head under the water, into the murky red, and let my gripping hand slide under the waves down the branch.

I got to my ankle and found that there was something encircling my foot, but it wasn't a branch. It felt like... felt like fabric.

I got my fingers through the loop and unhooked my foot, being careful not to let go of whatever had been holding me back. My lungs were burning, wanting my next breath, but I couldn't let go of whatever this was. What if it were something from Cherokee? Something that I could use...

I hefted the fabric strap up and my foot came free in the rushing water. I brought my head out of the water and took a huge breath. My chest heaving and my eyes smarting with the gritty water.

I was still holding whatever the fabric loop was, as I dragged it up past my body so that it broke surface.

It was a large nylon holdall. One you might fill with clothes or whatever to store in the hold of the Cherokee. It wasn't my bag and I don't remember Dad having one like it, but the chances of it not coming from the light aircraft were very slim indeed.

I would have spent more time examining the outside of the bag, but that's when the dinosaur, all pink mouth and huge white dagger teeth, decided to bite my head off.

TWENTY-ONE

The alligator burst through the surface of the water, hissing like an over-boiling kettle and turning the surface of the water white. The splash shocked me more than the gaping jaws, as I had to wait for the water to clear from my eyes before the chill breath of the reptile rushed over my face.

If the alligator hadn't misjudged its attack and not smashed into the branch I'd been using to hold on to while I retrieved the holdall, then it would have torn off my head off at the neck and left me floating in a pool of my own disappointment.

The jaws worked at the branch, ripping off the bark, I let go of it—obviously—which had the effect of dropping me lower in the water. I was looking up at the head of the creature, its scaly bulging yellow-striped throat heaving, its claws thrashing. I pushed myself back, but a branch behind me, shifted by the force of the alligator's attack, hemmed me in.

The alligator was in a proper frenzy, shaking its head from side to side. It was trying to push itself back, its eyes whirling in their sockets, water blown in clouds of spray out of its nostrils, but like me, it was held by some of the shifted tree behind. It was wedged in a thick V between tree trunks. I suppose it hadn't thought about making a plan when it leaped at me from beneath river water, and its excitement at there being a nice easy kill had taken priority over navigation.

The whole platform of branches was shaking as the alligator writhed. The teeth, white and dagger sharp, were crunching into the surface of the branch between its jaws at a steady rate of destruction. I could see that even now the branch would either be bitten clean through or break away with the ferocity of the alligator's attack.

I had to get away.

If I went under the water, I wouldn't be able to see a thing in the red cloudiness—which was even more turbulent now the alligator was thrashing madly in it. If I misjudged my route, I might get a claw across the face or get gutted by its hind legs or knocked unconscious by its tail, left floating in the water to drown, or immobile until the alligator got free just waiting there, like a McDonald's in a brown paper bag.

The alligator was big. Well, it was the biggest alligator I'd ever seen in real life, so I didn't know if it was an average-sized specimen or anything, but it looked way big enough to eat me with just a few mouthfuls. I might have thought it was way cool if I was looking at it through the safety glass of a zoo, or on a TV, but up close this thing was terrifying. All black scales, yellow stripes, and hissing jaws.

The branch it was biting into was crumbling, and wouldn't take more than a few seconds to fall in half. That would give the beast free passage towards me. There's no way it was going to worry about not going backward when it knew it was going to get to its dinner in a matter of seconds.

I reached up towards a branch, gripping it, trying to bring myself higher in the water. The branch was thick but it was loose at one end. It came free in my hand and I was no better off. In my frustration, I made to throw the useless branch aside, and then I saw the end of it. It was splintered and sharp. Could it be used as a weapon?

I stabbed at the alligator with it right in the face, aiming for the eyes.

The branch bounced off the alligator's nose as the rushing currents of the river destabilised me. I stabbed again.

This time the branch broke into two pieces and the alligator redoubled its efforts to bite through the wood jammed in its jaws. One bit of my attack branch was caught by the current and whisked away. The other I threw into the alligator's mouth where it served as another wedge between jaws.

It slowed the alligator's forward progress a little, but only by a few seconds. The teeth were relentless and the creature didn't look like it was going off the idea of ripping me into tattered red shreds of cripple boy.

I tried pulling at more branches to use as better weapons but they were all stuck fast. I pushed myself back, but the solid wall of broken tree behind me was going nowhere. I could go back out into the open river, but the currents were so strong I would be whisked away and drowned for sure.

Why hadn't I stayed with Tree Face and Kik-Kik?

If I could have controlled my temper, not cared about the bloody watch, I wouldn't be in this sodding predicament now.

It had been the same since the accident, since losing my ability to walk. I got angry much quicker. I was more stubborn, more argumentative. Especially with Dad, or when I went to stay with Mum in her new place. It was like I couldn't stand the idea of everyone else having legs and me not.

I wish I'd thumped Escobar now, back at the ranch in the hills.

I wish I pushed that smug arsehole's nose right back into his face.

He bloody deserved it…

The alligator, however, was a more pressing problem and there was no way that I was going to be pushing his nose anywhere. The attack branch slipped from the side of its mouth and it went back to sawing through the branch it couldn't shift. Splinters went up everywhere, as if a chain saw was cutting through the wood. Teeth slashed and crunched. The yellow neck inflated and deflated as the huge reptile breathed and shipped water.

I had no more dice to roll.

Either I risked downing or I waited for the animal to get through the tree branch and eat me.

The holdall.

It was big, black, and hefty. Perhaps I could use it in some way? Stuff it into the alligator's mouth and hook its legs through the handles. Something. Anything.

Who was I kidding?

This wasn't a Road Runner cartoon.

I didn't have a stupid ACME bag of tricks to catch the stupid bird like stupid Wile E. Coyote in those stupid cartoons. I was dreaming if I thought I had the dexterity, speed, strength, and ability to tie the alligator up in the bag. I might as well have prayed for the paint and brushes to draw myself an escape route on the air and run off down it. In this situation, I was Wile E. Coyote (see how stupid the name is?) and he was the one who always lost, right? The one with all the speed and the aggression and the ability to outsmart me was the alligator. I couldn't be the Road Runner.

For a start, I didn't have the legs for it.

The branch broke.

The alligator surged forward.

I pulled the holdall up and shoved it between me and the jaws.

The material wasn't going to last long and if the alligator kept pushing forward, it wouldn't need to kill me. I could feel a splintered piece of branch digging into my back from the force of the alligator's thrust. Much more of this and I was going to be impaled.

The alligator bit into the holdall, its teeth ripping into the material. The bag was waterlogged and jets of water spurted out as the alligator pressed against it and squeezed it with its claws.

I was holding the back of the bag as best I could, but it was hopeless.

The animal was biting and the zips were bursting. The bag was big and unwieldy, but it was no thick Amazon branch. It was going crazy now, sensing that it was close to the kill, its little yellow eyes filled with the fervour of the hunt, the blasts of excited air from its nostrils, the hiss from its cavernous throat.

Now was the time to make the decision.

Now it was time to decide to die here, or in the river.

In the end, it was no decision, was it? At least drowning might be serene and relatively painless. Being torn apart by a wild animal?

Not so much.

I let go of the bag, letting myself go to the current, hoping it would just carry me away.

The branch in my back had snagged deep onto my tee-shirt.

I could feel the current pulling me, but the tee-shirt was

betraying me. I couldn't sink lower into the water, and the current was no longer able to carry me away.

The alligator seemed to pick up on my sheer sense of defeat. It knew its next meal was just hanging there waiting. All it had to do was get the bag out of its mouth and I would be there. Like a side of pork hanging up in a slaughterhouse.

The alligator bit down one last time on the raggedy bag.

The side of the bag blew out on an explosion of white powder with a loud metal-rending crack that set my teeth on edge.

The alligator, dead, its face blown off in a tangle of bloody froth and ragged flesh, rolled back in the water, surrounded by a spreading pile of one hundred dollar bills.

TWENTY-TWO

Anyway, all the cracks that were in my parents' relationship before the accident, which knitted together for a while with the shared goal of getting me out of hospital and supporting me on the road to recovery, started to widen again after about six months.

Once I was back home, was getting regular visits from the physio-terrorist (I called her that because she was terrifying and held me hostage for an hour five times a week). And when all the alterations to our house were completed, the alterations to make it easier for me to get washed, dressed, exercised, rested, and fed with the minimum of fuss and the maximum amount of independence, they only had themselves to focus on again.

I could get myself into and out of bed. That was easy. I had a trapeze above me that I could hold onto to swivel my useless legs back and forth into the wheelchair. With a bit of struggling I could get pants and tracksuit bottoms on and change my Ick Bag from a set of supplies kept in a drawer-unit next to the bed. The bed itself was an all-singing, all-dancing, motorised up-down thing with a remote control for moving the various sections about and lifting the foot or the head of the bed to suit.

I had a 4K screen over the bed on another actuated motor-arm, so that I could look at it lying down, or sitting up, changing the angle for films, TV or gaming. The screen also doubled as a mirror for my PC screen for browsing, Facebook, and chatting. There was a webcam integral to the TV too. Dad said it cost the same price as a war between two African dictatorships. Wasn't sure what he meant, but it sounded expensive.

A section of the bedroom had been fitted out with a low-level marble-topped kitchen counter, with a small fridge, microwave, store cupboard, and kettle, so that I could still make myself drinks or heat food up when Dad or Mum weren't around.

It was like having my own self-contained flat.

It was a couple of months before I was strong enough go back to school, so along with the physio-terrorist, I had a tutor come in to keep me up to date and keep me busy. I didn't mind the schoolwork to be honest—I'm not exactly the big-brain around town, but I did like to keep busy now that I couldn't just pick up a football and go out for a kick-about with my mates.

When I wasn't being tutored or terrorised, I got bored really quickly. There's only so much you can take of being trapped in the house with no one to take you out. I mean yeah, I could go out in the garden and that, but the house was in large grounds in Finchley where all the kids were at school all day, and the only place to go in the wheelchair was the shopping centre, and doing that on your own was no-fun-city Arizona.

So I was stuck at home most of the day. Dad was working long hours at the office building his Property Empire, and Mum, who got bored as easily as me, went out. She told me she was going places and that I was welcome to come with her, but as most of them seemed to consist of her going around to some other rich woman's house to have coffee and chat, I really didn't fancy the idea. I mean, there's also a limit to how much to can take the cow-eyed-pity stare. Even when you were feeling nothing but self-pity for yourself.

I did my crying on my own. Made sure no one could hear me, stuffed my face in the pillow, made it wet with sobbing.

A couple of times I searched for "painless methods of suicide" on the internet.

Yes, it did get that bad in the first few months—I'm not ashamed to say that I contemplated the idea of checking out. Usually about three-thirty in the morning when I'd been up all hours, riding waves of bitter insomnia. Bitter that my life was over at fifteen. Bitter that my friends were too embarrassed to come and see me.

Bitter about Jen...

It was school, weirdly, that turned my mood around. When

the necessary arrangements had been made and I was strong enough to last the day away from home, Dad arranged for me to be taken to and from school in a wheelchair taxi. The taxi would open at the back and I could just be wheeled in and locked into place in my chair. No buggering about getting in and out of normal car seats and collapsing my wheelchair—that would mean someone would have to be available to reduce my levels of independence. The wheelchair taxi felt just like me getting myself to school almost under my own stream.

School, to begin with, was exciting.

Everyone, now they saw that I wasn't disfigured or gone mental and was basically a normal kid in a wheelchair, flocked around to ask me questions, and push me about and generally take a bit of interest.

Of course, this had only lasted just a few weeks. Once the realisation that hanging with me, while a football went begging, or there was smoking to do 'round the back of the language lab, where the path was too narrow or uneven for a wheelchair, or there were girls and boys to chat up when having a Dalek around might cramp your style, my days started to become less exciting. So I made myself enjoy the schoolwork. It had been a while since I'd wanted to engage my brain before my feet, and I was surprised at how much better it made me feel.

I might have been an idea to read some books about the wildlife of the Amazon, but you can't have everything.

So, yeah, my parents.

I was more self-sufficient so that made their problems bob to the surface again. There would be rows. There would be things thrown that I heard smashing from my rooms. There would be Mum crying and Dad shouting and there would be Mum spending more and more of her days out, and Dad throwing himself into work, and travelling here there and everywhere, spending weeks overseas, trying to set up some property deals in South America.

Mum hated the time that Dad was away on business, not because he wasn't around—she hated the sight of him by then— but because it meant she couldn't live her own life, because I couldn't be left.

I mean she never said it in those terms, but I could see the way she deflated when she looked at me. It wasn't the pity look of the cow-eyed; it was more the trapped eyes of the zoo animal.

This destabilised me a lot.

I started getting tearful again in the middle of the night.

One night I must have cried so hard that Mum had heard me. I heard her outside the door hovering, but she didn't come in.

After that, I didn't cry. Not out loud anyway.

I just kept it inside. I didn't want to risk her not coming in again.

Mum left eight months after I came home from hospital.

She didn't leave a note or tell me she was going. It was a Sunday, and Dad was due back from South America that evening. I heard Mum leave and it was only afterward that I guessed the sound of dragging I heard on the drive was her getting a fully packed suitcase into her car.

Dad came back on time, and it was good that his flight hadn't been delayed otherwise I'd have been stuck here on my own for God knows how long. He dumped his bags in the hall, came into my room, and told me that Mum had left and that I'd need to start coming with him on business trips from now on.

I blinked a bit.

My mouth went dry.

The complete matter-of-factness of it blew me out of the water. It was just as if someone had flicked a switch in his head. I suppose the marriage had been over a long time before tonight, but I couldn't believe how calm and how... professional he'd been about it. There was no discussion. No attempt to break it to me gently, or shield me from any more grief being piled on top of the grief I'd already been dealing with over the last ten months.

Dad got up from the bed and headed for the door without another word, and then stopped. He reached into his pocket and pulled out some sheets of paper and a small pamphlet. He scratched his head as if he was just remembering something important, and turned back. Threw the papers on the bed and said, "Start filling those in, will you. I'll get us a curry ordered."

I picked up the paper and the pamphlet, one was a complicated-looking form and the other had a Piper Cherokee on the front.

"What are they?" I asked.

"One's an application for a pilot's licence."

"And the other one?"

"That's a picture of the plane I've just bought you."

TWENTY-THREE

I actually started collecting handfuls of sopping wet hundred dollar bills before I realised what I should be doing is getting out of the water. Most of them were stained pink with alligator blood, but it still took a few seconds for me to shake my head clear of the automatic desire to pick up money. It dawned on me that if there was one alligator around here, there might be others, and I was floating in an inviting wash of delicious blood and tasty flesh.

I put the loops of the holdall over my shoulder and dragged myself past the carcass of the now even uglier alligator. Its body was rough and scaly against my skin. To get out between the branches I had to haul most of my body clear of the river and roll over its lumpy, dinosaur back. Halfway across its stiff spine, the tail moved and my heart stopped. It flicked and curled with a ripple of skin and muscle. I was on the creature's back. How unlucky was my day going to be? Was it still alive? Was it like the headless chicken that kept running around for a minute or so after it met the slaughterman's axe? Or was it still firing primitive impulses from the ruin of its prehistoric brain? Still searching for the unthinking, automatic kill? Like me when I hadn't thought about my own safety and instead had reached for the money?

It was the river current.

The tail flopped this way and that on the rising waves. Water slopped at the side of it and when the wave was big enough, broke over it. Now I could see the alligator was over three metres in length. I still had no idea if that was a big one or not, but it still sent a shiver through my guts.

I slid off the alligator back under the waves on the other side of it, pulling myself through the water on the branches of the platform. About a metre out from the bank, my hands could reach down to the squelchy riverbed and the buoyancy of the water on my body started to dissipate.

The bag was weighing me down.

I unhooked it and threw it as hard as I could towards the bank. It went through the air dripping a curtain of river water and a long puff of white powder from the jagged hole that had been torn in the side by whatever had exploded.

It occurred to me that perhaps it had been the alligator's head that had exploded before the bag. That the hole in the bag had been caused by a high-velocity rifle round fired from a rescuer trying to save my life.

Maybe I was being saved!

I scrambled to the bank, hauled myself out of the water as I had just a couple of days before, and looked around as best I could, pushing myself up on my hands.

I figured that in all the mad flailing rush away from Kik-Kik and Tree Face plus the fight with Jurassic Park I might not have heard a rescue helicopter, or a bunch of marines out looking for me.

Maybe I was just waiting for them to come out of the jungle, wave at me with big white grins and let me shake the hand of the sniper who had taken out the alligator.

Nothing happened.

I was alone on the beach, a dead alligator behind, and a holdall that had exploded in front of me.

Ok.

What do I do?

I had no supplies, no Ick Bags, no weapons, and no way of making a fire to signal to anyone flying overhead.

I was in a slightly worse position than I was back when I was with Tree Face and Flipper Girl.

The sun was drying me and the muddy sand was warm beneath me. Could I risk a little sleep out here to take the edge off my exhaustion?

No.

I began moving up the beach to the relative safety of the tree line, dragging the holdall with me one body-heave at a time.

Once in the trees, a few metres from the edge of the jungle, I looked back down on the platform. The alligator as bobbing gently on the waves, caught fast by the branches in which it was wedged.

I didn't know if you could eat alligator, but seeing as Kik-Kik had fed me snake, it was a reasonable bet that you could. There was a lot of meat down there that would keep me going for a few days at least before it went off. It seemed silly to waste it and leave it for other alligators and the animals of the forest.

There's no way I'd be able to retrieve the carcass, I'd have to rely on Kik-Kik. Not entirely sure how I was going to make that happen. Her god had gone off in a huff, screaming like a girl, I may have done massive harm to my reputation in that direction.

Screaming like a girl.

Yeah. The one girl I'd met around here hadn't done any screaming. Even with a flipper hand, she'd killed a snake, made fire, brought me food, and cooked it for me. I may have to reconsider the phrase "Screaming like a girl," in the future. Maybe change it to "Screaming like a Sam Coker who's lost his watch."

Ok.

The bag.

Yes, I had been putting off looking in there. Don't ask me why. My dad didn't normally carry hundred dollars bills, explosives, or white powder around with him. I was no expert, but I didn't think the white powder was going to turn out to be duty-free talc he was going to be taking home as a present for Grandma Coker.

I set all thoughts of the white powder aside for a moment.

I looked into the hole ripped in the side of the bag by the explosion. It had definitely blown out from the inside. There were burnt hundreds, ripped apart that looked like they'd been in a tight bundle before they'd got drenched in the crash, in the centre of the hundreds was a bag of powder that had ripped open in the explosion. On the outside, it was covered in brown packing tape, and on the inside, there looked to be layer upon layer of cling-film protecting the powder.

The powder had solidified where the water had got to it, but there were cracks in that dry plug that told me I wouldn't need to pick at it too hard to get at the fresh stuff behind.

Past the money and the powder was a black, fist-sized piece of metal, torn, jagged. The whole side of it had been ripped open by an explosion that looked like it had emanated from the piece of metal itself.

It was a black, semi-automatic pistol that had been blown apart. The handle was destroyed, and there was a tangled mess of steel and plastic where the magazine had been. The barrel of the gun had been opened up as if someone had been with it with a chisel and a lump-hammer.

I was no expert but it looked like the gun had got wet, the alligator had bit down on it, then triggered a bullet which then exploded in the breech, setting off the other bullets in the magazine and having the winning argument with the alligator's face.

Face.

Tree Face.

Maybe Kik-Kik's praying to her god had done something after all, eh? It might not have fixed her flipper but it had properly saved my neck.

I shook my head, and told myself to stop being a total melt.

This had nothing to do with Tree Face or the Flipper Girl.

I thought about undoing the zip and having a proper rootle in the bag but I was genuinely scared of what I might find in there. This wasn't my bag, and if it had been stowed in the plane at Carlos's place then either my dad knew about it, and he was in on it, or he didn't. If he didn't then Carlos was just waiting for us to go through customs, for the bag to be opened and the sweaty, trigger-happy guards to have marched us away, snapping their rubber gloves to their wrists.

Either way, this wasn't good, and if I'd seen this much of the bag, Tree Face knows what I'm going to find in the rest of it.

I noticed my breathing then.

It was hard and it was ragged. I was getting myself worked up with anxiety, and I needed to remain calm and level headed if I was going to make some plans, and try to use what I had to get me out of here.

Something touched me on the shoulder, and screaming like a Sam Coker, I turned my head and fell backward from the tree that I was using to wedge myself into a sitting position.

Kik-Kik was there, on her knees, holding out a bowl of fruit, praying.

TWENTY-FOUR

Kik-Kik dragged me back to Tree Face. Then she went back and brought me the holdall, and then she went back again, returning with armfuls of alligator meat, which she cooked over the fire.

Kik-Kik had propped me back between the roots that may have been Tree Face's legs, given me water and fruit while she made the other journeys. I had time to replace the Ick Bag I'd lost somewhere between Tree Face and the alligator and to void my bladder.

The flange in my stomach was a bit messy with my waste and jungle mud. There was nothing I could do about anything that might have gotten inside. I cleaned it the best I could with a wet wipe and put a new bag in place.

I drank the water, ate the fruit, and stared at the holdall.

Kik-Kik came back the final time with the alligator's tail hung over her shoulders like a scarf. She proceeded to skin it expertly with a knife in her good hand and holding the rest of it down with her feet, twisting it around with her toes and heels. Within a few minutes, the tail was out of the skin. It was light pink, muscly, and glistened like a larger version of the snake meat. Kik-Kik carried on without looking at me, carving the meat from the cartilage and putting strips of it on a stick, which she then hung over the fire. The smells from the cooking meat were helping me forget the holdall and not to fixate on it. My mouth was watering. No wonder these jungle tribes decided to live out here away from Wi-Fi and TV and football. It was like living in the world's biggest free larder. As long as your dinner didn't decide to eat you first, that is.

When Kik-Kik finished cooking, she carried out the ritual to which I was going to become very familiar. First the offering to Tree Face, who ate the meat while looking past us both without chewing. Then she prayed to me and then lastly, sitting back cross-legged on the ground, she mouthed a small prayer for herself, looked up longingly at Tree Face, rubbed her flipper, offering it up to the dead-eyed, wood-faced god and then ate the scraps of meat that were left.

I tried to give her some of my meat, because the last bits she'd saved for herself looked gristly and grey, but she was having none of it. The meat that I left, she gave to Tree Face. He wasn't complaining. He ate it all.

After the meal, Kik-Kik made another fire a few metres away in the clearing. This time though, she piled fresh leaves on top so that it made much more smoke. I thought maybe at last she was using it to send signals to speed up my rescue. Unfortunately not. She took more of the alligator meat, threaded it onto branches. She then hung over the fire. It was clear she wasn't signalling she was smoking the glistening flesh. I remembered from cookery classes at school that for bacteria to multiply in meat it needed three things—food, warmth, and moisture. You couldn't do anything about the first two out here with no refrigerators, but if meat was dried and smoked it wouldn't go off.

Kik-Kik was making alligator kippers.

I couldn't get my head around how brilliantly suited she was to life out here, even with her obvious disability. Everything her flipper couldn't do her feet could, or she'd find a work-around that meant survival was assured. I started to wonder if she had any wigwams to go back to anyway. Maybe, like me, she was all alone. Maybe, like me, nobody wanted her around because she was an embarrassment.

I bet her dad, if he was still around, wouldn't be teaching her how to fly, he'd be teaching her how to smoke alligators.

Kik-Kik made one more trip back to the riverbank and that was to bring back the alligator's broken head. She'd used twine made from thinned-out vines to tie the jaws back together from where they'd been splayed apart by the gun exploding. The alligator had lost an eye and most of the right of its face. Kik-Kik stripped the leaves and branches from a two-metre wooden pole, and stuffed the head on top with a sickening crack of bone. Then stuck the other end of the pole in the wet earth, twisting it in with her good hand. When she'd finished the alligator looked scarier than it had when it was alive. A pirate-ghost alligator head, almost hanging in mid-air, lit by the light of the fire. Scales shiny and slithery, the exposed socket of the dead eye black and mysterious.

I shuddered.

I realised I'd been looking at the alligator head for some time and when I looked down, Kik-Kik had gone.

I thought I heard her moving off through the jungle, and half-expected her to bounce back in a few minutes with another piece of the alligator jig-saw, but she didn't.

I settled into the hollow between Tree Face's legs. I was warm, fed, and dry, and felt as okay as anyone could feel under the circumstance. I knew I wasn't in any way at all safe, and was glad that Kik-Kik's snake-killing spear was still close by for me to use if any jungle residents decided to follow the smells of cooking or smoking meat to Tree Face's clearing.

I placed more twigs on my fire and listened to them crackle and pop. In the flames I imagined I could see faces or places. Dad or Mum. Home. London. School.

Jen…

I looked away from the fire. It was hurting my eyes.

But I didn't look at the bag. No. I didn't look there either.

And the clouds and the plane and Kik-Kik and the alligator who was Carlos and the bag and the gun who was Escobar and the snake and the fire who was Dad flew through the air and the jungle was below and the river was bursting with blood and the river was full of white-topped waves and the white tops of the waves became the powder and the white powder blew up into the sky and then the alligator, the one-eyed pirate-ghost alligator, was coming for me with the gun and it was up on its hind legs because it no longer had a tail and it could walk like a man in it was Carlos the alligator and it was Escobar the Gun,

and the Snake who was my dad, snakes bastard snakes, was burning
the in the fire shrivelling up, making white powder smoke which went
up into the endless blue, and became clouds through which we flew,
flew in the tiny dot of the Piper Cherokee towards the jungle in the
Tree Face's mouth.

And it was morning, but of course I couldn't tell what time it
was. My watch was inside Tree Face. I bet he knew what the
time was. And when I looked up at him, that side-eyed smirk
was there in the morning light. He was probably looking at the
watch in his stomach now. Admiring the workmanship, the
accuracy, the price it had cost.

Oh yes.

The price

The price it'd cost had been properly expensive. And I'm not
just talking about how much Dad had paid in money.

"Screw you, Tree Face," I said by way of good morning.

He didn't answer, but then a cloud shifted over the sun for
a few seconds, making his mouth a droop-sided frown. Either
that or it had given him a stroke.

So… what to do?

The holdall was right beside me. The torn and exploded
hole in the side facing me like an injured eye. As the sun began
to warm the night damp forest and the morning mists began to
form around me in their chill smoky curls, I undid the zip at the
top of the bag with a long smooth rip.

A bird startled by the sound launched itself into the air
from Tree Face's mouth, like he was spitting out a bitter gob of
phlegm.

Inside, the bag was ruined with river water. A lot of it had
drained away but the bag was still saturated. The top layer of
stuff in the bag was all clothes. Tee-shirts, dress shirts, pants,
socks, and jeans. They filled pretty much the top half of the
holdall's space. They didn't necessarily look like my dad's
clothes, but then he wasn't exactly a clotheshorse—they were all
fairly generic, good labels, but nothing remarkable.

The next layer was a bunch of cardboard folders that had
ballooned to mush at the edges in the water. There were three of

them, and as I peeled one corner up I could see they contained pages from yellow legal pads and were covered in Spanish or Portuguese or whatever language was spoken at Carlos's place.

Spainuguese for all I knew. Whatever it was, I couldn't read it.

There were some photographs in the folders showing various white concrete buildings in a city I didn't recognise. I put the folders to one side as the paper was starting to come apart in my hand. I'd have to dry them out by the fire if I was going to try to make sense of them.

Then came four brown-taped packets. The fifth had been blown open in the explosion throwing out all the white powder. I didn't know if it was coke or heroin. I'd seen enough cop shows to know it was one of those at least, and I wasn't going to dip my finger in to find out which one it was. Not because I was scared but tasting it wouldn't tell me which drug it was. How would I bloody know? And quite frankly, I didn't want to know.

I took the packets out and left them at Tree Face's roots

Next, there were four packets of closely packed one hundred dollar bills. I'd never see so much cash in one place. I couldn't even begin to guess at what the final value would be, even discounting the notes that were destroyed or floating downstream from what was left of the alligator.

There was a coldness growing in the pit of my stomach. I was having thoughts about my dad that I really didn't want to have. What was he mixed up in for all this to have been on the plane? I suppose I could still just about cling to the hope that this was all a great big mistake, but who'd put a bag full of drugs and money on a plane by accident? I just wouldn't happen.

Whatever was going on Dad was mixed up in something.

I took the wreckage of the snubby but completely destroyed semi-automatic pistol from the bag. My idea that the alligator's thrashing about with the bag had made the gun attempt to fire and then blow up because of the water or the enclosed space or whatever, seemed to be a good guess.

There weren't any unused bullets in the gun. It was useless to me as a weapon. Not that I would have known how to use it.

Then a thought hit me.

Why did I assume the bag had come from our plane anyway? Maybe this bag had come from somewhere else upriver. Maybe it had just been snagged on the tree platform. Maybe I was putting three and six together and making ninety-nine.

The holdall might not have anything to do with Carlos or Dad at all.

There was a transparent Ziploc bag below the gun. In it were some traveller's cheques, documents with various official seals, and a Brazilian passport.

The cold in my guts spread further out to my whole body as I retrieved the passport and opened it.

The passport was in the name of Victor LaSalle, a 41-year-old Brazilian national from São Paulo.

And the picture of Victor LaSalle was John Coker. My dad.

TWENTY-FIVE

"Run up check.
    Nose Gear straight.
Parking brake Set.
Engine up to 2000 rpm.
Mixture is rich.
Electric fuel pump. On.
Magnetos. On both. One. Both
Carb heat on.
Throttle. Retard
Engine 1000 rpm
Carb heat. Off
GPS on.
Suction one in five.
Circuit Breakers all in.
Alternator. Positive.
Temps and pressures all green.
Flight instruments check.
Fuel selector. Proper tank.
Southend Tower Information. Yankee 1954X Winds 300 at 11,
Visibility 10. Ceiling 8,000 overcast. Temperature 19. Dewpoint
9. Altimeter 3011. Expect the ILS or visual approach, runway 29.
Runway 15 REILS out of service. Advise on initial contact you have
Yankee.

    Southend tower. Cherokee 8720 Foxtrot. We have Yankee.
Flight instruments check.
Fuel selector. Proper tank.

Flaps Set.
Trim Set.
Doors. Latched.
Strobe On.
Landing Light. On.
Fuel Pump. On.
Mixture. Rich.
Carb heat. Off.
Cherokee 8720 Foxtrot. Runway 29. Track Bravo. Hold short of Runway 29.
Southend Tower, Cherokee 8720 Foxtrot holding short 29 at Bravo, we're ready to go for closed traffic.
Runway 29 cleared for take-off. Make right traffic first time around. Right traffic.
Cleared for take-off. We'll make right traffic.
Full power.
Strobe lights are on.
Right rudder
V1
V2
Rotate.
Maintain steady climb rate. Don't lose the horizon beneath the nose.
900 clear abort.
Begin turn onto crosswind.
Climb rate 700 feet per minute."

A light aircraft, all propeller noise and crackling radio, lifts you from below. Like you're in the palm of a giant's hand. The pressure comes from underneath and suddenly you're riding a tower of acceleration. If I'd had feeling in my legs and backside, I would have felt that push against gravity there first. But for me, because sensation in my back and guts starts just above my pelvis, it feels like I'm being pushed up from the inside. As if the elevator is running up my spine, its floor lifting my intestines, stomach, and lungs up with it, to squash them against the underside of my shoulders. It's not an unpleasant feeling to have that sense of movement and lift running through my body once more. It's like waking up from the grave.

It's not like getting up and walking or setting off on a run.

It's better.

Five lessons in and I was handling the plane, with its hand rudders to replace the pedals that I would usually use, like a professional. Yes, there would be a lot of maths to learn, and navigation to get my head around, but those initial weeks free flying with Dad in the other seat, teaching me the stuff he'd known since he was a kid, were some of the best weeks of my life.

Blue-sky flying was my favourite. Breaking through the cloud—there's nearly always low cloud over England—up into the clear air, where, during the day it's always summer. When the sun is a bright spotlight in the sky and the blue… the blue goes on forever, right over the edge of the Earth.

Up above the rain. Up above the fog. Up above everything. You didn't need legs up there. You weren't going to need them. The plane became the extension of your skin, you flew and soared dived and turned.

I was free.

Free of the ground.

A stuffed, lethargic belly of cloud below, a clear blue head of sky above. Passing through it like the sharpest, clearest idea with perfect clarity. Thinking through the atmosphere. An arrow of lucidity.

It felt like coming home.

I mastered the specifics and jargon of landing almost as quickly as I mastered take-off. The jargon and the routine. Easily learned. The sense in my stomach that I was leaving all things beautiful and descending to a place that was only a holding pattern in my life until the next time I could walk, and run and fly through the air.

My air.

The world I owned. The map of the heavens.

Me. Dad. Everything.

I didn't imagine that I would be in charge of an aeroplane, taxiing it to the runway and lifting it off the ground into the air on my first-ever lesson but that's the way to do these things apparently. Taking off is a "piece of piddle," my dad said. "Landing's a bit trickier," he'd continued, "but we'll come to that eventually."

And we did. Flying two or three times a week, every week when he was able. He moved appointments and meetings around when he could to make sure we got the time together. Silly Sally was pulling her hair out with his diary, especially when she'd arranged something, and he'd change it at the last minute. Petra, his girlfriend, got the right ache that he wouldn't move flying lessons with me aside too. Getting proper moody when she stayed over at the weekends and he would take four hours out with me at the airfield.

But in the end, she got it.

Wherever possible the flying lessons would take precedence over everything else, not just Silly Sally and Petra. It didn't feel like Dad was compensating initially, but over time, it became clear he was trying to give me back something that could not be returned. In a way, he was giving me something more freeing and vital, something that levelled every playing field between able-bodied and disabled flyers. Up there were no pitying looks or cow-eyes. Everyone was the same.

I wasn't left behind up there, or my head talked over.

I was just Sam—or Cherokee 8720 Foxtrot as I had to identify myself to the Control Towers of the airports we flew to and from. Dad had our planes stored at Southend Airport out on the Essex coast. As soon as you were up and cleared the brown and red-tiled roofs of the town, you were out over the Thames Estuary, with Kent a yellow-brown line dead ahead. London was on a right turn, and the North Sea and Europe with a left turn.

Just brilliant.

We didn't really talk about Mum leaving. Dad didn't bring it up and I didn't either. It's not that I didn't care. Of course I did. But it was just something that had been coming a long time before the accident and had only been delayed by it rather than the idea extinguished.

To talk about it would have been pointless. I still saw her about once a month. She would come to the house while Dad was out at work, or away on a single overnight business trip. He trusted me to be ok on just the one night. Mum would come, bring dinner and we'd watch a film or something. She didn't talk about Dad, and I didn't offer anything.

To be fair it was very much like it was before the accident. We'd rarely did anything together as a family then. I always spent time with one or the other. I noticed that Mum had taken off her wedding ring, but Dad hadn't, even when he started seeing Petra. Mum didn't tell me that they were actively getting divorced, but Dad would often tell me "Halliday is coming over and we'll be discussing legal stuff, so keep the noise down and sort yourself out for dinner."

Gordon Halliday was tall and gaunt and looked like you'd imagine a middle-aged solicitor to look like. He was okay I suppose. He didn't look at me with all Pityface or anything. He'd ask me about Chelsea if I opened the door to him if Dad was already in his office at the back of the house waiting for him.

I'm not sure if he was really into football or if he'd just looked up the latest news on his smartphone while parking the car on the drive. Other than Mum, and Petra, Halliday was the only visitor we had to the house before the trip up to Carlos's place in the mountains of the Amazon and I certainly wished it had been Halliday who had travelled with my dad up there, instead of me, that's for sure.

So Dad taught me to fly the plane he'd bought for me. A blue Piper Cherokee 180, single prop, static undercarriage, four-seater light aircraft. It was the best toy you could imagine, and I loved to take it out to play. Southend was just a forty-minute drive from home so it wasn't a huge pain in the bum getting out there. And when Dad told me that we'd be flying from Southend direct to Brasilia (by jet), and that waiting out there, on the edge of the rainforest, was a rented and modified Cherokee that he'd help me navigate out to Carlos's place, I was just bloody ecstatic. If I could have leaped up and hugged him from the chair I would have—but Dad wasn't really the huggy-type, and since the accident and Jen... neither was I.

We flew from Southend in Carlos's small private jet. I guessed it was his because the pilot was Brazilian and didn't speak a lot of English. Dad could converse with him so that was okay. Halliday saw us off at the airport, saying he had some papers for Dad to read and sign on the plane—probably about the divorce I thought.

I asked Dad to ask the pilot if I'd be allowed up into the cockpit and watch what he was doing for some of the flight.

The pilot said no.

TWENTY-SIX

Kik-Kik didn't come back that day. I had no idea if she would come back at all. On the plus side, I had fruit and meat and wood for the fire—on the downside I had a passport that showed me that either my dad wasn't John Coker, or John Coker wasn't my dad.

I felt cold all day.

The papers in the folders dried out by the fire and the passport rested on my dead leg, on the thigh. I couldn't open it again, but I couldn't put it out of my sight. It was like a scab that you knew if you started picking you wouldn't stop—that you knew was going to hurt when you ripped it off, but that you couldn't help yourself staring at it. Waiting to pick.

To put it back in the bag would have being trying to deny its existence, and there was no way I could do that anymore—keeping it out kept the reality of my situation in sharp focus, but I still couldn't bring myself to look at the picture and the name.

Was it a false passport or was John Coker his false identity?

Who was my dad?

Was he even my dad?

Was he smuggling drugs, or was he so much of a threat to the drug runners they'd planted drugs on the plane to ensure he was captured and put into jail?

That didn't make sense. We'd been up in the mountains in Carlos's place. He had armed guards. If Carlos wanted my dad out of the way all he'd had to do was have him... I swallowed... and me just taken out and shot on the veranda.

Why would Carlos send us off with all those drugs?

I blinked.

Why had the plane crashed?

Clang.

Crunch.

Was it really a simple mechanical failure in a plane that we didn't know that well or was it something more sinister? Had it been sabotaged to crash in the jungle so that Dad's and my bodies could have been found with a ton of drugs, discredited and not linked to Carlos at all? I mean we hadn't logged a flight plan. The only people who would have known we were flying were the sleepy airport workers at the airport on the edge of the jungle, and we'd certainly not told them where we were flying.

Had it all been a big set-up?

The chill sat in my guts and refused to shift.

As the jungle fell towards evening, I cooked some more alligator tail and refused to make eye contact with Tree Face. I could feel his woody eyes, boring into the top of my head, and imagined his accusing hissy laugh, but I wasn't going to give him the satisfaction of looking at him.

No way.

The alligator tasted bitter and I couldn't eat it all. This hadn't been the meat that had been smoking steadily overnight; this had been fresh, wrapped in leaf parcels by my side by Kik-Kik. I guess everything went off quick in the jungle if it wasn't preserved. I threw the leftover parcels of meat away from me because even the thought of them was making me feel sick.

It's not every day that you find out your dad wasn't who you thought he was, or that there was a good chance he was a drug trafficker. Or that someone wanted him out of the way so badly they'd sabotaged his aeroplane with his son inside at the same time.

Clang.

Crunch.

The tee-shirts from the bag that I'd taken out and spread on the ground near the fire felt as near dry as anything got in the jungle. I took off my shirt, which was, of course, filthy, torn and covered in mud and a fair bit of Ick from when my mad crawl to the river had torn it from my side and put on a fresh one. It was a bit big for me, obviously. My dad was an XXL after all, mostly muscle, a little bit of fat, and I felt a bit tiny in the folds of the material. But it was nice to be wearing something that didn't look like it was the "before" picture in an advertisement for washing detergent.

I took off my current Ick Bag, emptied it where I'd emptied the other, cleaned the flange with a wet wipe, and reattached the bag with extra tape.

I felt my forehead. It was cold and clammy and there was a buzzing in my ears that didn't match up with the insects flying around me.

Obviously, the cold, chilly feeling in my guts wasn't just the surprise about my dad's secret identity and his not so fabulous friends.

I was ill.

Now, being a sickly paraplegic kid, with a case of the jelly belly in good old London Town was a pain in the backside (no pun intended) at the best of times. You could rely on someone at regular intervals to bring you nice drinks and bland food, possibly an aspirin or whatever. They'd let you stay in bed, and maybe have a couple of days off school and everything would be fine and Jim Dandy.

But being ill out here.

Man. I didn't even know where to begin.

Was it the food? The off alligator? Or had the bitterness just been my imagination? I didn't think food poisoning came on that fast. Had it been something else that Kik-Kik had given me? Had there been an insect burrowed into the fruit that I hadn't noticed? Or worse still, had some alien insect laid eggs in the fruit and those little bastards were at this very moment hatching in my gullet, making me feel like vomiting and about to burrow out through my armpit?

I cannot tell you how much I didn't know about what could possibly have happened to me.

In all reality, once the horror films had stopped playing in my head, it was my flange and nub of intestine being exposed to the river and riverbank that made me ill. I'd only been able to clean the site with a wet wipe, there's no telling what had already made it inside me from the killer-jungle-of-death.

I wanted, more than anything, to see Kik-Kik coming through the trees.

I was properly scared.

I had a decision to make—if I had a whole load of unpleasantness going on inside me right now, stuff that was going to want to get out through the surgical hole provided, I was going to get through my spare Ick Bags in a day. Maybe even sooner. You know what it's like when you have the jelly belly, mate, when you can't get off the toilet for an hour at a time?

Yeah, double the trouble here my friend.

So do I remove the bag that was in place on the flange, let nature take its course, and use Dad's spare clothes as wadding to clean myself up or do I keep the Ick Bag in place and hope it's not something serious and it'll pass overnight?

I had no idea what to do.

To be honest I stopped thinking about it then, because as I looked way over to the left of the clearing, the sound of something scrabbling across the jungle floor froze me. Right there... RIGHT THERE...was a fat-looking leopard. Bold as you like, stalking out of the undergrowth, claws drawn, and pawing at a parcel of alligator meat.

A bloody bleedin' LEOPARD!

His paws looked enormous and the claws ripped open the alligator parcels with ease. Fat Leopard—much stockier and compact that the ones I'd seen on telly, lay down and munched on the meat. It was gone in a second. Fat Leopard didn't even look up at me.

It didn't really need to consider me, did it? If you think about it? I'm not a threat in any way shape or form. I must smell exactly like the jungle around me now, so I'm not out of the ordinary. I was sat up against Tree Face, trying not to breathe in or out, resting my hands at my side in the stupid big shirt; I tried very hard not to draw attention to myself.

Fat Leopard worked his way through three parcels, pretty much sucking the meat and slices off the leaves into his flat face then licking his paws clean.

He yawned.

Yup. Just yawned. Then he put a paw behind his ear, scratched his head as if he were a bloody domestic cat after a bowl of Katty-Kit or whatever. He looked around, seeming now be looking for the best place to curl up and sleep off the freebie dinner he'd just scored.

That's when my tummy, full of Sickness-Ick, rumbled and bubbled like the loudest thing in the jungle.

Fat Leopard looked up.

Looked at me.

In the breeze, I could hear Tree Face rubbing his branches together with glee.

TWENTY-SEVEN

Fat Leopard took a step forward, sniffing the air. He was close enough now for me to see his whiskers trembling. I could see spit glistening on his teeth. There were pieces of meat between them, alligator meat.

Soon to be Sam Coker meat.

He took another step and growled at me.

My stomach growled back. Sweat started to dribble off my forehead into my eyes. The leaves up above in the branches hissed Tree Face's laughter at me. I wanted to look up, shout and scream at the prick, tell him to just shut up and get out of my freaking head. But my eyes were fixed on Fat Leopard's eyes.

He took another step.

One more and I would be able to reach out an arm and feed it to him myself.

Fat Leopard was regarding me oddly. Still sniffing. Licking his nose as if to get an extra taste of my aroma. I could see Fat Leopard suddenly at a table, with a napkin around its neck, holding a knife and fork, like those stupid paintings of dogs eating a banquet or playing snooker up on the wall of Dad's local pub. Instead of a sumptuous roast beef dinner on the plate in front of Fat Leopard, it was me, a tiny me, lying on the plate with paper chef's hats on my hands and feet, and an apple shoved in my gob. My eyes though, my eyes were wide and terrified, my eyes knew what was coming as Fat Leopard's fork descended like a claw...

Fat Leopard made up his mind then that I smelled good enough to eat and he jumped at me, claws outstretched and mouth wide as a bear-trap, and just as deadly.

I had no time to think or process, I just held up the spear Kik-Kik had left by my side and waited for Fat Leopard to hit it.

The point of the spear went deep into Fat Leopard's neck. I could see the skin folding back and ripping open. Fat Leopard seemed to hang in mid-air, legs splayed, like Wile E. Coyote running out over a ravine before noticing there was a 2000-metre drop below him.

Fat Leopard howled and hissed, falling to the ground, pawing and twisting at the spear, almost pulling it out of my hands. I pulled the spear out, ripping more of the fur-covered flesh on the back of the sharpened stone and then stabbed at the cat again. This time the spear went in deep in Fat Leopard's belly.

The cat scrambled up, didn't look back, and bounded away into the jungle, just leaving a trail of swaying leaves and the sound of a diminishing howl.

The end of the spear was dripping with dark red blood.

I stayed awake all night and didn't let go of it once.

And I stayed awake all night so Fat Leopard couldn't get me and the spear was in my hand and the bag was in the clouds and the money was rain and the gun was the sun a black sun in a red sky and Fat Leopard was screaming and the plane came out of its mouth and I was home and Mum was back and Dad was there and I could walk and I could run and the paths were covered in drugs and in the back garden and there was a tree and the tree had a face and on the face was a mouth and in the face was time and time sat there like a frog in a cave and the frog croaked the seconds and Kik-Kik had two good arms and a wheelchair because the alligator had eaten her legs even though I had eaten the alligator maybe I'd eaten her legs and I was an alligator and the black sun fired bullets and Carlos caught them in his hand and Escobar was a cloud and he had a huge laughing mouth but Escobar was only a mouth and he rolled inside out and the frog was there in the clouds made of money and it ticked out the time and it wept money and Mum and Dad were at the table eating snooker dogs and eating at the pub and Kik-Kik was made of fire and smoke and the embers of her eyes

*burned like the reddest and brightest things in the jungle sky and I felt
sick and I felt like I'd been kicked in the stomach and my stomach was
in the clouds and it was full of money and drugs and they hurt and I
was sick and the sick came out of my mouth with a song and the song
hurt my ears and the sky was full of sick and my nostrils were full of
sick and I was drowning in...*

I'd been sick in my sleep.

The sleep I'd tried to stay away from, because I knew that
if I slept then Fat Leopard would come back and finish the job.
But he didn't and I woke up covered in sick, and with my guts
churning like a washing machine. I felt hot and cold at the same
time and my eyes were full of sticky mucous.

It took me a few seconds to realise that I was properly ill
now.

It was as much as I could do to pull the wet tee-shirt over
my head and throw it away from me. I hurt too much to put
another one on so I leaned back against Tree Face bare-chested.
Sweat was running down my neck and as I wiped the sleep
from my eyes, I could see in the dim morning light that the
hand resting on my thighs had a slight tremor. When I brought
down the other hand, it was shaking too.

I was just able to lean sideways before I deposited another
puddle of vomit into the undergrowth. That taste in my mouth
was foul. Acidy and rich with sicky flavours. My eyes watered,
as my guts pushed the stuff it needed to get rid of out of my
mouth and nose.

I was sick again.

I pulled myself back up to a sitting position on one of Tree
Face's creeper dreads.

"Ouch," Tree Face said.

I looked up. My eyes swam. My throat stung. Tree Face was
immobile on the bark as usual. He wasn't even looking at me.

Something rustled some bushes over to my left; I snapped
my head away from Tree Face to see if it was yet another jungle
threat. The jungle was suddenly twilit and full of deep shadows.
It was day, but it was night too, and one by one the normal
sounds of the jungle began to fall slowly towards silence. All

that was left in a few seconds, once the birds had stopped calling, and the leaves had stopped rustling, and monkeys had stopped whooping, and the beetles stopped scuttling like whispers in the undergrowth and the flies had stopped buzzing like faraway telephones…all that was left was the creaking. The creaking directly behind me, the slow and woody and squeaky creaking as I heard Tree Face climbing down from the tree.

I dare not look.

I could hear him standing there. His root legs creaking with disuse. His breathing crackling like leaves in a stiff breeze. His neck squeaking and protesting as he moved it from side to side, getting the life back into it.

I dare not look.

I concentrated on the darkening jungle in front of me, where I suddenly heard the rustling of branches.

Was it Kik-Kik or Fat Leopard?

"It's neither," said Tree Face.

His voice sounded like a limp foot being dragged through jungle undergrowth. Thin plants snapped and broke in his voice, beetles scuttled in it, earthworms twisted through, and woodpeckers hammered in the distance of it. It was a voice that sounded like the jungle had grown a mouth and had something to say.

But I wasn't going to look at him.

The jungle moved and swayed in front of me, the smell of my sick replaced by something earthier, something sweeter even. In the place where I had thrown up, small blue flowers were growing.

"You can't stop life," Tree Face said, his chest groaning like a wooden ship out at sea in the night. "The rainforest is made of life."

I closed my eyes. I was not going to turn my head. I was not going to see what was there. The rustle of the voice was enough. My stomach was a twist of aching muscles, my throat burned and sizzled in my neck. My eyes were tearful then clear, tearful, and then clear. My vision went pink and for one panicky second I thought I was crying blood, but as I looked through the trees I could see the edges of the rising sun were boiling and flaring and the jungle was blossoming from darkness into that red light.

"Look at me," said Tree Face. A twig bushed my shoulder. It could have been dropped by a nesting bird above, or it could have been one of Tree Face's black bark fingers brushing my flesh. It felt brittle and I could swear I could smell his mulchy breath on the air as Tree Face bent down to whisper into my ear. "Look at me, Sam."

"No," I managed to say through clamped tight lips, afraid that if I opened my mouth fully my stomach would send up another gush of vomit.

"Please, Sam."

"No!" I put my hands over my eyes. My stomach lurched, and jungle roared with a gale in my ears, leaves whipped against my face and even though my eyes were closed I could see the blue flowers dissolving on the air and falling back to the jungle floor as vomit.

Tree Face placed a hand directly on my shoulder.

Terrified, I opened my eyes and looked. The fingers were gnarled and shiny, knuckles like buds for new twigs to grow, slimy moss in the cracks on the back of the hand. The fist was wet with rain from the forest, it glistened and shimmered. Then it squeezed my shoulder.

"Look at him, Sam," said my dad, stepping out of the trees.

TWENTY-EIGHT

"Look at him, Sam."

Dad was pointing through a window at Carlos's place up in the mountains. I wheeled myself over to the window. We'd just been shown to our rooms and Dad was making sure there were no problems with mine. Carlos had assured him that the bathroom and loo had been adapted, and that the bed had the necessary grips and rails next to it so that I'd be able to get myself in and out of it.

Through the window, out beyond a courtyard lit by clear mountain light, I could see the football pitch. A boy I hadn't met yet, tall and stocky, with curly black hair, was dribbling a ball with considerable skill up and down. He flicked the ball up onto his knees, bouncing it from left to right, hardly breaking sweat. Moving with the spare efficiency of a metronome.

I watched him for as long as I could until I could take it no more. Dad carried on for another minute or so. I don't think he did it to annoy me or anything. For a start, he couldn't know what was going on inside my head or feel the ache of depression clutching at my heart. Less than a year ago, that boy with the curly black hair and the madskillz with the ball was me. I could freestyle better than anyone in my school, probably as good as anyone in London. Not that I'd enter some lame-ass competition or anything, that was definitely not my style—my style was the Crossover, Toe Bounce or a properly sick outside Around the World—that's where you kick the ball up and circle your foot around it so the same foot bounces the ball up again. I was pretty good at the Palle Around the World too, which was the same, only your foot went around the ball three times in the air before you used the same foot to flick the ball up—seven times out of ten I could pull a full Palle, and just before the accident I was getting better.

I wheeled myself over to the bed and waited for Dad to come away from the window. He pointed his thumb back over to the window. "Pretty good, yeah?"

I nodded but didn't say anything. Dad didn't take the hint and just rubbed the top of my head with the palm of my hand. "Carlos says we should go down to dinner in about twenty minutes. You need help unpacking or anything?"

"No. All good," I said without looking at him.

Dad got up and, whistling a tuneless tune, left me alone in the room.

I went back to the window. Looked at the boy out on the pitch.

Had a little cry.

The boy I'd seen through the window was Escobar, and he had a younger, bouncy, always 110% little brother called Ramos. They both shook my hand as Dad introduced us. Carlos came up behind them, putting his hands on their shoulders and shook my dad's hand. He didn't shake mine.

Through a long line of floor-to-ceiling windows, which gave a view out over the gardens below the mansion, I could see the Cherokee parked up and some of Carlos's men tending to it. Carlos was a flyer too, Dad had said, and kept men around to service his planes. Carlos was planning to have a runway cleared in the jungle at the foot of the mountains so that in future he'd be able to fly his private jet in and out of the country without the dogleg through the two other airports.

I wondered just how rich you had to be to own your own jet.

Dinner over, I went back to my room. I didn't really feel like hanging about with Escobar and Ramos, telling Dad I was tired after the flight. He gave me the cow-eyes and patted me on the shoulder; I guessed he wanted to get down to business with Carlos. If Carlos was building runways, that meant he was successful and Dad wanted a piece of the action. Although Dad seemed comfortable that I was here with him, I suspected deep down he'd wished he'd made the journey alone.

I thought back to when we left Southend how Halliday had looked at me weird—maybe none of them wanted me around.

I showered, changed again, and watched TV until I was tired. I hadn't been able to find any channels in English, and I was effed if I was going to ask Escobar how to do it.

All through dinner, I could hear Escobar sighing whenever Ramos asked me to explain anything about my school or my friends or Chelsea. Ramos followed the Premier League, watched all the games, and sitting there in his canary yellow Brazil kit gave me a full rundown of the Brazilian players in the English League. He knew his stuff, he knew his stats, and I could see that Escobar didn't like not being the centre of attention. He rarely made eye contact with me, and when he did it only lasted a fraction of a second before I could swear that his eyes were looking straight at me like I was invisible.

After dinner, Carlos went off with Dad, throwing a meaty arm around his shoulders. Escobar followed them. Ramos, whose English was much better than my Spainuguese or Portish or whatever they spoke when they didn't want us to understand what they were saying, politely said goodnight, and he was going to bed.

Once back in my room, via a ramp that Carlos had had made, and a lift that had been built when the jungle mansion had been constructed, I went back to the window to look at the night sky over the mountains. With the bedroom light off in the room, the sky lit up with messy swirls of stars. I couldn't tell you what all the constellations were, but I recognised a couple. There was no moon to light the land around us, so the whole scene through the window reminded me of when we'd gone to Hamburg on the night ferry, the mansion, and the boat both glittering constellations of light adrift in a sea of black.

Something caught my eye.

A torch flashed on the ground and illuminated the wheels of the Cherokee. I squinted and pushed my head forward from the wheelchair as far as I could go. The windowsill dug into my chest.

Carlos's men were still working on the plane.

I awoke in the middle of the night in a cold sweat. The bedroom was as dark as the sky outside the window and I couldn't make out anything. I guess I'd been woken by a troubling dream but I couldn't for the life of me remember what it was. I used the rail to pull myself up to a sitting position, and peeled back the duvet. My head was cold, but body was warm, too warm.

I took off my tee-shirt and threw it onto the bedroom floor. It disappeared into the dark

Shouldn't my eyes be accustomed to this my now? I screwed them up and rubbed them with my hands.

With a groan of disgust, I took my hands away from my face. They were slick with a liquid that stank like a puddle of vomit. I wiped them on the duvet. Had I been sick during the night? Had it been the change in altitude and the food? Was I ill? I didn't feel ill.

I didn't feel anything at all.

Clang.

Crunch.

I swung my legs over the side of the bed and stood up.

I…

I…

I was back in the bed, under the cover and lightning flashes were going off outside in the windows. Was it lightning or was it…

I walked across the room.

I sat on the bed.

I bent over and picked a blue flower growing in the carpet.

"Look at him."

Dad was standing by the window smoking a big cigar, one of Carlos's finest. The smoke moved around his head, and there was just enough light to see the shape of his face against the window. I wheeled myself over to him in the wheelchair. I'd find out why blue flowers were growing in the carpet later, and where the vomit had come from.

When I got to the window, it was now too high for me to look out, Dad was pointing, but either I was smaller or the windowsill was suddenly higher.

"Look at what?" I asked Dad, trying to push myself up on the side arms of the wheelchair. I couldn't work out why I couldn't walk any more. I'd been able to walk to the flowers after all.

My head lifted up as I pushed hard with my arm, my whole body coming free of the wheelchair.

Up and up I went, as if I was going up in Carlos's clanky, metal elevator.

Clang.

Crunch.

There was a flash of lightning through the glass again, and the face made of twigs and bark and eyes of cut branches with the screaming red mouth and the broken wooden teeth loomed out of the dark.

"Tree Face," said Dad.

TWENTY-NINE

I screamed and ran back to the bed, ran *and* wheeled. I was running and wheeling at the same time. My legs had wheels, my wheels had legs. I couldn't see the window behind me but I could hear Dad opening it and Tree Face climbing into the room.

I jumped off the bed and was in a corridor. The corridor was in my house in London and in Carlos's house in South America at the same time.

I ran and wheeled down both simultaneously. Hearing the dirt-dribbling footsteps of Tree Face behind me. He was running on sticks. Even though I didn't look back, I could see him. Huge and made of branches and bark, in place of his heart a golden wristwatch and in his stomach a ball of rotting alligator meat.

I tried a door. It was locked.

Again.

Locked.

I ran-wheeled on. I could feel Tree Face's whispery breath on the back of my neck. I could hear the leaves rustling in his twiggy hair. I felt a wooden, splintery finger catching at the collar of my shirt.

I tried a door.

It opened.

Carlos looked up from his desk, where he was sat writing.

We'd been here a couple of days now, and as I'd been left to my own devices and was trying to avoid spending any time with Escobar watching him on the football field, I'd taken to wheeling myself around the mansion where I could, having a nose. I would sometimes draw squinty glances from the machine-gun-toting guards if I came upon them unannounced—the wheelchair's bearings were so smooth I could literally glide around silently—showing how jumpy and nervous they were. I guess the rebels that Carlos had told us about up in the hills were getting closer or whatever.

Carlos put down a thick gold pen. "Can I help you, Sam?"

I waited in the doorway, hands on the wheels ready to turn right 'round again and continue my mooching elsewhere. Carlos had been writing on a piece of yellow paper that he slid inside a buff cardboard folder in front of him.

"Sorry," I said. "Just having a look around, I didn't know you'd be in here."

"So you only want to look around when there's not a chance of you being discovered?" Carlos's smile was wolfish and his voice dripped with sarcasm.

"No, 'course not. Just loving the house. It's great. And I'm nosy."

"Nosy. An English word. I am not familiar with this word." Carlos reached into a box on his desk, flipped up the top, and pulled out a jumbo sausage cigar. He lit it while pushing the folder away with the other hand. His cheeks puffed up a few times. He looked like a sweaty frog with a big moustache.

"Oh, right, yeah. It just mean curious I guess."

"Then why not say curious?"

"I dunno."

Carlos stood up. "Nosy implies something negative." He tapped the side of his nose. I got the impression he was playing with me. "It implies deceit."

"Does it?"

"Yes."

Carlos was walked towards me across the wide expanse of carpet in front of his desk. Still puffing, sucking hard to get a good draw on his cigar. All he'd have to do to complete the image of a human frog would be to start croaking.

"What are you looking for? With this... nosy?" Carlos pressed a sweaty finger that smelt of cigar against my nose. He pressed a little harder than could be considered friendly. I had to move my head back to relieve the pressure.

"I'm not looking for anything. Honest."

"I am making a very important deal with your father. The negotiations are... complex and time-consuming. I hope that neither of you are disrespecting my hospitality. Perhaps you came here to find information that would help your father in these negotiations. Perhaps that is why you are nosy. No?"

Carlos's eyes swirled with darkness—the rest of his face might be totally froggy, but his eyes were sharp, and drilled right into me.

I wheeled myself back. He was enjoying making me feel uncomfortable far too much.

"I'm sorry. Really. Didn't mean any harm. Just bored, you know."

"Bored? Go and spend your time with Escobar and Ramos. They are never bored. They will teach you."

I looked down at my legs, at the wheelchair.

Carlos nodded and made a small "hmmm" sound. "You are jealous. Jealous of their legs no?"

I couldn't look at him. It gave him all the answer he wanted.

"They have more of an advantage over you than your legs, my little compadre."

That stung. I looked up.

"Yes?"

"Yes. They are my sons. And they have no need to be nosy."

I flew back on my wheels then and the last thing I saw before the door slammed shut was the buff folder on the desk, the pages flicking but also at the same time, weirdly, dripping with red river water... The water was coming out of the folder, sloshing across Carlos's desk, pushing his box of cigars to the edge...

BANG!

And the door slammed closed and the corridor was here, and London, and I was flying along it again in the wheelchair. But I wasn't pushing, my hands were still in my lap. I looked over my shoulder to see who was pushing me. On the thick rubber grips of the chair back, was the wooden, twig-boned, mossy hand of Tree Face.

He was pushing me down the corridor at maximum speed.

His feet thudding on the tiles, leaving splinters.

A wall was approaching. I was going to crash into it face first. There was nothing I could do. I was helpless. I couldn't even bail out of the chair because my waist safety belt was across me. I fumbled with the catch on the release mechanism, but it was slippery and kept dropping from my desperate fingers. The wall was getting bigger and bigger. That's it! I was going to crash!

I threw my hands over my face.

And I was home.

In London.

In Westfield, and Jen was walking by with Steve.

They were holding hands. She had her head on his shoulder.

I'd gone there on my own after school. Getting the taxi driver to drop me off there against his orders with a promise of a big tip. I assured him I wouldn't tell Dad. He who wouldn't be home for four hours yet anyway, and I told the driver I would get home before Dad. No worries.

Jen and Steve hadn't seen me. Possibly because I was sitting in one of the open coffee shops that glut the main concourse, making the shoppers streaming past walk nearer to the shop windows unable to escape what they were selling. But mostly I assume they didn't see me because they were pretty much eating each other's faces off.

My palms bit into the wheels of the chair. The pain in my hands keeping me focussed. Stopping me from crying like a girl (… crying like a Sam Coker…) in the middle of town.

Jen and Steve carried on towards the escalators.

I could have wheeled after them, could have followed. I could have screamed at them for the betrayal, but how much of a betrayal was it really?

Before the accident Jen and I had been for a coffee a couple of times, hung out in the shopping centre, had a kiss and a grope in the car park, and winked at each other a lot in school. It's not as if it was the romance of the century or anything, but… but…

I should have known that things weren't going anywhere when Jen was the only one in our group who didn't come to see me in hospital or at home when I got back. Oh, we chatted fine on Facebook and that, but it was just general chit chat and stuffs. I thought it was because she didn't want to put any pressure on me while I was supposed to be getting better. What I didn't realise it was because she was doing anything she could to cut whatever bonds we might have had before the accident as kindly as she could. Without coming out and directly saying, "No legs. No fun, buddy."

Steve was someone I knew well but he wasn't someone I'd call a close friend—after the accident, I didn't really have anyone. He might not even have known what had gone on between Jen and me.

What had gone on?

Did anyone know?

Was I getting worked up over nothing?

Maybe. But it didn't stop it hurting, like a spear cut across the shoulder or a belly full of sickness.

Tree Face's whispery leaves rustled as he sat down in front of me in the coffee shop. His woody eyes fixed on me as he picked up his coffee and drank slowly. Small insects and worms moved in his hair. His lips were red and bright. To look at them hurt my eyes. Tree Face reached a bramble-like hand across the table and touched my hand.

As I looked up from the hand, I saw that everyone around us had the bodies of humans and the heads of alligators.

I pushed back, bumping into an alligator-headed girl. A naked, brown-skinned girl. It was Kik-Kik but she had the body of an alligator. Something burst and popped in my shoulder. There was a savage pain as if I'd just been bitten by something. I tried to reach up but my hand came away wet with pus-streaked blood. My shoulder stung and screamed hotly. I looked up at Kik-Kik's alligator face. She was pulling a tooth from her dead jaw. Levering the sharp canine out by rocking it on its hinges in the rotten gum.

As the tooth came free, Kik-Kik shoved the tooth down into my shoulder and burst the infection there properly this time. Blood, pus, and watery serum gushed down my chest. I screamed in agony, wanting to claw at Kik-Kik and her alligator face, wanting the pain to stop.

All around me, the alligators were laughing. Their huge jaws flapping. And all of them were Jen and Steve and they were all holding human hands and laughing and kissing with alligator faces.

The laughter went on and on and on...

From here to the end of the world.

THIRTY

"Another two days at least," Dad said as I pleaded with him for us to go and get back in the Cherokee and fly away. I didn't care. I just wanted to get away from here. It had already been five days of hell with Escobar, and if didn't look like it was going to get any better, especially after I'd beaten him with the arm-wrestling contest. He had the same level of cancerous pride as his dad, as I was to find out later in the jungle to my cost.

Dad was annoyed I'd stopped him in his room. He was due to join Carlos in the conference room for a Skype call to some blokes who were also throwing into their business venture or something. Dad had his suit on and his tie done up and his hair slicked back and gelled. He only dressed like this when he wanted to make a good impression. He'd even shined his shoes.

"But Dad, Carlos gives me the creeps. He was properly nasty to me yesterday."

Dad growled. "What did I tell you about looking about here? Carlos is a man you don't want to get on the wrong side of, believe me. And I don't want you messing up things for me, is that clear?"

I side-eyed Tree Face who was sitting on the bed, leaves littering out of his head on the breeze, curling through the air to fall like a slice of autumn around Dad's feet. Dad just kicked through the leaves without noticing them. He was ignoring Tree Face too.

Tree Face didn't seem to mind; he was intently making a necklace out of alligator teeth.

"Look, Sam, I know you hate hanging about when I'm in business mode, but I thought letting you fly up here and back, as well as hanging out with Carlos's kids would make it worthwhile."

"Have you met Escobar?" I said sarcastically. "All he wants to do is kick a football around, in front of me. Not exactly my idea of fun."

"And what about Ramos? He's alright."

"He's ten."

"Okay, okay! I'll see what I can do, but things are at a delicate stage… I just needed you… well…"

"Needed me? What do you mean?"

Tree Face put the necklace around Dad's neck. The teeth were still wet and bloody like they were still in the alligator's mouth and on the necklace at the same time.

Then it dawned on me what Dad meant. "I'm window dressing aren't I?"

"No…"

"Oh come on Dad I don't believe it! You thought me being here, all wheel-chaired-up and sad and crippled would make Carlos like you more. Make a better deal with you. Make you more money."

Dad fiddled with the alligator tooth necklace, and Tree Face stood behind him, looking over Dad's shoulder at me, his hissy laugh snickering out between the twigs.

"No, Sam. Of course not."

"Yeah, well it didn't work. He hates me."

"Perhaps if you didn't go snooping around his rooms making him suspicious he may not have done!"

Dad let that hang in the air. Before I could speak, there came a blunt knocking on the door.

"Mr. Coker?" It was Escobar.

Dad opened the door. Escobar was there in his full football kit with a ball underneath his arm. "I have been looking for Sam, is here?"

Dad stood aside and Escobar came in. "My father sent me to fetch you. We are to go and play."

Keep me from snooping you mean, I said as Tree Face wheeled me from the room.

A jungle had grown up around the football pitch overnight.

Piper Cherokees flew above us at regular intervals and Escobar kicked the ball up and down. I sat and boiled by the touchline. Escobar would occasionally kick the ball into my hands and expect me to throw it back to his feet so he could continue freestyling. Escobar didn't want me there, as much I as I didn't want to be there. He'd been given the duty of keeping me from roaming the mansion while Carlos and Dad were doing their business in the conference room.

Escobar didn't want to talk, either. And I didn't offer to talk to him. We were a million miles apart in the same place. Tree Face sat in the centre circle of the pitch looking up at the Cherokees circling above. One was my blue one from back home, the other was the red one in which I'd flown up to the mountains five days ago, and the third was just black. It buzzed around, banking and rolling. Whoever was flying it knew what they were doing.

Ramos came out after an hour, trailed by Maria, his mum, holding a tray of cold drinks. When Maria had poured the cokes, given me the cow-eyes, and departed, Ramos sat next to me on the bench.

"Are they still in the conference room?" I asked.

Ramos nodded "They will be in there all day. It is boring."

So at least one of Carlos's boys got bored. I bet I wouldn't get the same admission from Escobar. The older brother was on the other side of the pitch to us now. He'd taken the arrival of Ramos to mean he didn't have to babysit me too closely anymore and was enjoying the limited freedom it gave him

Tree Face wandered off into the jungle, leaving Ramos and me alone.

"So what does your dad do?" I asked.

Ramos shrugged. "I don't know. Exports things. Export means send things out of the country."

His ten-year-old earnest face really believed he was telling me something I didn't know.

"Oh right," I said encouragingly. "Dad said he was a property developer."

"I don't know what that it. Please explain."

"Someone who buys land and builds things on it."

Ramos shrugged. "Maybe. I do not know."

Escobar had come back, he was standing very close. "Be quiet Ramos. You don't talk about father, OK?"

Ramos clammed up.

"Sorry," I said. "Just making conversation."

"No," said Escobar. "You were making nosy."

Escobar went back to freestyling the football and the red Cherokee circled another couple of times before coming in to land. The windows were smoked over, so I couldn't see who was piloting it.

The door opened, and Tree Face got out.

The dealings in the conference room didn't end until gone ten pm that night. Escobar, stiff, near-silent, boiling angry, had been stuck with me for the best part of thirteen hours. The only time we'd been out of each other's company had been for comfort stops and Ick Bag changing. We'd moved inside in the late afternoon for sandwiches and some kind of rice dish that looked like an octopus had been sick in it.

I stuck to the sandwiches.

I sat at the table looking out through the long range of windows over the garden to the airstrip. A black Cherokee was parked up next to our plane and two of Carlos's guards were standing by near it. Their hands on their machine pistols, scanning the surrounding area, on the lookout for trouble. One of them waved a hand to someone I couldn't see and a few seconds later another guard came into view pushing a low, wheeled trolley over the rough ground towards the black Cherokee. It was stacked with several dark holdalls of a kind I recognised, but couldn't place.

When the trolley got to the plane, one of the other guards opened the door in the side and jumped up. The trolley guard started throwing the bags up into the plane, waiting while the guard inside stowed them evenly to distribute the weight. When he came to the last bag, the trolley guard unzipped it, and pulled out a small black box. He pressed a button on the side, turned a dial, held it up and around like someone trying to pick up a mobile phone signal. When he was satisfied, he put the box back in the bag, zipped it up and threw it into the Cherokee.

"What are they doing?" I asked, not expecting an answer from Escobar.

"Exporting," Tree Face whispered in my ear. I looked around. He was sitting right next to me. He sneered his wooden grin and sat back. Showing me that Jen and Steven were sitting further along the table, eating the rice and kissing each other between mouthfuls.

"I reckon we'll be able to go home tomorrow," Dad said, sitting down across from me. Carlos picked a cigar out of Tree Face's belly and lit it with an enormous onyx desk lighter.

The smoke blew darkly from his froggy-cheeked mouth.

I wheeled myself away from the table, made my excuses, and went back to my room. I could take Escobar and Carlos, and even my dad who'd used me as a business advantage, rather than a son, but I wasn't going to share a table with Jen and Steve.

When I got to my room, it had been changed completely. It had been made to resemble my lounge at home in London. It felt a little bit weird, but Carlos's people had had all day to do it, and so I wheeled myself in.

Halliday and Dad were sitting on the sofas discussing papers in buff cardboard files. Halliday and Dad looked up as I came in. They didn't say anything, they just looked at me. Tree Face, who had been digging his finger into one of the many pot plants dotted around, sniffed his finger and then ate the dirt that was clinging to them.

Kik-Kik with her alligator head took the alligator-teeth necklace from around Dad's neck and started to put the teeth back into her own jaw.

For the longest time, with everyone staring at me, the only sound in the room was the teeth being screwed back into place. They squeaked and protested, as if it was a real effort to get them in or as if they were being put into the wrong mouth. When Kik-Kik had finished with the teeth, everyone in the room, including me, was holding a buff cardboard folder.

Dad and Halliday were still staring at me. They weren't even blinking. Their mouths drooped open with a dry clack—like they were made out of wood—and a trickle of red liquid started to run out of the side of their mouths. A first I thought it was blood, and then I realised it was river water.

And it was coming out of Kik-Kik's alligator mouth. And from between Tree Face's branches. And when I looked down, at the papers open in the folder on my lap, I realised the water was also coming out of my mouth. It was running over the papers, across the words, blurring them, but also sloshing up against the black box with the greyed-out screen.

And over the dial on the front, and around the satellite aerial, like a thick finger of rubber, folded up along one side.

THIRTY-ONE

Drums. Darkness. Firelight. Voices. A language I did not understand. I didn't even know if what I heard were words. They could have been anything. The sounds shivered through me. Fires from torches cast crazy shadows over the vegetation. The sky was filled with smoke from the fires and a hundred legs danced about in the clearing, attached to cannibal bodies and cannibal heads. The dance was fast and the dance was frantic. The feet stormed to a stop in a hush. Jumped, landed with a synchronised thud that rattled the ground beneath me, and then began to dance again.

The gyrating cannibals whirled in a circle around a shadowed figure. It was bent over and kneeling down. Fists in the dirt, head bowed. The light from the torches and the fires didn't reach it. It was as if whoever was there had the ability to reject light and push it back by sheer force of will alone. I thought I could smell a trace of it, blown to me on the gentle breeze. It smelled of decay and mulch and compost.

It was Tree Face.

With a roar, Tree Face leaped up and let the light hit him. He was all branches, glistening moss; the vine-dreads of his hair whirled, and his bright red mouth opened wide onto his creaking wooden throat. Tree Face screamed at the sky, threw his barky arms wide and the dancing cannibals stamped to a hush of stillness again, looking up at Tree Face with a mixture of awe and fear. One by one, they vibrated their lips with breath and pointed their spears at him. As the last spear rolled into place through the smoky air, a Piper Cherokee at full throttle burst out of his mouth and shot up towards the sky, swirling the smoke into spiral vortices and curls of grey vapour.

"You have control."

Dad took his hand off the flying yoke, and the Cherokee was mine. Grey England below became the grey estuary of the Thames. I turned the yoke, operating the rudder and flaps with my thumbs on the modified control column.

The plane was mine.

Dad was letting me take it where I wanted.

The cloud ceiling was 6,000 feet and climbing at a steady rate of 700 feet per minute, I'd be up above them in about eight minutes. Up there it would be a different world, above the grey and the drizzle; above the clouds it is always summer, the sky is always blue. Below us, there would be no ground, just the sunlit puffs of white, powdery clouds all the way to the horizon. Grey England would sink below that fast-moving, glutted wake of weather and would be lost to me until I decided to take us back.

This was my last training flight before going to South America. Dad said that flying over featureless clouds was very much the same as flying over featureless rainforest. I'd have to rely on instruments rather than landmarks or coastline. There would be no fancy Instrument Landing Systems to ping my navigations in the right direction either. I'd need to keep steady headings based on the compass and flight controls. There'd be no beacons to lock onto, and there'd be no friendly voice of Ground Control to talk me through any difficulties.

I would be piloting by the "seat of my pants," Dad had said.

"I hope it'll be ok if I wear some trousers," I replied.

I thought it was a good joke. But Dad blanked me and didn't respond. Just like he had in the hallway a month ago. Before I even knew I was going to be flying anywhere outside the UK. Like now, his thoughts had already moved on as his phone was ringing.

We paused in the hallway of the house. Dad looked at the screen of his phone as I wheeled myself to the door, ready to get on my way to school. Dad was taking me today; he didn't need to be in the office until eleven.

"Carlos!" Dad said in to the mobile, then something Spainuguese or Portish I didn't understand. Dad held up his finger to me, motioning me not to open the door. It was an important call.

"Sure, all set to go on the 30th. No bother."

Dad listened and his face changed, as if he didn't understand what was being said to him for a moment, "I'm sorry?"

Dad looked at me hard.

"Sam? Come with me?"

My ears pricked up at the mention of my name. I didn't know a *Carlos*, did I? I thought back. Nope. Didn't mean anything to me, except it was the first name of that Teves geezer who used to play for CITEH. All hair and face like a shaved monkey who'd scraped his head across tarmac.

"Well, come on Carlos. This is business. I've arranged for my ex-wife to..."

Carlos cut him off. I couldn't hear the exact words, but the voice on the other end of the line rose a little in pitch and sounded agitated.

Dad took a deep breath. Closed his eyes. "Yeah, ok Carlos. He can meet your boys and stuff while we set things in motion. Fine. Cool. All good."

There was a quick, steely question.

"Yeah, mate. It's fine. He'll love it."

Love what? I thought. Dad hung up the phone. For a moment his face sagged and I thought he was terrified. Then he painted on a smile and said, "Just got to make another call, but guess what?"

"What?"

"You're coming to South America with me."

Wow.

"South America? Brazil?"

But Dad was already retreating towards the kitchen, and slamming the door shut behind him, mobile glued to his hear. The last thing I heard was him saying "Halliday please." Before there was a knock on the door behind me.

I reached up and opened it, wheeling back in horror.

There was a man made of trees on the doorstep.

Tree Face stalked in on a rustle of dead leaves, bringing a gust of mulchy wet autumn with him. His mouth moved with wood beetles. A fat black centipede hung from his ear like an earring.

I could hear Dad shouting into the phone in the other room but my throat was constricted. Tree Face left a trail of dirt across the hall carpet, got behind my wheelchair and pushed me as hard as he could towards the front door. I crashed out, over the steps onto the gravel and up into the air, breaking through the five hundred feet of grey could into the sparkling sunny blue above.

"I said 'I hope you'll let me wear some trousers!'" I thought maybe repeating the joke would get a reaction from Dad but he was too busy looking at the screen of his phone reading a text. His eyes flicked up to the instrument panel. "Watch your heading. You're off course."

I made the correction as Dad thumbed through the text on the phone. I looked out over the cloud, levelled off at seven and a half thousand feet, and watched the blurry indistinct horizon.

Dad's face was concerned. He turned off his phone, put it back in his pocket, and then rubbed his face with his hands.

"You okay?" I asked, concerned.

"What?"

"Are you okay? Did you get bad news on the phone? Do I need to land so you can get back to work?"

Dad shook his head. "It's okay; I'll take care of it when we've finished up here."

Someone prodded me in the shoulder, I took off my headset and turned around as the circle of cannibals circling Tree Face began to dance and sing and shake their spears towards the sky, where a huge moon was rising through the smoke above the silhouetted skeletons of the trees. The Cherokee flew across the face of the moon like a tiny black shadow. I found myself waving at it, wishing that it and my dad would come back and pick me up from here. I wanted more than anything to go home. I wanted to stop sweating and I wanted the ache in my shoulder, the throbbing red pain that lived there now to go away, to leave me alone. I wanted Kik-Kik to give me some water because my mouth was so dry and there was nothing I could do now the alligators, hundreds of them, tiny baby alligators were swarming around my legs and over my lap and then Fat Leopard...

I lifted my head from the pillow as Fat Leopard licked my face. I didn't know if he was tasting me or just trying to wake me up. He jumped down off the bed and went and sat in the corner of the bedroom I'd been given in Carlos's mountain mansion. I could see the wound I'd made in the side of his neck. It was open and bloody, weeping onto his black and yellow fur, darkening it. Fat Leopard licked at the wound and looked at me as if he forgave me.

I got out of the bed and walked to the window.

In the distance,—the hot, white, midday distance—my dad and I were about to leave the mansion and fly away in the adapted Cherokee. Dad was making the pre-flight checks, and I was looking at the Brazil shirt in the crinkly cellophane on my lap. Although I wasn't really taking notice, wanting to get away from Escobar and his legs that worked and kicked and ran. I noticed that one of Carlos's mechanics was under the engine cover on the other side of the plane. I couldn't see what he was doing, but because I was in the chair, I was low enough to see his legs.

I didn't really want to notice him, maybe this time it was important to notice him, I didn't know. I just wanted to get away from Escobar and this place, where Carlos was a bit of an arsehole and had wanted me there for a reason. Maybe it wasn't Dad using me; maybe it had something to do with that phone call in the hall. I heard the mechanic closing the engine cover and the crunch of his feet walking away. And I rolled myself forward, waiting for Dad to lift me up and put me in the plane.

And that's when my throat closed.

The engine cover clanged shut again.

The mechanic's feet crunched on the hard dirt of the airstrip.

My throat closed and I couldn't breathe, Dad was reaching towards me, bent over, his hands spread, but however much he reached, however much he bent he never touched me, and the engine cover clanged shut...

And the feet crunched away...

And Tree Face, behind me, tightened his thorny forearm across my throat.

And Carlos's face and Escobar's face both as big as the moon in the jungle sky loomed towards me through the firelight.

And the engine cover clanged.

And the mechanic's feet crunched.

And Tree Face started to strangle the life out of me.

And high above the Amazon, in that endless blue sky, when I was flying and Dad was sleeping, the Piper Cherokee's engine clanged and crunched to a halt, and we began to drop out of the sky.

THIRTY-TWO

The jungle drums rattled the sides of the wigwam. The walls bowed, flexed, and flapped.

Tree Face didn't relax his grip on my neck. However hard I scrabbled at the bark and moss-covered arm across my throat I couldn't pull it far enough away to let me breathe. Dark spots filled my vision like dozens of tiny fruit flies. They spiralled and swooped. Sometimes they were birds. Sometimes they were flies. Sometimes I was in the wigwam. Sometimes I was being strangled at dusk on a quiet autumn night overlooking the Essex marshes, where Dad sometimes took me fishing. The sky was streaked with clouds, purple, red, yellow. Beautiful sunset in one eye, wounds, bruises, and tears in the other. The jungle drums beating out a headache in my skull and the tides in my belly washing up and down, up and down.

Sometimes I was flies. Sometimes I was birds.

The purple was inflating my head like a balloon, distorting my eyes. The wigwam went crazy then. The fire, surrounded by stones leaped up as if it had become a flamethrower. I could feel it burning my skin. I burned all over. I needed water. I needed to breathe, but Tree Face was intent on squeezing every last atom of air out of my lungs.

I could taste his breath in my dying mouth. It was putrid and thick, like the smell that comes off fox shit. That stench you can never get rid of if you get it accidentally on the wheel of your wheelchair and then onto your hand if you're pushing yourself across the grass to where Steve was leaning against the goalpost in the park. Waiting for the others, waiting for the game.

Steve unslouched as I approached. It would be a few minutes

before I realised I had the fox shit on my hand. I was intent and focussed on Steve. I was wheeling towards him. I wasn't going to stop.

He didn't realise what was happening. Steve only got halfway through "Wotcher Sam..." before I clattered into him hard with the footplates of the wheelchair. They smashed into the skin above his ankles and he yelled. I pushed forwards with my hands trying to carry the momentum through his body, trying to get him to fall over so that I could wheel straight over his lying, cheating face.

Steve did go down, but not in a way that I could roll over him. He fell to the side and whacked the side of his head on the cold metal goalpost. When I thought back, I imagined him going down like a cartoon character, eyes crossed and birds and stars swirling around his head.

Steve's arm was trapped between the axle and the wheel. He hissed again with pain, but his arm was stopping the chair moving backward or forward. But I wasn't going to let that stop me. I undid my seat belt and bailed out of the chair. Steve groaned beneath me as the weight of my body crashed into his chest.

I started to pummel his face. Steve had regained enough of his senses to grab my wrists. But however powerful he was, he wasn't a match for my super-strong, wheelchair-exercised arms. I easily pulled his hands aside and head-butted him on the nose.

"Stop!" Steve yelled, turning his face to one side.

I head-butted his ear, my forehead splitting the top curled edge of it. As I came away, blood welled in the wound.

"What the bloody hell are you doing?" Steve screamed at me, trying to roll out from underneath me.

"Jen. You... bastard..." I managed to spit out, still trying to break my wrists free of his hands.

"What? What do you mean Jen?"

"I saw you!"

"What are you talking about, you mentalist!?"

"I saw you at Westfield! I saw you kissing her!"

"She's my girlfriend you utter prick! What else am I supposed to do?"

"But..." I couldn't find the words.

"But what? You've been in hospital and at home for three months, you've only just come back to school. You had three coffees, a kiss and a go on her tits. That does not make her your girlfriend!"

I stopped trying to break free.

"She told you?"

"Yes. Of course she told me. She's my girlfriend."

"But..."

Steve wriggled out from under me and rolled away. I was face down in the mud of the goalmouth, my hand covered in fox shit, and the sliminess against my stomach I prayed was the mud and not my Ick Bag coming loose.

Steve got up. Aimed a kick at me and then, whether feeling a stab of compassion or embarrassed by the visual of a big lad like him kicking a cripple who was already down, let his foot drop.

"You and Jen weren't a thing, were never a thing, and were never going to be a thing. She'd stopped seeing you four weeks before the accident. Remember?"

I thought back.

But...

Yes. It was true.

It had been four weeks since we'd been for a coffee or anything. She was just being nice on Facebook for ages before Dad totalled the car on the way back from Birmingham. I'd been so caught up in feeling angry that she'd dumped me because of the accident I'd forgotten that our relationship, even if you could call it that, was dead a long time before my legs died. Anger and self-pity are funny things. They can make you remember stuff that hadn't happened in an order you thought they had. Or they could make you think things that hadn't happened, or worst of all make you miss things that were important that had happened, only you'd been too wrapped up in yourself to notice.

Clang.

Crunch.

Steve left me there in the mud, next to the overturned

wheelchair. I watched him walk away for a good few minutes before the others arrived and helped me back into the wheelchair.

I had burst my Ick Bag.

I could smell it, the thin stench rising up, as the fire in the wigwam burned even brighter and redder. The tribe were coming into the huge, hide-covered space. Smoky with magic and crackling with energy. I'd given up on the idea of ever breathing again and was now welcoming the idea of death. It had to be better than this. Let Tree Face choke me to death, see if I care!

Among the dancing, rhythmically chanting cannibals, I could see Carlos, naked to the waist, alligator symbol painted all over his fat, sweaty, hairy body, down to where his huge, flabby belly hung over the top of his loincloth like a half-punctured balloon. In Carlos's hand, instead of a spear, a large cigar burned brightly with a red ember of ash on the end that could have been a landing light. In fact, through the billow of smoke coming off the end, I thought I could see the shadow of a Cherokee darting across the surface of the hide wall of the wigwam.

Clang.

Crunch.

Behind Carlos was Escobar, a small bone through the septum in his nose, naked to his loincloth and also covered in symbols and signs. Half of his back was given over to a crude painting of Fat Leopard. In his hands, he carried a football covered in tiny representations of Tree Face. He was chanting loudly with the rest of them; he knew the words off by heart. Behind him, I had expected Ramos, but instead it was a man, big and powerful. The entire top of his body was in shadow, and I could only see his legs. He carried a small black electronic box in his hand, and his feet clanged and crunched as he walked.

Then more cannibals followed. The wigwam, big as it was, seemed to be filling to capacity. And yet still more and more of them entered in an orderly precision, into the dimly lit interior, their eyes sparkling with tears of ecstasy as the communed with their god.

Their Tree God.

The forearm tightened again around my throat.

I could feel the bones compressing, the skin losing any resistance, my windpipe flattened against itself. Deflated. A barrier to breath. A darkness was seeping up from my guts. Like black ink dripped into the clear water, a cloud of black nothing. An emptying, a draining of me, to be replaced by nothing. I heard the muscles creaking in Tree Face's arms. His branch-biceps swelling against the side of my face.

Then into the closed, warm, stinking interior of the wigwam came Jen and Steve. Naked and painted. Holding each other in a cuddle of possession. They didn't look at me, they didn't see me. They just went on to join the swelling ranks.

Sparks floated up from the fire; two cannibals came towards me holding bowls of paint. They sat by me as I died, painting on my skin. Painting Cherokees, painting Rolexes, painting my dad dead in his chair with a branch through him, painting snakes, painting an alligator whose teeth were arranged in such a way it looked as if he was eating my arm.

My eyes flicked up. Dad and Halliday were entering the tent. Dad holding parcels of white powder wrapped in brown tape. Halliday clutching buff cardboard folders to his chest. The folders were covered in symbols I didn't recognise. There might have been a white building by some water that had a green roof. It sort of seemed familiar but I couldn't place it. My dad showed me he was carrying the exploded gun in his other hand. It sparkled there as if the inside had been sprayed with gold and the bullets were tipped with diamonds.

Suddenly Kik-Kik was in front of me, pushing away the cannibals who were painting me. She was holding a bowl up to my lips. She wanted me to drink.

Tree Face tightened his armlock even more, I thought he was about to pull my head away from my body.

The bowl came to my lips.

Tree Face heaved.

I drank the water.

Tree Face pulled my back into his thorny chest.

I drank again.

Tree Face howled.

My legs were suddenly working. I dug them into the ground and pushed with all my might. The feeling in my legs was amazing. A combination of pins and needles and adrenaline. Tree Face resisted, but in the same moment, he'd put so much pressure on his arm across my throat that the brittle wood of his elbow snapped and his arm fell down loose in my lap.

I could breathe!

I pushed and pushed with my newly healed legs. Tree Face went back, unable to resist me.

We ripped through the side of the wigwam and were back in the clearing. I pushed and pushed, Kik-Kik followed with the bowl, giving me sips of water as I heaved and pushed and fought.

I turned around. There was a look of panic on Tree Face's features and I thrust out with both my arms. He crashed into the tree and was swallowed by it. The bark of the tree ran around his body like liquid and locked him back inside the trunk.

I fell forward exhausted.

The ground smelled sweeter. The air fresher. There was water on my lips and the taste of fruit in my mouth.

I opened my eyes.

THIRTY-THREE

An alligator loomed towards me, blinding light in its eyes. I threw up my hands and screamed.

Kik-Kik laughed.

I put down my hands. It was the alligator's head on the pole that I'd seen, the morning sun behind it in the trees, blazing through the empty eye sockets. Kik-Kik sat next to me; there was a bowl of water in her hand which she was offering up to my lips.

I drank. The water was cool and clean.

Kik-Kik placed a chunk of fruit into my open mouth and nodded.

I chewed.

I blinked.

I swallowed.

I could see Tree Face on the opposite side of the clearing, his face lit brightly in the morning sun. His mouth was freshly painted and small green and red birds were flying in and out of his mouth, with bits of straw and twigs in their beaks, making a nest in his throat. Good, I thought, maybe that would stop up his mouth and whispery wooden voice...

I blinked.

Kik-Kik placed a cool hand on my forehead and smiled and nodded.

I felt properly rubbish, but the ache in my guts had gone and so had the white-hot pain in my shoulder. I looked at skin there out of the corner of my eye. There was a brown and purple mound of what looked like chewed up vegetation that had been shaped like a mud pie and slapped onto the wound. I moved the joint experimentally and although there was a dull shadow of pain still there, it felt manageable. I looked down my body. I was naked.

Great.

My skin also glistened with painted figures. Tree Face. The alligator, Fat Leopard. The alligator was eating my arm like it had in the dream...

The dream.

God.

It all came back in a rush of memories. The mansion. The Cherokee. Jen. Steve. Dad.

Clang.

Crunch.

I tried to shift my position to sit up, but I felt so weak. Kik-Kik, a big smile made from ruined teeth, reached under my arm with the crook of her elbow and lifted me back up against the tree that I was leaned against.

That's when I saw I wasn't wearing an Ick Bag.

The pink nub of intestine was exposed but clean. It was surrounded by leaves that had been stuck in place with what looked like the same stuff Kik-Kik had put on my shoulder. The leaves were draining a thin sludgy line of Ick down and away from my skin. Kik-Kik wiped at the opening with a soft downy leaf, screwed it up, and threw it into the trees. She got another leaf ready by my side ready to clean me again when the need arose.

I had no idea how long I'd been out of it in the grip of the double whammy of shoulder infection and stomach poisoning, but it was clear that Kik-Kik had undressed me, moved me, kept me fed and watered and clean for the whole process. She'd come up with a reasonably ingenious solution to the Ick Bag problem and she had kept me alive.

I felt so rough and it wasn't a great leap to assume that without her looking after me, I would have died up against that tree, while Tree Face looked on and did nothing.

"Thank you," I tried to croak, but all that came out was a dry whisper that hurt the muscles of my throat. I guess the dream of me not being able to breathe hadn't been that far from the truth.

Something wet moved against my shoulder and I flinched.

Kik-Kik laughed again and held up her finger. It was covered in yellow paint and she was continuing a half-finished snake there on my skin. She waited for me to nod, and then continued putting yellow dots all down the green body of the snake. Its eyes were red, and its mouth was wide and bared with white fangs. Kik-Kik wasn't a bad artist either.

For a cripple with a learning disability, she wasn't doing at all badly in my book.

I picked up some fruit and popped it into my mouth, enjoying the fresh feeling of it on my tongue.

Kik-Kik finished the snake and sat back to admire her handiwork. The snake, the alligator, and Fat Leopard. I was painted with the animals that had tried to kill me, which between us we'd beaten by death or by fear. She was painting the last few days' adventures on me. It was a book of our time together. I'd never liked the idea of tattoos before, but if I ever got out of there, I think I'd quite like to get something done to commemorate what had happened.

Then it hit me what she'd missed out.

She would need to add pictures of Carlos and Escobar to the animals that had threatened me.

The delirious fever dream rumbled through my head again.

Clang.

Crunch.

The mechanic I'd been too wrapped up in my own misery to notice, working on the engine on the other side of the Cherokee, was planting a device in the fuselage, wasn't he? Something that would go off at a pre-determined time and crash us in the jungle miles from anywhere.

How would they know when to detonate it though?

Then the dream exploded again. Watching through the window, that night, when I was feeling too sorry for myself and thinking about the ways I could pee-off Escobar, it hadn't even registered on my thoughts the guys loading the plane, and the one putting a device with a satellite aerial into one of the bags. They'd used that to track us, and then when the time was right, when we were the furthest we could be from civilisation, they made the plane crash.

Oh, God, I promised I would never be so wrapped up in my problems and myself again. Maybe if I'd noticed all this in the first place Dad would still be alive.

Kik-Kik got up and started to dance and sing.

I had no idea what prompted it but she danced, touched my forehead, ran to Tree Face, danced in front of him, popped some fruit into his mouth, and jumped up to pat him on the forehead too.

Then she jigged back to me and performed the same process all over again.

Then she started to sing.

Well, at least I think it was singing. It seemed to be some sort of celebratory song. There was a lot of smiling and laughing and pointing at me. Lots of touching me and pointing at Tree Face and touching him. There was quite a bit of her rubbing her good arm against Tree Face's tree, whispering up at him and then rubbing her flipper vigorously and then punching it a bit, and then slapping it and then doing the whispering dance all over again.

This went on for about an hour.

I think I dropped off at one point as the exhaustion of recovery overtook me again.

When I awoke, Kik-Kik was building me a shelter. Which wasn't easy with one hand and a flipper. First, she emerged from the jungle with four long branches, which she proceeded to stand on, then pull the young thin branches away with her good hand. Then using her feet and hand she tied the top of the branches together with endlessly curling vines. Next, she stood the frame up over me, kicking the bottom of it out around me until I was in a roughly shaped pyramid. For the next hour, she went back and forwards to the forest and came back with a collection of huge, flat leaves, which she began to attach to the frame with thorns. Soon, the leaves, forming a pattern that looked like roof tiles, surrounded me on three sides, with a tree at my back.

It would keep the rain off and it would block me from the view of any passing predators.

When she'd finished, she surveyed the shelter.

It was an excellent piece of work. I wish I wasn't staying in the jungle, but if I had to, then I supposed that to have a shelter—to keep the rain and maybe the worst of the direct sunlight off my body—was a good thing.

However grateful I was of the shelter though, I couldn't stop myself having moments of anger and sadness at what Carlos had had his men do to us.

It was a horrible thought, the idea that someone valued your life so little that they wanted you dead, and it took a special kind of evil to want to do it in this way. It was like something out of a stupid film or something. A dastardly plan to remove someone who would potentially cause you problems—I mean why not just shoot them on the spot? Why make a scheme and a plot? What did you gain from knowing someone was going to crash in the jungle, and even if they survived, die a slow horrible death from starvation or a quick violent death at the teeth of a snakogatoleopard?

I imagined Carlos, sitting at his desk. Glee all over his sweaty frog face, with Escobar throwing his head back, rubbing their hands and giggling as they watched a radar screen showing us dropping stone-fast into the jungle, like villains in a rubbish Bond movie.

Kik-Kik was waiting, and I'd drifted away. She hadn't moved since she'd finished the shelter and was now looking at me expectantly.

I smiled. Pointed at the shelter and put up my thumb.

She got the message and clapped her hand awkwardly with her flipper and made a thumbs-up sign. Then she ran away in the direction of the river without looking back.

"Kik-Kik!" I called but she didn't stop running. Soon the trees swallowed her up and I could no longer see her brown back running between their trunks.

The shelter was keeping the sun off, the fire was still alight, I had water and fruit and my Ick was draining thinly away on an aqueduct of leaves, but I suddenly felt very alone and vulnerable. When the source of your safety, Kik-Kik, runs away and leaves you, a churning of anxiety in your guts starts up almost immediately. I became in that moment, acutely aware of how much I was relying on this girl now. How I was helpless without her.

If anything happened to her down at the river, if anything happened to her between her village and here, I knew that was curtains for me.

For the last year since the accident, I'd done everything I could to regain my independence, to acknowledge that losing the power to walk and run was not the end of everything, that I was not defined by my legs. But now, here, as the jungle closed in, Tree Face, by the action of the sunlight cast shadows on his face, began concentrating on me hard. His mouth became a dark hole of mockery. The leaves in the trees whispered his predictions at me. You're going to die. You're going to die. You're...

I put my hands over my ears, but I could still hear him. I couldn't shut him out.

You're going to die.

You're going to...

"Kik-Kik!" I screamed into the jungle. "Kik-Kik! Please! Please come back! I need you! Don't leave me!"

The panic rose like bile inside me, I didn't know if I was going to faint or vomit, or both. It was as if a black knife was sticking into my heart and Tree Face was twisting it. He knew it wasn't just in my dreams that he could kill me, he could kill me here, with terror.

All he had to use was the wind, and the sunlight and his screaming, deadwood face.

"Kik-Kik! Come back!"

And she did.

But not in the way I was expecting.

THIRTY-FOUR

Jen...

Okay. I can say her name now. Let's do this.

Jen came to see me the day after I'd attacked Steve in the park's muddy goalmouth. She hadn't told me she was coming, hadn't texted or Facebooked me. Nothing. It was Saturday morning but Dad had had to go into the office for a few hours or something. He'd promised, on his life though, to be back to take me for a flying lesson at four. Normally I'd check the entry phone to see who was at the door, but as I was in the hallway anyway picking up some letters from the cage behind the door, I couldn't be arsed to wheel myself back to the kitchen to check, so I just opened it.

Jen stood on the doorstep. Bobble hat with the knitted earpieces tied under her chin against the cold and the fog. Overcoat done right up to the neck, gloves on. Wellies. Her face in the tiny oval of space between the top of her hat and the start of her scarf.

I wheeled myself back. I didn't know what to say.

She stood there. I seemed as if she didn't know either.

I hadn't fully processed what had happened yesterday, other than to suffer the embarrassment of people picking you up, putting you back in a wheelchair and them realising that they had fox poo and my Ick from the torn-away Ick Bag all over their hands. I bet both of them had really regretted coming to help. I'd mumbled a quick "Thanks" and promptly turned the chair around and pushed hard all the way home. I'd got in the shower and turned it on, still fully clothed and undressed as the warm spray hit me. It washed the Ick and fox shit off my hands and the wheels at the same time. The clothes could stay wet in the corner until the housekeeper came in the next morning to do the cleaning.

Anyway, I'd spent the rest of the day pretty much feeling like an idiot, shaking a bit, noticing a tremor in my hands. I put it down to an overdose of adrenaline or something. I hadn't eaten and I told Dad I just wanted to stay in my room. He was cool with that. Halliday was coming over for something and he wanted to use the lounge for that. Every time the landline or his mobile had rung, I tensed, expecting someone to be ringing him up to complain about me attacking their son, or the police wanting to talk to me about an assault in the park yesterday. But no one complained, the police never called, and by the time I was yawning and ready for my bed I'd calmed down enough to fall into a solid sleep in which there were no dreams, or at least any that I remembered.

I'd heard Dad going at 7am, when the banging of the front door, which was at the end of the hallway outside my room, woke me. There was a voicemail on my mobile from Dad telling me he was on his way to the office but would be back. And it had turned out to be a fairly normal morning until now, with the fog swirling, and the milky sky not looking like it was going to shift from the cold and grey, here was Jen.

Standing on the doorstep.

Saying nothing.

"Shall Do I you go want Sam to or come shall in I stay?" we both said at once. I nodded.

"Which one?" Jen said.

"Come in." I wheeled back further and Jen came in, unwinding her scarf and pulling off her hat.

I took her to my bedroom. It was the first time she'd been there. I got us cokes from the fridge and she sat in the armchair near the window. There was yet another uncomfortable silence in which I had the chance to look at the girl I'd fought for. Jen didn't make eye contact and just sipped at her coke.

"It wasn't because of your legs," Jen said suddenly, almost blurting it out. She'd been holding it inside. This was her primary reason for coming here, and the silence had all been about the pressure of those words building up inside of her until she could contain them no longer.

I nodded.

"You don't believe me?"

"I just nodded, didn't I?"

"Yeah, but you could be nodding either way."

"I believe you."

That seemed to relax her. Her hair was tied back in a ponytail, there were dark rings around her eyes and she wasn't wearing any makeup. Usually you wouldn't see her dead without makeup. I suppose she hadn't come here to look attractive to me.

"I just wanted you to know that. I didn't come to see you because I didn't know what to say. We never actually said that we'd stopped seeing each other, not that we'd really started or anything, I mean it was just a few coffees and you know..."

Her face reddened.

I knew.

"And then it just didn't feel right. I was going to tell you. I promise. And then you had the car accident and then there were your legs and everyone saying how you were paralysed—"

That word cut across my guts. It was a word I never wanted to hear again.

"—and there's me thinking maybe he still thinks we're going out, and I couldn't really just come to the hospital and tell you, 'Oh by the way Sam, sorry about the legs and everything but you're dumped and that,' could I? I mean you could see how difficult it was for me, can't you?"

Honestly, my heart was bleeding for her.

"So when I found out what you did to Steve yesterday, I realised that you still thought that what was happening before your accident was still happening after the accident, and I couldn't believe it! I felt like such a slime that I hadn't told you or got someone else to tell you—"

Oh, well thanks for the consideration.

"—not that I would have got someone else to tell you that you were dumped; that would have been cruel. And I didn't say anything to you on Messenger or Text, because that would have been unfair too, but I promise I was building up to tell you, I promise I was. I know you've been back at school awhile—"

Two months, Jen. Two months.

"—but you were still settling in. Well, that's what I was telling myself. And I suppose you didn't want to say anything because you needed to concentrate on getting better, and I suppose you thought that we were still a thing and that, and like I was waiting for you, like one of those women who marry serial killers and wait for them to get out of prison—"

Serial killers.

"—not that I'm calling you a serial killer or anything, but you know what I mean. And I just couldn't come up to you, so I was waiting for you to bring it up so that I could tell you and of course you never brought it up because you thought nothing had changed, but yes it has changed, everything has changed and that—"

So it is about my legs.

"—but that's not the change I'm talking about. I went on my first date with Steve the night you had your accident and you were in Birmingham and that, and I kind of fell for him that night, and he kind of fell for me and that, and so even if you hadn't had the accident I would still have dumped you—"

That's comforting.

"—And really that's what I came to tell you because I definitely didn't want you thinking it was because of your legs. Because it's not. Swear down."

I blinked.

Jen really was sitting there telling me that even though it wasn't my legs, which was great, she was cheating on me, whatever cheating in the context of whatever relationship we had or hadn't had, meant.

I blinked again.

I think it sunk into Jen, what she'd just admitted to during in her rush to tell me that it was nothing to do with me becoming a cripple that stopped her from seeing me.

"You don't think it might have been a good idea to tell me you were going on a date with someone else then?"

Her face was doing the reddening thing again.

She played with the hat in her lap. I could tell that this wasn't how she'd expected things to turn out this morning.

"I thought that if I told you it wasn't about—"

She pointed at the wheelchair.

"—that it would all be okay and we could be mates and you wouldn't be attacking Steve again or anything."

This time we had the longest and most awkward silence in the history of the human race. It was so long, I bet a new species of insect evolved somewhere in Africa or something.

In some ways, this was even worse than hearing that she hadn't fancied going out with someone in a wheelchair. This sounded like I was a loser before the accident, that I couldn't have Jen as a girlfriend even if I could still walk, or take her clubbing, or freestyle a ball around the field while she looked on admiringly (OK, that one was a bit of a stretch, but you never know). It really hurt. I actually thought that I couldn't sink any lower in my mood since the accident, that the idea that I was stuck in this chair for the rest of my life wouldn't be the worst possible thing that could happen to me. But the accident hadn't been my fault, it was just the unhappy consequence of a lot of things that were out of my control. Jen and me, well that was in my control, well at least partially. I thought we had got on really well. I thought she liked me. I thought I liked her—I didn't want to admit to myself then that the like had turned into something else—but with the distance of hindsight, it may well have. I had to face up to that. Well, I'd bloody gone off food, and my heart had leaped any time her name lit up in Messenger in the four weeks before the accident. She'd been the last thing on my mind before I got up and the first thing on my mind before I went to bed. So yeah. It was tough hearing this.

In some ways, it would have been easier if she'd told me that the reason she'd stopped seeing me was because of the leg thing.

But she hadn't.

Jen got up. "Anyway, I need to, yeah—" She pulled on her bobble hat and did the straps up under her chin. "About Steve…"

I looked up at her, "Yes?"

"I just wanted to make sure that everything is going to be cool at school, that you're not going to be going for him again or making trouble and stuff."

I shook my head. "No. I'm done with that. No more fighting."

She puffed out her cheeks with relief and put her gloves on, "I'll show myself out, yeah?"

And with that she was gone.

The door slammed and I was left in my room alone. It took a few moments to steady my breathing, and wait for the new adrenaline tremors in my hand to subsist before I wheeled myself to the gym.

The gym was part of the new build extension on the back of the house and had been fully adapted for someone who couldn't use their legs. I went to the bench press and lowered myself into the body cradle, latched the straps, and set the weight to 100kg, which was the upper limit of what I could deal with. I began pushing.

Hard.

Harder.

Hardest.

Every push becoming at first a breathless sigh, then a shout and finally a hoarse scream.

I knew I wasn't supposed to use the gym when Dad wasn't around to supervise. But I didn't care.

Dangerous places gyms.

Easy to have an accident.

Easy for something to go wrong.

And would I care if it did?

Right now? No.

THIRTY-FIVE

There was a fabric strap across Kik-Kik's chest. She was also pulling something bulky and black through the undergrowth behind. Her hair and skin glistened with water. Her eyes were bright and the graveyard smile was as wide as the river she'd just come back from.

She marched up to the shelter where I was sitting having my frankly girlie—well Samlie really—panic attack and swung a holdall around from behind her, and then unhooked the one over that she was carrying with the strap on her back. Both bags thudded down in front of me like black sacks of anxiety. I half-expected both of them to explode, like the one that had killed the alligator. But they didn't. They just sat there, water dripping from their zips and corners like fear-sweat.

Kik-Kik sat down. Made the thumbs-up sign and didn't stop smiling.

I searched the clearing for the first holdall. It was still underneath Tree Face with the piles of clothes, papers, and brown packets of drugs stacked neatly beside it. Kik-Kik had weighted down the pages from the folders so they wouldn't blow away and had shaded them from the rain with big leaves threaded onto sticks. As I studied the area beneath Tree Face I couldn't help thinking that it looked a bit like an altar made out of my stuff. The closer I stared at it, the more ordered it became in the way it was arranged.

Kik-Kik moved her head in the way so that I could no longer see Tree Face and his altar. She wanted my attention. Thumb up, gormless expectant smile, eyes sparkling with emotion.

I reached forward, patted the bags and gave her the thumbs-up.

More than anything, I was glad that she was back. The bags were just a dark bonus leading me even further away from what I knew about Dad, but at least Kik-Kik was still around to keep me alive. That was the main thing.

I recognised one of the bags, at least. It was mine. It still had my airport tags on it although the biro-written label was smudged and unreadable. I undid the zip and Kik-Kik thought the sound was highly amusing, waving her hand next to her bottom as if she was wafting away a fart. I had to admit it was funny and the first joke that we had shared since I'd washed up in her life.

It had never occurred to me before that tribespeople of the darkest Amazon would have a sense of humour, or that they would make fart jokes. It just seemed so out of place in the jungle, where survival was the number one consideration every day, all day.

But then, even in my predicament, a laugh felt good in my throat and belly. I did the zip up and undid it again, making the ripping fart noise and wafting my hand in front of my nose. Kik-Kik, laughing then rolled onto her back kicking her legs in the air as if it was the funniest thing she'd ever seen, beating at the ground with her good hand. Tears of laughter ran down both our cheeks.

I didn't make the situation any less upsetting, but man it felt good.

Once we'd finished the fart gags, I started going through the bag. Plenty of my clothes, with underwear and even a couple of Chelsea tops—home and away. I thought about pulling on the away kit, but for a start, Kik-Kik wouldn't get the joke and I realised that I kind of liked the animals she'd painted on me. They were a better expression of where my allegiances lay right now. With Kik-Kik and not with a football team a billion miles away.

There was a bag of my toiletries which when I opened it was dry inside, so it had been watertight at least. I couldn't think of a need right now for underarm deodorant or even toothpaste, but it was nice to see something that hadn't been ruined by river water.

I remembered that I'd packed the bag in a bit of a huff because Escobar had been outside the window of my room, kicking a ball up against the wall for some time. He knew that's what I was up there doing, as Dad and I had told them our plans for leaving at breakfast that morning. I couldn't help thinking that Escobar looked the happiest at that news, so him being outside the window, doing something with the football that I could never do again was his way of twisting the knife just one more time. So I'd wheeled myself between the bed and the drawers where my stuff had been unpacked, grabbing what I could and trying to knock chunks out of the furniture with my footplates and wheels.

So most of the bag was a jumble of stuff, once I'd got past the clothes and bag of smellies.

And once I'd cleared the next layer of tee-shirts, socks, and puffed and exploded football and car magazines, I found the box.

It felt wrong in my hand as I lifted it out. The outside was rubberised but still felt cool and metallic. It was heavy and solidly constructed. There was a dead-grey LCD screen at one end, and below it was a dial that could have been an egg timer or a radio tuner—it looked like it was from another age—the nineties or something. What the box reminded me of, was my dad's old iPod that he refused to throw away because "They don't make them like this anymore," except it was five times as big and had a satellite aerial on the side. I experimented with twisting it up and down like the guard had before he'd slipped it into the bag in the dream that wasn't a dream, that was me remembering stuff that had happened that I hadn't noticed.

I had definitely not packed this box in my stuff. Even by mistake in a huff. This had been put in my bag later.

There was a rubberised switch on the other side of the box. Chunky and thick.

Kik-Kik's face appeared between me and the box. Her smile could light up the night if she'd had more teeth. Now she had my attention she pointed at the magazines and then pointed at her chest.

I didn't know if she wanted them for the fire or if she wanted to check the latest results from the Championship, but I nodded.

Kik-Kik literally punched the air, scooped up the magazines, their pages fat and puffy with water, and took them off to where the sunlight was uninterrupted by the surrounding trees. She lovingly laid the magazines out in a square. Opening one page at a time, studying a photograph, laughing and pointing back to me, then her, then Tree Face, and giving me the thumbs-up. If it kept her amused while I looked at the satellite box then all well and good. There's only so much insane smiling I could take in one day, even if it was Kik-Kik.

I returned my attention to the satellite box and pressed the button.

It buzzed in my hand, the screen lit up and a series of black LCD numbers ran across it as the mechanism inside booted up.

The numbers resolved into a globe that spun around, and zoomed in on the bulbous head of the South American tadpole.

It zoomed in a bit more, there was a grid superimposed over the map, and in the centre of that grid, a black dot started to blink.

The satellite box was a GPS—Global Positioning Satellite—device and it was showing me exactly on a map where I was.

I was a very long way from anywhere, but at least I now knew how far.

The box had been tracking the plane for Carlos. And when the plane had reached the back of beyond, this literal middle-of-nowhere place on his computer screen, Carlos had pressed the James Bond button which had blown up our engine and sent us down into the green and brown and red hell of the jungle.

I looked at the menu on the screen and turned the dial, a load of stuff came up in Spainuguese that I had no hope understanding, and when I pressed the button in the centre of the dial, a night light came on for the screen. But that was it.

I put the box down. It was if I was suddenly holding my dad's true murderer in my hands. I mean I know it had been my decision where to put the plane down, but this box was the tell-tale grass who had put me in that position.

For a few moments, I felt like chucking it against a tree and smashing the bloody thing to pieces, but the sense that there might be a way I can use it to get out of here—not immediately apparent, it had to be said—niggled at me. I also didn't want it to fall into Kik-Kik's good hand. She'd probably have posted it into Tree Face's belly like the watch.

Kik-Kik was still having a cracking time with the magazines. Turning a page, looking at the picture eyes wide in wonder, then putting her hand across her mouth as if to stop more laughter from leaking out. Her thin shoulders shook with mirth as she explored a world as alien to her, as hers was to mine. Except, my world wasn't as dangerous.

Or maybe it was. Some of the things I heard in the crowd, some of the stuff I knew some people thought about people who were different, would certainly mark Kik-Kik out as a figure of fun or hate.

I suddenly felt properly ashamed of the things I'd called her. The stuff I'd heard on the terraces, or in school from the white kids who repeated the shit their parents told them. I didn't think I was a racist up until now, but I realised it then. I was. As Kik-Kik looked at the magazines, she'd be way less welcome in some of the places I liked to go, than she had welcomed me here.

I wanted to wash my thoughts out with bleach and yet Kik-Kik howled with laughter, oblivious to how shrivelled I suddenly felt inside. She pointed at the magazine and gave me the most enthusiastic thumbs-up yet.

I didn't feel so great about me and bits of my recent past right now, but the idea of Kik-Kik enjoying what she looked at appealed—if not entirely making me feel less of a slime-ball, shite-hearted racist-dickhead.

"Sorry," I said. Not really meaning to say the word aloud. Kik-Kik looked up, her eyebrows raised questioningly. "For what I called you. I know you couldn't understand me then and can't understand me now, but I'm sorry. Really."

I thought the words were going to start tumbling out of my mouth like Jen's had when she'd visited me after my attack on Steve, but they didn't. None of my earnest apology was getting through. So I just gave her a smile and a thumbs-up.

Kik-Kik understood that.

THIRTY-SIX

It began to drizzle and Kik-Kik gathered up the magazines as best she could with her one usable hand and came back to the shelter as the rain dribbled down out of the sky. The water ran in little streams over the leaves above us and washed away the puddle of Ick that had been leaking from me. Kik-Kik had carved a small channel downhill from my position for just this purpose, and the sludgy yellow-brown Ick floated happily away. Kik-Kik was also an awesome plumber. I couldn't believe how much I'd underestimated her skill; even if she wasn't the brightest chisel in the toolbox, she was one of the sharpest, and if I needed a chisel rather than a torch, she was my girl.

Kik-Kik continued looking through the magazines. They had dried a little in the warm sun, and I knew that the rain shower would pass almost as soon as it had begun. The relentless sun would soon be beating down on us again. As if on cue, the rain stopped as if someone had turned off a tap and Kik-Kik laid down dry leaves around the fire, putting the magazines on them to dry quicker. She turned the pages gingerly, looking closely at the players in the action shots, and at the cheering crowds, or the players in the dressing rooms, or showing off their houses. She stroked the silky paper and I swear at some point she pressed her nose right up to it, not to get a sense of the words written there but to smell the paper.

The magazines were as fascinating to her as holy relics and she revered them in the same way I'd seen history professors in documentaries my dad watched treat ancient manuscripts. All she needed was the white gloves and the little round specs and she'd be set.

Over her shoulder, the afternoon sunlight was hitting the altar.

Tree Face was silent above it, shadows covering his whole mouth. He wasn't looking at me, but he kind of might have been looking at Kik-Kik. There was a sort of jealous greenness to the moss on his bark and maybe he wanted more stuff for his altar. Maybe he wanted the magazines; maybe he wanted everything fed into his mouth. Maybe he was always hungry.

Kik-Kik finished the last magazine, and then happily began turning the pages of the first one again, laughing as if the jokes inside her head were completely new ones.

I opened the other holdall. Kik-Kik was too wrapped up in the football magazines to make any fart jokes. This holdall was packed with brown packets of drugs. I took the bricks of brown-taped powder out of the bag and built myself a little pyramid out of them next to me. I suppose I was hoping there was another gun inside the bag. If there had been I might have felt better being alone at night when Kik-Kik went home, as I knew she must.

There was no gun.

There were more papers in the bottom, this time in a blue folder. The writing was unintelligible to me as usual. If only I spoke any other language other than pampered London teenager, I might have been able to make head or tail of what was in the folder, but they were as obscure to me as algebra. The paper inside was wet through, but the typing on it was solid enough. There were a few photographs inside the folder. They were of Escobar and Ramos playing football, and of Carlos looking proud next to one of his aeroplanes on his private airstrip. The mansion glistened in the background. I wondered why Dad had pictures of Carlos in with the drugs.

It didn't make a huge amount of sense, but then so little did about any of this.

At the back of the folder, there was another passport. I held my breath as I opened it. This passport was the identification for the man I knew as my father, John Coker, but it wasn't a British or EU passport. It was Swedish. Apparently, my dad was a Swedish national and well as a Brazilian national with a different name. According to his Swedish passport, Dad had been to the US five times in the last year. Which was rubbish. I looked at the dates; three of them were for times he'd definitely been in the UK giving me flying lessons.

What the bloody hell was going on?

I threw the folder and the passport down.

While I'd been reading, Kik-Kik had been taking the parcels of drugs and putting them on the altar below Tree Face. There was no point in me intervening. What was I going to do with sixteen parcels of heroincoke?

It occurred to me then, that if I got really ill again, or Kik-Kik abandoned me, at least they might be a means by which I could check out and avoid the pain of starvation. Suicide really wasn't my preferred option you understand, but there's no way I'd survive more than a week here without Kik-Kik. The drugs, suddenly, became a comfort in the same way that finding a gun might have.

I shook my head.

How had I come to be thinking like this? Was everything really this hopeless? I looked again at the GPS tracker. Surely there was a way I could...

Kik-Kik, underneath Tree Face, making her little drug pyramid, suddenly spun around and crouched low. Looking to the trees to my right. She held a finger to her lips. She was speaking the universal language of SHUT IT. I clamped my jaw shut and tried to breathe as quietly as I could through my nose. Kik-Kik took two careful steps forward and picked up the spear that was lying in front of the altar.

The sun blazed down, breaking up the last of the afternoon's drizzle clouds. I could hear birds singing in the distance, but nothing close by.

Keeping low, Kik-Kik took two more steps towards me, her feet making no sound in the drying mud. She was looking intently to my right, her eyes narrowed, lips pursed shut so as not to make a noise.

I looked into the trees where she was staring. In the dappled shade between the branches, I could see nothing untoward. I could look deep into the forest, past the bushes, and through the leaves. I could see as far as the green and brown moss-covered tree trunks crowded together to frustrate sight of anything beyond thirty or so metres. What wouldn't I give right now to be up above the jungle, piloting an aeroplane at three thousand feet, with an open vista of jungle to look down upon? The trees, the plants, the animals, the streams, the rivers the tracks—to see it all from the safety of the fuselage.

Fat Leopard walked from left to right in my field of vision. He was twenty-five metres away but I still flinched and made a soft moan of distress. Kik-Kik was waving the spear point at me. KEEP QUIET!

I'M SORRY, I faced back at her.

Fat Leopard had completely disappeared into the forest again, but he had unmistakably been there. I could feel my heart banging about in the top of my chest, flapping there like a fish pulled from the water, dying on a riverbank. Any second now Kik-Kik was going to tell my heart to SHUT UP too.

Kik-Kik swivelled on her heel slowly. Her head moving in the direction Fat Leopard had. She could still see him, make him out in the jig-saws of vegetation, even though he was totally lost to me and my city eyes.

She followed him around in a slow circle. Pointing at him with the spear again. I caught the occasional glimpse of him padding silently along. Not getting any nearer but totally letting us know that it was there. I knew it was Fat Leopard I'd stuck with the spear. I could still see the black blood on his fur from the wound I'd made. Was he just trying to scare me? Get his own back? Was he telling me that it wasn't scared and that he was going to come back and he was going to finish the job?

Kik-Kik moved with him. Eventually, Fat Leopard became obscured from her view by the shelter she had built for me. She waited patiently for him to come around the other side and soon he did. The end of her spear twitched as she caught sight of him again. I supposed he didn't come close enough for her to use the spear on him and Kik-Kik wasn't going to go in the jungle to hunt him.

It was a stand-off.

Fat Leopard went around us fully four times. Winding

his noose of terror four more times around my neck. Kik-Kik
followed it on the spot, grinding up a curl of wet mud with her
feet, never wavering from the cat with her spear. As it walked
away, she stood for fully fifteen minutes looking in the same
direction it travelled. I got one brief glimpse of its tail, but I
got the impression Kik-Kik's eyes followed him for a thousand
miles.

I was chilled to the bone even though the heat of the forest
was hitting me like a migraine and my throat was as dry as a
mouth full of cream crackers.

The other animals that had been a threat since I'd arrived,
had just stumbled upon me. The snake was probably up the tree
minding its own business when it had noticed my nice juicy
neck and decided to eat out. The alligator hadn't known I was
going to be buggering about under the platform of branches.
The reptile had chanced on me like some kid had dropped his
packed lunch running to catch the bus.

But Fat Leopard? All thick muscles and spear-cut anger?
He'd come back to where he had lost his battle. He'd walked
around me. He'd made sure I knew that he knew that I knew
that he was there. And he didn't sneak about. He just did his
do. Walked around, bold as you like. It was a message. He was
making his point.

It was a declaration of war.

THIRTY-SEVEN

Before Kik-Kik left for the night she built two more fires in the clearing, dragging thick logs from the forest which would feed both fires for many hours. The fire nearest to me she built up, and she brought me stacks of branches so I could keep that fire going until morning. Her intentions were clear as she stood by the fire and turned a circle with her spear outstretched; the fires were to guard against Fat Leopard until she returned tomorrow.

When all three fires were roaring and twilight was approaching under a grey expanse of sky, she spent many minutes on her knees in front of Tree Face, praying solemnly to him. Raising her hand, singing incantations in her strange reedy voice. She ate berries. Spat the juice into her hand and used it to put three palm prints on the bark below Tree Face. She reddened his lips again with freshly prepared paint and arranged his dreads into straighter tidier lines.

Tree Face just looked awake into the darkening jungle. Taking no notice.

At the end, Kik-Kik hugged his trunk and walked backward away from him with her head bowed.

She came and knelt by me, chewed more berries, spat the cold juice into her hands, and put a fresh wet palm print over the painting she had made of Fat Leopard on my arm and shoulder. Then Kik-Kik went back on her knees, bowed her head and prayed to me.

It went on for ages.

Totes awks to be honest.

There was a note in the prayer that seemed to be questioning, asking for something. Kik-Kik held out her hand and bowed her head even lower. She wanted me to do something. But what?

Was it to complete the magic? Three hands. Me, Kik-Kik and Tree Face linked by markings and paintings and prayers. Kik-Kik putting her palm prints on Tree Face, putting them on me and now holding out her palm to me…

Kik-Kik had put the magazines on the altar under Tree Face, so she couldn't want those. I looked about. All I had next to me was a bunch of clothes and deodorants. Then I remembered how much Kik-Kik had enjoyed looking in the football magazines— how she'd laughed and pointed and smile and got excited. I had no paint to put a picture on her skin, but I could leave my mark on her. I reached into the damp pile of clothes. Pulled out a Chelsea away top. It had a twenty-seven on the back (my birthdate) and my name, Coker, across the shoulders. I shook out the creases and folded it back up neatly.

Then I put the top in on her hand.

Completing the magic. Finishing the prayer.

Kik-Kik stopped the incantation, looked up, at the shirt, and then at me. A look of religious wonder on her face.

I'd done the right thing.

She needed help to put the shirt on and she didn't care that it was still damp from the river water. Everything was damp in the rainforest. She stood and looked down at herself. The shirt was too big for her, in similar proportions to how my dad's tee-shirt had been too big for me—it was more of a dress and the sleeves completely enclosed her flipper. Just the tip of those crooked fingers appeared. This seemed to fascinate her most off all.

The magic hadn't cured her, but it had covered up that which made her different. I kind of got that. The wheelchair gave me mobility and independence, but it was still a wheelchair. If my back had broken lower down, near the bottom of my spine, I might have still been able to walk with calipers or prosthetic legs. When I'd been in the physio-terrorist department of the spinal injuries unit, being told which ways to move my dead useless legs with my hands to stop the muscles contracting and the legs curling up under me, there had been other people there learning to walk for the first time since their own accidents. It was hard not to be jealous. Hard not to look at the wheelchair and think it was the only thing that made me different. If you looked at me otherwise, sat in any other kind of chair I'd look... okay.

Kik-Kik pulled the sleeve down on the Chelsea shirt right over the flipper and looked at me like all her Christmases had come at once.

Do they have Christmas in the rainforest?

I didn't know what religion Kik-Kik was praying to with Tree Face and me. It didn't feel like a Jesus-thing. I mean, I'm not religious—how could I be, if there was a God he'd taken a huge piss on me over the last year or so—but the times I had been to church for marriages, christenings and stuff, I could see the parallels. A place to worship, check. A Jesus or a Tree Face. Check. An altar. Check. Prayers and singing. Check.

All I needed now was a miracle to complete the set.

Kik-Kik left as twilight really started to close in. She was still unable to take her eyes off the shirt or wipe the smile off her flat brown face. She left me the spear and also a pile of fist-sized stones. Miming that I should use them to throw if anything approached the shelter while she was gone.

I ate some of the dried smoked alligator, which was tough but tasty, and ate some fruit. I needed to do a bit of bladder pressing and changed the leaves around the Ick Site. I thought about getting a new Ick Bag from my ruckkie but the leaves and the poultice thing seemed to be doing the trick. Maybe there were some antiseptic properties to the mulch of leaves she'd stuck to my abdomen. It was certainly working on my shoulder. The wound site there was feeling a whole lot better.

With darkness, the night shift in the jungle started up. I could see clouds of insects reflected in the firelight. The fires were attracting them, but the smoke was stopping them, it seemed, from taking a great interest in me.

Tree Face flickered and wobbled through the heat haze coming off the flames nearest to him, animating his mouth and eyes. There was a look of indecision about him now, as if he didn't know how this was going to play out. I'd survived a lot longer than either of us had anticipated and maybe he was now an angry God. Angry that he hadn't got his own way. The shivers that run up and down his face could have been from rage I suppose. His mouth was still screaming. He still looked at me like I shouldn't be here.

"Up yours," I said and chucked one of the stones at him.

It hit him square in the face and bounced off into the darkness.

Something growled, spat, and shook a bush on the left side of Tree Face.

Fat Leopard emerged from the bush and began rubbing at his head with his paw. Perhaps he'd been sitting there watching me for ages. Perhaps the stone had bounced off Tree Face and cracked him on the skull.

Fat Leopard stopped rubbing his head and stood up. His face was lit orange and red by the fire. Through the flames, his face shimmered and shifted like Tree Face's did. Rivers of shadow ran over him in a constant rush. His eyes glittered and they were looking straight at me.

I could see the open wound on his neck I'd opened up with the spear. It was weeping, and full of pus. It was in a place where he couldn't lick to clean and protect it, so it was beginning to fester. I couldn't smell the infection from the twenty metres between us, by I imagined I could. It clawed at the back of my throat. Made my stomach turn over.

I picked up the spear.

Fat Leopard didn't blink.

I wondered if his infection was affecting him in the same way my infection had affected me? Was he dreaming? Was his delirious dream making him come here? Was the infection driving his brain to madness as mine had? Is that why he was going against his natural instincts—fear of fire, fear of humans—to keep coming back here to taunt me or torture me?

Was he mad with illness?

I held the spear out in front of me with my left hand and looked down to pick up the sharpest stone I could find to throw at the cat if should come closer.

When I looked up again Fat Leopard had gone. Disappeared back into the night and Tree Face shook and shimmered with fire-light-shadowed laughter.

I stayed alert for as long as I could. Listening intently to every chirrup and rustle. Every night call and howl. The spear and stone ready in my hands. Ready to defend myself if I needed to, but Fat Leopard did not return. As the first fingers of dawn started to streak the sky above Tree Face, I allowed myself to sleep.

I did not dream.

When I awoke, the fires were right down to the embers but they had done their job. Tree Face was asleep; sunlight was not yet hitting his face and so he would exist in a gloomy shade until the sun cleared enough of the forest to make him open his eyes.

I properly preferred the ugly sod when he was asleep.

A rustle.

I grabbed the spear and scanned the bushes. Something was approaching, but it was not a sound I recognised. It was halting. It sounded like it was dragging something through the sticky mud. I licked my lips, which had suddenly gone dry.

The Kik-Kik who came from the trees, dragging her injured leg behind her, was not the Kik-Kik who had left here in such great spirits as yesterday. The Chelsea shirt was ripped open along the front exposing her chest; the arm had been ripped off, so that the flipper was fully exposed. Kik-Kik's lips were split and swollen, and her right eye was blackening.

I thought for a moment she'd been attacked by an animal on her way here, but then I realised, looking at her injuries—the finger marks on the arm above the flipper, the red blotches on her neck (those sickening parody of hickeys), that the animal that had attacked her had been human.

THIRTY-EIGHT

Kik-Kik looked like she'd been hollowed out. The excitable, devout, crazy girl who had kept me alive for the last week, who had fed me, worshipped me, cleaned me, and protected me looked transparent. As if she'd become a ghost. She was just a memory of Kik-Kik, an impression of her on the air.

And yet, with her injured leg and bruises and cuts and hickeys she'd dragged herself through the jungle—I had no idea from how far or how long it had taken her. But here she was. She couldn't make eye contact with me. Her head was cast down, like it had been last night in prayer but now it spoke of something else. Shame and defeat.

Her hand trembled and I could see the nails on her fingers were broken and cracked. There was a small bald patch on the side of her head where it looked as if a handful of hair had been torn out.

A tear balanced on the edge of her nose. Glistening in the morning light. As I watched, it grew and dropped when the surface tension would no longer keep it there. Tears blinked in her eyelashes and her shoulders trembled like her hand. Kik-Kik's skin was blue with sorrow and shame and guilt.

I reached out a hand. Pointed in front of me. "Kik-Kik. Sit down. Please. Warm yourself by the fire."

Kik-Kik flinched as my fingers came up. The palm of her good hand coming up to cover the fresh hickeys on the side of her neck. Those marks which we laughed at and joked about in school whenever they were seen on someone's neck. The evidence of teenage fumbling and date-play. But there was nothing to laugh at here.

Kik-Kik was ashamed.

I pulled myself onto my front, feeling the leaves stuck to my stomach rip away on the earth. I'd have to deal with that later, but right now I couldn't just leave Kik-Kik standing there. I pulled myself towards her, over the leaves, over the mud, grabbing onto whatever I could. Roots, stones, branches. Anything.

Soon I'd dragged myself to her feet and looked up. I could see right to her upside-down face. Two of her tears fell onto my cheek. I reached up and held her hand. There was a moment of tension, as if the last thing in the world she wanted was to be touched, and then her hand relaxed in mine. I pulled on her hand. "Come on. Please. Sit down."

Kik-Kik took off her jungle-made rucksack and laid it on the ground.

She didn't so much sit as have her legs suddenly collapse beneath her. She came to a rest in front of me cross-legged.

And that's when I saw the finger and palm print bruises darkening on the insides of her thighs. At some point in the last few hours her thin brown legs—with considerable resistance from Kik-Kik—had been forced apart - and the full realisation the nature of the attack which had happened to her hit me like a brick in the head.

The anger rushed up inside me like a hot terrible beast. It was in that moment I realised that not just how much I depended on Kik-Kik but how much I had grown to care for her. Her crazy ways, her loopy laugh, and her clever-in-her-own way eyes. To think that anyone could... do... that.

I almost wished she'd been eaten by the Fat Leopard.

She'd put up a fight though. There were bruises blossoming on the tops of her arms. There were scuffs and cuts on her knees that had only recently stopped bleeding. Her lip had been split by a punch or a hard slap, and her eye had been blackened by a heavy blow. These were not the injuries of a girl who had rolled over, given up, and let horror take its course.

In a strange way, I felt pride for her. Pride like you'd feel for a teammate who'd pulled off an incredible tackle on the pitch or had overcome something terrible and lived to tell the tale—maybe a car accident where their back had been broken. Kik-Kik was a fighter.

And oh... God... she had fought.

I didn't let go of her hand for a long while, and she didn't stop crying for almost an hour. Her head bowed. Shoulders trembling. The tears running in a slow stream from both her eyes and making the journey to the tip of her flat nose.

When the crying stopped, I let go of her hand and she helped me back to the shelter and into my usual sitting position against the tree. She built the fire up and sat with me in there for the first time, rather than being outside, on her knees worshipping.

The sun didn't wake Tree Face up until way past midday. It was as if it knew he'd be no help here. I was glad that I didn't have to deal with him as well. If he'd looked at Kik-Kik in a way that hadn't transmitted full-on compassion and sorry, he'd have got a couple more stones in the gob.

The sun kept Tree Face's eyes firmly closed.

Kik-Kik got up and began tidying the leaves I'd dislodged and cleaned me up. Placing new leaves about the nub of intestine, sticking them down with more poultice that she made of a collection of berries, some straw, and a particular leaf with yellow-tipped edges.

When she'd finished, I offered her another Chelsea shirt from the pile drying by the fire, but she shook her head, said something I didn't understand, and pulled the ripped shirt around her shoulders. Tying a knot in it so she was no longer exposed.

I took a chance, picked up the bowl containing the poultice, and used it to coat the wounds on her hands and knees. Kik-Kik didn't stop me or pull away so I guessed it wouldn't do any harm. I didn't know if she was letting me because I was a god, or because it was the right thing to do. It didn't matter in the long run—as long as her wounds didn't become infected that was the main thing.

I could only guess at the infections growing in the wounds of her mind after what had happened. There was no poultice for that, and they would not be easy to see or treat, but I knew they were there.

I'd had that poison in my head too.

Kik-Kik peeled fruit and we ate it with the last of the smoked alligator. If we were to have more meat Kik-Kik was going to have to go and source it, but to be honest, I'd rather she sat here with me until she felt better. Until all the rubbish inside her, the tear-forcing, tremble-making rubbish had floated away like the smoke from the fire.

Kik-Kik cried a little bit more as the sunlight moved across Tree Face and he became more visible to us. Maybe she was feeling the shame and guilt again in the same way she had when I'd first emerged from the bush this morning. Maybe she felt both her gods were going to be displeased with her.

I put a hand on her shoulder and gave a little squeeze. She turned from Tree Face to me and I gave her a small thumbs-up.

She looked away into the jungle.

It's going to be quite a while before I saw that smile again.

The day moved on slowly. At one point, my stomach rumbled louder than the forest noises around us. Kik-Kik got up automatically and went to the river to get more water in the bowl, foraging close by for some fruit and berries too. I ate and drank gratefully. But didn't hassle her for any more food.

Kik-Kik didn't eat.

She built up the fire, and she got more firewood to relight the other two warning fires.

As the day began to die in the pinky-grey sky, Kik-Kik relit the other fires with embers from the one by the shelter. Her movements were stiff, and I could see she was limping harder now. Favouring her left knee. It was more swollen than the right and had been injured in her struggle. Going to the river for water and foraging for food and firewood had made it worse, and the pulpy swelling around the joint looked pretty painful. When she brushed against my shoulder, coming back to sit next to me, I could feel the heat coming off the joint. It probably wasn't broken or fractured, but it had suffered a severe and agonising sprain.

Kik-Kik reached for her own ruckkie and began taking out objects, placing them carefully in front of her.

First was a beautifully smooth white stone. Perfectly flat and oval-shaped. It fitted in her palm exactly, as if it had been made for Kik-Kik alone. This wasn't a tool; this was an ornament, something precious to Kik-Kik. She kissed it before putting it down on the ground.

Next out was a small statue made from a chalky material. The handiwork was rough and the stone wasn't hard and strong like the white stone. This was a carving of a woman. It looked like something you'd get in a museum, a fertility figure. Its stomach bulged out in a pregnant lump, the breasts above looking swollen. This piece Kik-Kik kissed as well but in a strange way. She kissed its round head, its belly and then both its arms. This was a ritual I thought she probably did to the statue every night.

Next, there was a flash of baby pink and she pulled a woman's tee-shirt from the bag. It was covered in gold writing and there were spangled sequins on it. The picture on the front was not what I was expecting.

The golden outlines went right around the face of some blonde popstar who I'd seen on MTV but couldn't remember his name. It if had been someone playing striker for Arsenal or Chelsea I'd have been there. But this guy. Nope. Justin? Dustin? J-Dustin? Dustin-J? He was one of those interchangeable pretty-pretty boys who has more talent in his haircut than his voice box. I vaguely remembered he'd been in a boyband or something. Then he hadn't, and then they'd reformed and well…who cares?

But a name for the purpose of telling you who it was? Nope. Not.A.Scooby.Mate. I'll just call him *P-Star*. But you'd know him if you saw him. Possibly.

She kissed P-Star. Put the tee-shirt down next to the statue and the stone. She smoothed her hand across P-Star's face as the gold around him flickered in the firelight.

I looked up. It was now full dark.

Kik-Kik had never been out this late before; usually she was well on her way back to her wigwam by now. I tapped her on the shoulder and pointed to the sky. She just shook her head and pulled the last object from the ruckie.

It was a dog-eared, ripped, stained celebrity magazine,

bloated from at least one time being submerged in water. The pages were waxy and stiff. They crinkled as she held up the magazine and kissed the picture of P-Star on the front of it. The headline in Spainuguese was meaningless to me, but P-Star was pointing at a mansion, so I guess he was about to show the reporter and photographer around his home.

Kik-Kik opened a couple of pages, and indeed, P-Star was indeed showing us his huge marble bathroom, his garage full of cars, and his bedroom the size of a football pitch.

It kind of reminded me of Carlos's place up in the mountains. Then the reality check.

I realised then I was looking at Kik-Kik's entire collection of possessions from which she could not bear be parted. Where I'd have iPhones and MacBooks and Games Consoles and Rolex watches, this girl, this tiny-in-the-scheme-of-things girl—who was now an enormous presence in my life—had left her village after what had happened, and had come here with her stuff.

Her tiny, wonderful, achingly beautiful stuff.

I felt the warm prickle of tears in my eyes.

Kik-Kik had left home and she was never going back.

The night was still. The moment perfect. Firelight the only illumination, and the crackles of the fires the only sound. It was as if the entire rainforest had left us alone for a bit to feel the weight of the occasion.

I knew I was trapped here. I knew I was going to die, but looking at Kik-Kik—her eyes shining in the firelight as she looked down on the only four things she owned, I couldn't think of a better person with whom to spend my last days. I wanted to put my arms around her and hug her so tight she might explode.

It felt like coming home. Like being saved.

So when, from the direction of the river, I heard the *thub-thub-thub* of the boat engine, I was more annoyed, to begin with, that it had intruded on the magic.

THIRTY-NINE

Kik-Kik was immediately alert. The pain and the sorrow fell from her as if she'd just shrugged a spider from her shoulder. We couldn't see anything past the fires, but the boat's engine was definitely getting nearer, the beat of it coming across the still jungle night like the beat of a native drum in that stupid King Kong film, the rubbish black-and-white one Dad had tried to get me to watch a million times.

Kik-Kik reached down and took a handful of earth. She extinguished the fire in front of us, then she leaped to the other two fires, kicking the big logs out of the flames and dropping on more mud. The fires flared briefly but all that was left was the glowing embers on the logs. The only other light came from a huge curve of the Milky Way over our heads, cutting the sky in half like a spine going up a back.

Kik-Kik came back and picked up the spear.

I could just see the outline of her in the shelter, and an acute brightness in her eyes. Instinct for survival had taken over and she was back to being the Kik-Kik I knew and admired.

Loved?

Dunno, but it was great to have her back. Especially now the flaming fires were no longer there to scare away any night predators.

I watched the tip of the spear in the near dark, moving, pointing. Kik-Kik was gauging the direction that the boat was travelling and it looked to me, as the sound grew louder, competing very well with the thumping of my heart in my chest that it was travelling upriver.

Then it hit me.

What was I doing?

I'd completely bought into the idea that everything was dangerous. That everything was going to kill me, to have trigger reactions like Kik-Kik, and now utterly had missed the point that it was a BOAT!

It might mean rescue!

"Hey! Hey! Over here! Over—"

Kik-Kik put me down onto my back with a vicious shove, and put her flipper across my throat and her hand over my mouth. Her eyes blazed.

The boat engine was not a welcome sound for her in the same way it was for me. The boat meant her God or the gift from her God might be taken away. I didn't even know if her people had met outsiders before. Maybe they were terrified of everyone and I was lucky I'd met Kik-Kik because any of the others might have killed me.

I nodded to Kik-Kik. Letting her know that I wasn't going to say anything. There was no point fighting with her. One slash of the spear and I'd be history. I was going to have to play this her way for now.

She released my mouth and throat. She put a finger to her lips, then my lips, and then back.

I nodded again.

She kissed my cheek and then ran away into the night in the direction of the boat.

The engine continued to struggle up the river. From the way Kik-Kik had pointed her spearhead, I was certain that the boat was travelling upriver, rather than down. So in the opposite direction to the way I'd come here on the platform of branches.

That meant, depending on how long I'd been unconscious after the crash, that at some point the boat would meet the wreckage of the Cherokee. They'd find Dad, might work out or already know that I was missing and start a proper search for me.

Perhaps they were already searching, and it had taken them a few days to get to this part of the forest.

Hope blossomed in my guts in a way it hadn't done for days.

There were people out there either looking for me now, or

would be soon. All I had to do was stay alive for a short time more, wait for Kik-Kik to leave me alone long enough to get myself back down to the beach and arm myself with a spear to protect myself from the alligators...

Oh yeah. The alligators.

Or from Fat Leopard who would eat me on the way.

Or from the snake that would drop out of a tree as I dragged myself past.

This wasn't as easy as it sounded. I would have to make sure I got to the beach when I knew the rescuers were in the vicinity, I'd have to hope they came in daylight, so that I had more of a chance of making it to the river, and I'd have to find some way to prevent Kik-Kik from stopping me.

Man, did I feel like a bag of scum even thinking that. After all she'd done, and what she'd been through. But at the end of the day she was keeping me here. Yes, she was looking after me and that, but I wanted out of this stinking place, away from everything that *www.just.wanted.to.kill.me.com.*

The urge to get away from here was stronger than any feeling I had ever known. Even the one to have my legs back in working order. I knew there was no hope of that ever happening, but now there was genuine hope that I might get away.

I just had to be patient.

Tree Face was hidden in the dark. He couldn't see what I was thinking, and I couldn't see what he was thinking. As I kind of sketched out a plan in my head of a way, if needs be, I would be able to get the stuff done I needed to, I was well glad that he couldn't see me.

I know he would not have approved.

The boat engine reached its closest point. I possibly caught the glimmer of a searchlight through the jungle, but it might just have as have well been my imagination or the dance of fireflies.

True to form, I didn't even know if there were fireflies in the rainforest. But they seemed like the kind of insect a rainforest might have anyway.

I was babbling. Yeah. My head was all over the place. I really felt that if I reached out I could touch the sound of the engine.

Put my hand on the deck and stop the boat from moving.

I knew that I could easily call out now Kik-Kik wasn't here, but she'd make it to me a lot faster than anyone on the boat if she needed to, and the madness-y threat in her eyes was clear. Almost as if, "if she couldn't have me, no one can."

I shook my head.

I was probably just inventing that as her motive. Perhaps she was genuinely concerned that the boat would put her and her people in danger. There's always some sort of Greenpeace, Friends of the Earth charity guff going on about the rainforests with has-been celebrities going on about saving the rainforest and that. I didn't really take a lot of notice—and why, when they talked about the destruction of the rainforest, was everything measured in terms of an "area the size of Wales"—since when had Wales become a unit of measurement anyway? I didn't take a lot of notice as I said.

But I suppose if you had to live here and were scared of logging companies, or oil drillers, coming here to ruin your world—I could almost understand. The *thub-thub-thub* of a boat engine at night might not have been the most beautiful sound in the world that I thought it was, but perhaps it was the beginning of something pretty rotten for Kik-Kik and her people. I didn't understand why they wouldn't want the jobs, and the tellies and the computers that would come with it. That had to be preferable than living in this shit, yeah…?

Yeah. I was babbling again. In my head I sounded like Jen. And that didn't improve my mood at all.

The engine note started to change as the boat carried on upriver. I thought I could hear the sloshing of the water against its hull or the wake it left behind breaking like blood-red surf against the banks. Probably my imagination too, but when you're in the dark, and the last embers of the fire were going out, all that you had left to fill in the gaps was your imagination.

I worked a bit more on my plan, but it would be difficult to finalise until there was enough light around for me to know that I could do what I needed to do.

I knew that I would need all my strength, and hoped that my arms hadn't lost too much muscle mass while I'd been the unwilling guest of Kik-Kik and Tree Face, because without that upper body strength, nothing that I wanted to do would be possible.

Kik-Kik didn't come back.

Dawn started to streak the sky and I'd purposefully stayed awake just in case Fat Leopard was in the vicinity looking for a sleeping Sam Coker Sarnie. It had been a warm humid night and the mist soon started to form and curl around the vegetation. When the time came, the forest mist would be a perfect cover for my actions, and I hoped that when the boat did come back, that mist would be my silent ally.

Tree Face was becoming visible.

Mist moved around his face like it was the smoke of a demon coming out of his mouth. The birds, dull in the lack of direct sunlight, came in and out of his mouth like the flicks of a darting tongue. He looked directly at me. There's no way that he could have known what was coming from me, but I could see in the half-light his mouth was taking on a sarcastic curl and sneer. The bird tongues flicked. The mist smoked from his mouth.

I was a little cold and stiff after the night, and Kik-Kik had so effectively extinguished the fire next to me that I could not find an ember with which to restart it. The ashes were warm so at least I could put my hands near them for much-needed heat.

A woodpecker started up then.

The *clat-clat-clat* of its beak against the bark of a tree sounded a long way away, but the sound moved sadly across the mist-deadened atmosphere as brittle as Morse code.

Clat-clat-clat.

Clat-clat-clat. Clat-clat-clat. Clat-clat-clat. K-k-k-k-k-k-k-k-k-*clat.*

Clang.

Crunch.

Clat-clat-clat.

Not a woodpecker after all I thought then, a new depression sinking hard and heavy in my guts.

It was the echo of a machine gun.

FORTY

It's the first time I'd heard a machine gun in real life. I mean, yeah, I'd heard them on TV and that, on the cop shows or the war films, but they don't sound anything like they do on the telly. In real life machine guns clatter like skeletons falling downstairs. They sound like death. In my head, bark exploded, vegetation was ripped apart and bloody great holes were torn in flesh.

I was still on my own; there was no sign of Kik-Kik or anyone else, thankfully. But the machine gun noise was enough to scare the living Ick out of me. The gunfire went on for minutes, maybe longer. It sounded like a fierce battle, and as the *clat-clat-clat* continued, sometimes covering up another blast of noise, I could tell that there were at least two people firing. Perhaps more. After that, it all got too difficult to differentiate. I didn't know if the screams I was hearing between the gunshots were real or imagined, but whatever, they stirred me into action. After attaching a new Ick Bag to the nub of intestine, I put on a clean black tee-shirt, pants, and black joggers. My Nikes were still serviceable so I put them on too. I scrabbled around in the dirt, picking up the things I'd need and dropped them into my ruckkie. I closed the guppy mouth of the bag and slung it over my shoulders. It was heavy, but the weight I'd lost since crashing in the rainforest would more than compensate for that. With the bag in place across my shoulders, I tumbled out of the shelter and began dragging myself across the mud.

I stopped. My skin was so white, even with the tan I'd got in the jungle, however well I thought I'd be hidden, judging by the way Kik-Kik had been able to see Fat Leopard long after I had, she'd see me straight away, wherever I was.

I began smearing mud on my arms and over my hands. It smeared it all down the side of the white Nikes and covered my face and eyelids in the brown smelly mulch. I wonder how much of it was just broken-down vegetable matter, and how much of it was animal dung.

Classic. As if I didn't have enough issues with Ick as it was!

Tree Face's black mouth laughed at the futility of what I was attempting, but I really had no other options, and soon his laughter would matter no more, whatever happened, because I was getting out of here.

Out of breath and sweating like I had never sweated before; I pulled my useless legs into place and rested my head on the vegetation. It wasn't a comfortable hiding place, and I was cramped in a hollow surrounded by leaves on all sides. I wondered if Kik-Kik would be able to smell me? I wondered if the mud I'd smeared all over my exposed skin would hide me from her nose, just as effectively as it I hoped it would from her eyes.

My plan had been simple: wait here hidden until she came back, had seen that I was gone, and hopefully she'd go off to try to find me out in the jungle. It wasn't much of a plan, but it was all I had. I didn't like the idea of swiping her around the head with a rock or tying her up. I just wanted to get her out of the way. I figured she'd try the beach first, so I only had to stay hidden until she went off into the wider forest to find me, then the plan was to wait for the *thub-thub-thub* of the engine and make my way down to the beach for rescue.

But the machine-gunning really had put the spanner in those works. If the gunmen were connected to the boat—how could they not be—and they found the camp, I'd need to remain hidden until I was sure it was ok to reveal myself.

The machine-gun fire had stopped, so whoever had been firing had won whatever battle they'd been fighting or wouldn't be firing anymore.

I swallowed.

That was an even worse notion. That there were other

people out here who could take on a bunch of machine-gunners
and keep them quiet.

Kik-Kik's people?

The flies and insects were very much attracted to the sweat
and mud on my body. A fat-bodied black monster thing landed
on my wrist and started snuffling about in the mud-covered
skin. I was just about to slap it into a flat dead thing when I
heard the voices.

The tribe moved warily into the clearing. There were six of
them. All male, potbellied, with the same flat faces as Kik-Kik.
In fact, a few of them you could say might even have been
related to her. They all carried weapons. Blowpipes, spears, and
bows. They were all breathing hard as if they had been running
hard to get here, and one of them was wounded. His arm below
the bicep was painted entirely red with glistening liquid. If I
hadn't seen the bullet hole in his arm, pumping out blood as he
moved, I'd have thought it had been Kik-Kik's handiwork with
the berry paint.

The lead tribesman, a thick, stocky bloke with straight black
hair that hung like a helmet on his skull raised a hand—the
party paused and they began to look around the camp. At the
shelter. At the fires. At...

I heard the audible gasp from the headman as he saw Tree
Face and the altar beneath him. He skipped forward, spear at
the ready. Four of the others formed an outward-facing circle
around him as he moved forward towards Tree Face. They all
had his back.

The injured tribesman, not more than a boy my age, sat down
on his haunches and held his hand over the bullet wound. The
blood still dribbled copiously between his fingers. If he didn't
get medical help soon he was going to bleed to death right in
front of me.

But I couldn't bring myself to let them know I was here. If
they'd offed the machine-gunners, what would they be prepared
to do to me? I kept my head down and tried to sink deeper in
the hollow.

The headman came back to the injured boy and looked at

the wound. He said something to the others and they relaxed a little and started going through the stuff on the altar—the magazines and the parcels of drugs. One of them looked Tree Face right in the eyes and touched his mouth; his fingers came away dry, telling him at least how long since the lips had been painted. Another was going around to each hearth, feeling the ashes, making an assessment that way. The last two were in the shelter, pulling stuff out of bags—the folders, the pictures of Carlos and Escobar, my iPhone and MacBook just dumped in the mud. It's not as if they were still in working order, but I still didn't like the violation of my stuff.

One in the shelter made a noise, like a grunt and a low whistle at the same time, then beckoned the headman over. The headman reluctantly left the boy and came to see what he was being shown. I could just make out what was passing through his fingers. A flat white stone, a small statue of a pregnant woman, a pink tee-shirt and a magazine about P-Star. The headman threw them down one by one and then spat into the trees. He returned to the boy and the search continued.

Once they had discovered everything that they needed to, and the headman had got the boy to apply strong pressure to his wound and had tied a tourniquet above the boy's bicep, the headman spoke to him in a hoarse whisper. The boy, although he looked terrified, nodded.

The five tribesmen departed into the jungle at that point leaving the boy in the centre of the camp. He was sat next to an extinguished fire looking properly sorry for himself. He waited for them to go off into the jungle before he allowed himself to cry. Men don't cry in front of other men in the jungle, obviously.

I thought maybe then I should make myself known. But something held me back. Was it the relationship between these men and Kik-Kik? If they were capable of allowing what had happened to her, and for her to be beaten for her troubles, what would they do to me for keeping her interest here and not at home? They didn't seem to have any love at all for Tree Face, and if they thought I was connected to him… well, I could do the maths.

So I waited.

After about half an hour I heard a rustle in the bushes on the other side of Tree Face, coming out of the jungle spear held out in front was Kik-Kik.

I almost called out but then I saw her expression...

It was one of pure hatred.

Was she coming for the boy? He didn't know she was there. Perhaps the blood loss has sapped his jungle-sense. I'd heard her, and he definitely hadn't or he would have turned around. As it was, he was sitting on the ground, slightly wavering, slightly rocking back and forth. Should I say anything, or should I just let her get on with it. Perhaps this was the boy who had done to her the thing that had broken her. Perhaps this was someone who deserved to die...

But... no... I couldn't. There had been enough death. I wasn't going to stand by and let this happen. If he was the culprit, he deserved to be arrested, go on trial, go to prison—not be speared through the back of his neck.

I picked a stone from the ruckkie and threw it as accurately as I could into the camp.

The boy with the bloodied arm turned around and just as Kik-Kik was about to strike, he fell back with a yell and kicked the spear away out of Kik-Kik's hand. She was over-balanced, and the boy rushed at her, pushing one forearm against her neck and with the other pulling her head viciously back by the hair.

He said something to her that made her eyes wide.

She said something that made him laugh. He pushed her back—even with his bullet wound she was no match for him— and as I watched they both thudded into the bark below Tree Face. Kik-Kik's back crunching hard in the gnarled trunk. He had her good arm pinned against the tree and his weight was on her shoulder. Her flipper moved uselessly in the air; even when it batted softly at his face it was ineffectual.

Jesus Christ. In saving the boy from certain death, I'd allowed Kik-Kik to get in even more danger.

What should I do?

The reasons for me not making myself known had not changed. What was more important—Kik-Kik or my rescue?

In the end, the decision was made a lot easier by the boy.

He didn't hit Kik-Kik or stick a knife in her or try to beat her head against the Tree Face's bark.

No. He did something much worse.

He undid the knot closing the rips in the front of the tee-shirt I'd given Kik-Kik, and with a filthy lust shining in his eyes, he started to reach inside the material.

FORTY-ONE

I pulled my legs from the hollow, gripped the branches either side of me, and fell feet first from the tree.

I landed directly on the boy's head. My knees buckled up, as my jelly-stiff legs splayed in all directions. My pelvis smashed into his face as my knees knocked him back and I speared down on him the whole weight of my body dropped from four metres above him. My trajectory crushed him as we clattered to the jungle floor. He ended up flattened beneath my body. I was now looking up at the sky so I began pummelling him with my elbows, hoping to catch him a lucky blow in the face before he rolled from underneath me and grabbed a rock and beat my brains out with it. All I hoped was that I'd give Kik-Kik enough time to get away.

The boy didn't move or resist.

I stopped the flurry of blows from my elbows and looked at Kik-Kik. Her hand was over her mouth and her eyes were wide.

The boy still hadn't moved.

Ok.

I rolled off him.

Nobody's head goes back that far and the twist in the skin around his neck told me that even if he was still breathing, he wouldn't be able to. His eyes were glassy and open.

His dead eyes.

I felt hands getting under my arms, pulling me up and leaning me against Tree Face's tree, moving aside the creepers that I'd used to pull myself up into the high branches to hide.

I mean, who would think of looking up in a tree for a paraplegic?

My muscles were still aching from hauling my body weight and the ruckkie full of stones up to my crow's nest in a hollow between two thick, moss-covered branches. There had been more than enough foliage to hide me, and the extra weight from the stones—which I'd taken in case I was discovered and had to defend myself—had sent me down at such a speed I'd broken the boy's neck at first asking.

If it hadn't been such a sick-making idea, I might have been amused at the number of people I'd killed accidentally this week.

Kik-Kik checked the boy with a trembling hand.

She closed his eyes with her palm. She looked at me with wonder and awe. She pointed at me, and then up.

I followed her finger. She was pointing at Tree Face's mouth.

She pointed at me.

And then the mouth.

Going up close to it. Putting her good hand in the mouth then taking it out and putting it first on my head, and then on the dead boy's head.

She thought that I'd been spat from Tree Face's mouth to come and save her.

What was the point in arguing? If the girl hadn't have been totally sure I was her God—the Jesus son, to Tree Face the father—before, she surely would now.

I had completely become her God in the Tree.

I closed my eyes. I couldn't look at the dead boy anymore. It was too much like looking at my dad, in the cockpit of the Cherokee speared on the branch. Every time I flew—someone died.

"I'm sorry," I said.

Kik-Kik didn't reply. She just stuck up her thumb and smiled. I guess she wouldn't be mourning the dead boy. Under the circumstances, seeing as I'd stopped her sticking a spear in his back, she wanted him dead anyway.

Clat-clat-clat.

Machine guns lit up close by. Coming from the direction of the river.

Kik-Kik's smile disappeared in an instant and she burst

into action as there came shouts and yells to complement the gunfire through the trees. I heard bullets ricocheting off tree trunks, I heard men shouting distantly in a variety of languages.

Kik-Kik ran to the shelter. Picked up her bag and stuffed the four things she owned in it, and then picked up some of the other magazines and stopped dead as if something had just kicked her in the face.

I honestly thought she was about to fall over with a stray bullet wound in the back of the head.

But no.

She picked up one to the photographs that had fallen from between the papers I'd taken from Dad's holdall. She screamed and hopped on the spot as if the photograph was burning her fingers. Stuffing the papers and fruit into her bag, she bounded back over to me. She reached into her bag and pulled out the photograph and held it up to my face.

It was Carlos and Escobar, standing next to one of their aeroplanes. Arms around each other, smiling, and their father-son frog cheeks split in big sweaty smiles.

Clat-clat-clat.

At the gunfire, she pointed at both Carlos and Escobar, then pointed in the direction of the machine guns.

Carlos and Escobar were here, in the jungle, and they were firing machine guns.

I looked at the wreckage of the altar, at the bricks of drugs, and felt like the world had collapsed around me.

I wasn't being rescued. The drugs were.

They'd obviously had to convince Dad that he had the drugs on board the plane before we left otherwise he might not have taken off—and they couldn't kill us there on the ranch because someone would have come looking for us, so they'd hatched the plan to blow us out of the sky. When the Cherokee ditched, and they knew the area, all they had to do was get here before the plane was discovered, retrieve the drugs and bingo.

But then…

What were they doing here? Why weren't they searching at

the crash site? Why were the shooting up the jungle here and getting closer all the time? How could they have known that the drugs were here?

The satellite box! I'd turned it on. I'd activated it. They knew the box had moved and that it was packed with the drugs so they could find them easily. I'd brought them right to me!

I pointed at the satellite box. "Kik-Kik! That! Bring it here!"

It took a few seconds of pointing and guessing before she picked up the box and brought it to me. It was still on. The battery had lasted. It would lead them straight here!

I smashed it with a rock.

I thought quickly. We had to get away from here. Kik-Kik was packed, I guess to run into the jungle with her stuff, get away, but there's no way I could stay here. If Carlos got here first, he'd have to have me killed. If the tribe got here first then they'd see the dead boy and put two and two together.

I pointed to Kik-Kik, then me, then away from the gunfire. "We have to get out of here!" I said stupidly. As if she could understand. I pointed around again. She gave me the thumbs-up.

I poured the stones out of my ruckkie and pointed to my clothes in the shelter. She nodded and went over, then picked up some clothes and the folders or papers, shoving them in. I didn't want them, but there was no point in arguing, I could dump them later.

I had one more thing to do before we left the clearing.

Kik-Kik pulled me as fast as she could with her one arm, taking me down slippery mud tracks that looked and smelt like they were animal-made paths. Maybe worn out by Fat Leopard or other land mammals.

As I bumped along, slithering and slippery with mud, Kik-Kik did her best to keep me off the worst of the stones and jagged rocks, but sometimes one would bark against my back with a painful thump. I did my best not to yell out and give our position away.

Eventually the gunfire diminished in the distance, and although Kik-Kik was still pulling me faster than I was comfortable with, and my shoulder was becoming numb from the wrenching of Kik-Kik's forward movement, at least I started to feel a little safer.

Well, relatively.

After nearly an hour, Kik-Kik pulled me under a bush. Motioned me to be quiet and disappeared into the undergrowth. I listened as hard as I could but the good couple of kilometres between Tree Face and us, seemed to swallow any sounds into the distance. Maybe whatever battle was being fought back there was over. I could not tell.

I took the opportunity to empty the Ick from the bag and reattach it, as well as pressing down on my bladder. It had been an age since I'd been able to do this, and it felt good to do something normal.

Being dragged through the undergrowth by a girl with a flipper for an arm wasn't the greatest experience I'd ever had.

I caught a flash of yellow moving about thirty metres away, back down the track. I squinted. But there was nothing. Were we being followed?

And by what?

Kik-Kik crashed back beside me, making me jump. She had been using the ripped Chelsea shirt as a pouch. It was full of berries. She pointed that I should eat them. I did. They were tart but edible. I scoffed as much as I could. Kik-Kik ate a few but her eyes were darting back along the track, and ahead.

Kik-Kik's head went still, and I felt her body go tense as she leaned against me.

She'd seen something back down the track.

"Kik-Kik, no!" I hissed, but it was too late, she left me and ran, back the way we'd come, keeping her feet light and her body low. Within a few seconds, she was lost to me. The jungle had a habit of closing in around me. It seemed weird getting claustrophobic outside, but this part of the jungle was denser than I was used to. I felt my chest tightening as my breathing quicken as my heart thumped.

BANG!

Kik-Kik was back but came at me from a completely different direction, as if she'd circled right around the area where I was lying and come back on herself. She was animated and trembling. I got ready for her to pull me again but instead she rolled back the arm of my tee-shirt and pointed at Fat Leopard.

That flash of yellow I'd seen had been the cat.

The war he'd declared was not over.

FORTY-TWO

We crashed through a bush and suddenly we were falling through space.

Kik-Kik hadn't made any pretence that she was not scared or that we should stay put. She'd collected me under the arm again and pulled me as hard and as fast as she could back along the track. It was only then I saw the bleeding double scratch mark on her skin beneath her right arm. It was from a cat's paw. Fat Leopard. Not only was it still after us but it was willing to attack in broad daylight.

I began regretting not bringing the stones or the spear with us, but both would have made our escape impossible.

So Kik-Kik rushed forward as best she could. I slithered through the mud and tried to relax my upper body so it hurt less when Kik-Kik crashed me into things.

Kik-Kik looked back occasionally but continued driving forward.

That was her mistake.

I saw the hard left turn the track made curve away from me as we left it at an angle and crashed through a bush, and suddenly the land below me disappeared. Again not my life, but an image of Wile E. Coyote filled my thoughts as his legs moved uselessly over the drop that he hadn't known was there.

Meep-Meep.

Clang.

Crunch.

We crashed to the ground, a fall of about five metres onto a steep slope that was running with water, which made the mud even more slippery. We both shot off like spinning bobsleighs.

I tried not to yell my fear and frustration, but "OOOFED" a couple of times as I slammed into rocks. I stuck my chin in my chest and tried to protect my head with my hands, the ruckkies I was carrying in the crooks of my elbows flying around as I slid and fell, one corner of my bag smacking into my mouth and drawing blood.

After a fifty or so metre slide, we both crashed into trees.

That properly hurt.

I didn't think I'd broken anything—my arms still had full movement, and really only ached under my armpit. As I looked up, my legs were twisted and odd. Of course, if they'd both been broken I wouldn't know. Couldn't feel a thing in them. If the bones were smashed from dropping on the dead boy, I'd have to check later. I didn't have time now.

Kik-Kik was getting to her feet, pulling me under the arm again, around the side of the thick-trunked tree against which I'd beached. She dragged me underneath a bush, her breathing hard, sounds that I thought were sobs vibrating through her lips. We got further and further into the undergrowth and then burst through into sunlight.

But this time there was no fall.

We were in a small clearing bounded on all sides by thick shrubs and bushes. The trees were tall and smooth and stretched right up into the suddenly blue sky. I felt the warmth of the sun of me for what felt like the first time in a thousand years.

I was cold and exhausted, but the sunlight took a lot of the pain and panic away.

Kik-Kik sat me against a tree trunk and collapsed onto her back. She didn't move for ages, not until her breath became something like normal and the sobbing stopped. The tears leaking from her eyes ran on for ages, a bubble of snot like a bullfrog's ribbeting throat inflating and deflating.

Carlos.

Clang.

Crunch.

The unhappy thought of who might be hunting us in the jungle made me look away from Kik-Kik, turning my face up towards the sun. Birds, just high black specks, circled above us. A black monkey-thing swung through the trees, picked a high-up fruit like someone carefully choosing an orange in a supermarket, and then swung away out of sight.

There were a few clouds, but it wasn't going to rain in the rainforest for a while yet.

Kik-Kik obviously thought we'd be safe here for a while, from who or whatever was chasing us—or she'd just collapsed from the sheer terror and exhaustion. She sat up suddenly and I thought perhaps we were going to go off again, but she just reached into the bag and pulled out a knife. I had no idea where she'd got it from. It wasn't an improvised jungle knife, it was the real deal—stainless steel, sharp edge and a wooden handle. She got up and went to a group of young trees growing on the other side of the clearing and started to cut down some branches that looked like she might be able to fashion into a spear.

She cut two of the makeshift weapons into vicious white points and gave them to me.

Then she started on the trunk of the tree against which I was leaning. She was furiously chopping at it. Curls of bark and splinters of wood fell down into my hair and I brushed them aside. She worked for about five minutes then stood back.

When I looked up, I saw that Tree Face had come with us.

Kik-Kik jogged away into the undergrowth leaving me with the freshly cut spears. I was limited in my range of vision because of the tightly packed undergrowth and the bushes, but I scanned the leaves and the grasses and the flowers and the branches and the trunks like my life depended on it.

Well it did, didn't it?

Bloody hell, how I wished I was up in the sky with the circling birds. Out of this stinking jungle, off this poxy continent. I just wanted to be home, in my house, in my room with my wheelchair jammed up against the door so that no one could get in. Not Mum, not Jen, not anyone. I just wanted to get under the covers and stay there for the rest of my life. Six or so days ago, I hadn't killed two people and I hadn't got myself on the kill list of an Amazon tribe, a bunch of murderous gangsters and Fat Leopard, who I'd sent crazy with infection.

Utter madness.

Kik-Kik was the only good thing about the whole mess and we couldn't even have a conversation.

I wondered how much longer she'd be able to keep me alive.

I didn't think it would be long.

Kik-Kik came back then; she was squishing red berries in her palm and spitting frothy white saliva into the middle of it. When the paste was the right consistency, she poured the mix into my cupped hands and then painted on Tree Face's new lips. She also made his eyes red and painted hair either side of his head. There were no vines hanging down to make into dreads, so Tree Face 2.0 was bald and I'd have no way of Rapunzelling myself up to the canopy again to avoid detection.

Kik-Kik finished the painting and wiped the blood-red juice paint on the side of her tee-shirt, where it covered the patch of drying blood caused by the claw scratch. She reached down, picked up one of the spears, and held it across her body. Her eyes were glassy, and her mouth moved as if she was singing without voice.

Then she began to dance.

Where Kik-Kik found fresh reserves of energy after dragging me headlong through the jungle for kilometres I had no idea, but she danced as if a thing possessed. Her head shook, spittle formed in the corners of her mouth. Tears fell freely from her eyes and were spun away from her head like individual drops along the front of a just-starting rainstorm. I felt them hitting my cheeks, I felt them drying against my skin. It was if Kik-Kik was seeping into me.

She stamped her feet and hopped.

Kik-Kik shook the spear and touched it to her forehead, and then, stamping to a silent stillness she lifted the end of her flipper on the shaft of the spear and offered it to me, looking between Tree Face 2.0 and me. Her black eyes steely and focused, the tears gone, the intent insistent and powerful.

She pushed the flipper towards my mouth.

I hadn't been this close to it before. The skin was gnarled and hard like an old woman's elbow. The scrambled fingers growing from the elbow looked like the top of a sea-anemone or something. Alien. Moving to its own purpose. I could see the dirt engrained between the fingers, I could smell the warmness of her skin, salty, like fresh sweat.

It came closer.

I knew then what she wanted the son of her God to do. She wanted me to bless the flipper.

I felt my eyes widening. Me? What power did I have to bless? Why was she so idiotic to believe that I, this crippled waste of space, the boy who'd killed his own father with his clumsiness and stupidity, who'd accidentally killed someone else by falling out of a tree onto them. How could she believe in me, when I couldn't believe in one thing about myself?

I was useless. I couldn't walk. I knew nothing about this place or its people. I'd been so wrapped up in myself I had closed my world down to a bitter skin around me that no one wanted to break into, or that I wanted to break out of.

I felt plastic.

I felt fake.

I didn't feel worthy.

"I'm nothing," I said. "I can't bless you, Kik-Kik. I can't help you. I can't even help myself."

She wasn't going anywhere. The flipper stayed put, her eyes imploring.

Even if I kissed it would I be giving her false hope? What I really needed to be doing was sending her away, telling her to save herself. I was going to get both of us killed, at least without me she had a chance.

I pushed the flipper away. "No. Leave me alone."

He face fell and she put the flipper back even nearer to me. I pushed it away again. This time harder than I had before.

She tried one more time.

I pushed it away.

Kik-Kik hissed and got up, just as the bushes parted behind her and the tribesman, who wasn't from any tribe I had already seen before, led Carlos, Escobar, and three men with guns into the clearing.

On seeing me, Escobar smiled.

It was the first time I'd ever seen him do that.

Carlos raised his machine pistol and pointed it directly at me.

FORTY-THREE

"You're harder to kill than I expected."

I was looking down the barrel of Carlos's gun.

The leading tribesman, who looked like a native of the jungle—with the same flat face, and straight black hair—but who was wearing combat fatigues and carrying a very large knife, began looking around the clearing. His quick eyes darting and assessing in the same way I'd seen Kik-Kik weighing up the dangers.

Yeah, I was trying not to focus on the gun thing. And anyway, what was I supposed to say back to Carlos? "Better luck next time"?

Kik-Kik moved between Carlos's gun barrel and me, holding up her spear.

Escobar took two quick steps forward, caught the spear in one hand, and punched her hard in the stomach with the other. Kik-Kik fell to her knees. Escobar must have seen the look of pure hatred on my face because he winked at me and then spat on Kik-Kik.

The gun was unwavering.

Kik-Kik got off her knees and stood between us again.

Combat Indian was still moving around the clearing. He'd reached Tree Face 2.0, and was tracing the line of it with his finger.

Escobar drew back his fist, readying to punch Kik-Kik again.

"No," Carlos said. "We don't have time for fun and games." He moved the aim of the gun from me and pointed it at Kik-Kik's head.

"If you kill her you'll never find the drugs," I said.

I had no idea where the words came from, no idea that terror would make me this bold, or that all I cared about now was making sure Kik-Kik walked away from this.

It was the one thing I could do to repay her.

"What makes you think I need you to tell me where they are? I might just want to kill you both for fun. And in any case, they can't be far, we just need to search the clearing." Carlos was the kind of man who enjoyed getting the drop on his opponents. His frog cheeks puffed out around a reptile smile.

"Why would you have followed us if you knew where they were?"

"Knowing one of you was alive complicated things. It was supposed to be simple, crash the plane, fly in, pick up the drugs, leave your bodies for the alligators or the jaguars…"

Fat Leopard. Ah right. Jaguar. I'd learned something about the animals of the Rainforest at last. Go me.

"… but you're alive and you need to be dead. We can't have you talking can we? So we're here to… what do you English say?… iron out that wrinkle."

It probably wasn't the best idea I've ever had to argue logic with a gangster, especially one with a gun, but all I had right now was my voice. If I could use it to delay Carlos, maybe make them release Kik-Kik, maybe it was worth a shot. I mean, I'm a dead boy anyway whatever way you slice it, what was he going to do? Kill me twice?

"If you knew where the drugs were and you wanted me dead, why am I still talking, Carlos?"

Escobar slapped me. Hard. My head snapped back and thumped against the tree. Tree Face 2.0 hissed in the leaves.

"The drugs are not here." It was Combat Indian. "They didn't bring them." His English was good, but I could still hear the tribe in his accent.

Carlos pointed the gun back at me, over Kik-Kik's shoulder. I could see the fury reddening his face.

A twig snapped behind us, everyone looked. Carlos's men raised their guns, none of them knowing which way to point.

Combat Indian was the only one who didn't look concerned. He looked…interested.

"They're back," he said simply.

Carlos yelled his anger and unloaded the entire magazine of his machine pistol into the trees over my head. Combat Indian leaped towards him and pushed his arm down. Bullets spat into the ground near my feet, throwing up gouts of mud. Carlos stopped firing and looked daggers at Combat Indian. "Do not touch me! You're paid to track, nothing else!"

Combat Indian was looking into the trees; he spoke to Carlos like he was a slow child. "When you shoot in long bursts I can't hear them moving. It compromises us. You have already lost two of your men. I do not wish to join them..."

For the first time, I saw a look of concern on Escobar's face.

"They only have bows and arrows. When I see them, I'll kill them."

"That's the point. You won't see them."

Carlos fitted a new clip into the machine pistol. He hissed at two of his men, "Find them. End them."

The two men exchanged glances. They were big, barrel-chested, henchmen types, but I could see from their faces they didn't like the idea. Carlos's face looked like a shiny tomato. Thinking probably that their boss would likely shoot them if they delayed any longer, the two gunmen moved gingerly into the trees and soon disappeared from view.

Combat Indian was alert. Carlos had said he was just there to track, and he didn't seem to be scared of Carlos. With just the knife, he'd be no match for a machine pistol so it looked like a delicate balance of power between the two of them. If Combat Indian was being paid by Carlos it seemed like a dead cert that he'd want to keep him alive.

And that left Escobar.

Why would Carlos bring his son out here?

Obviously, they hadn't expected to get attacked by Kik-Kik's tribe. I had probably been Carlos's equivalent of "Take Your Kid To Work Day"—except Carlos was a gangster and the work was drugs and murder. Escobar was doing a fair job of playing the hard man to impress his father—punching a girl and hitting a cripple.

What a man.

But I could see that at some point this mission to recover the drugs had spiralled out of control. They'd been attacked by the tribe—which was the machine-gun battle we'd heard, and all that seemed to have happened was that they'd managed to shoot one boy in the arm (the nasty piece of work I'd killed by accident), the drugs had disappeared and someone who needed to be dead, me, was still alive.

They're three-nil down at half time.

Although Escobar and Carlos were still properly dangerous, I took some comfort in seeing they were both on the back foot. Carlos was full of rage. I could see that he was regretting coming here in the first place, rather than just sending his men.

Carlos reached behind him and pulled a black semi-automatic from a holster on the back of his belt. It was a gun, very much like the one that had exploded in the alligator's face. He handed it to Escobar.

Escobar weighed the pistol in his hands. He licked his lips. I couldn't work out if it was with apprehension or anticipation.

"If you let the girl go, I'll take you to the drugs."

Carlos's eyes narrowed. "Or I could just cut pieces off her with a knife and feed the rest of her to an alligator until you decide to tell me where they are. Samuel, like your father, who tried to betray me, you are an amateur. I have been making people tell me what I want to know for many years."

Carlos pointed at Kik-Kik, who was still standing her ground between us, trembling with tension and determination. The muscles on her legs stood out, hard as rocks. She was ready for whatever was to come, and she would meet it head on.

"This... mutant... will suffer for you, Samuel. Is that what you want? Shall I start with the fingers of her good hand? I would start by breaking them one by one. I'd be sure to let you hear the crunch as every one of them snapped. I think you would try to be strong. I think you would last perhaps three fingers, maybe four because you'd know, deep in your heart that once I had snapped her thin little thumb at the knuckle, if you hadn't told me where the merchandise was and the papers your father stole from me were, I'd be reaching for my knife..."

Papers?

The ones I had in my ruckkie?

Dad had stolen them?

What this the betrayal that Carlos spoke of? Was Dad, crazy, idiotic Dad, trying to sell Carlos out?

Is that why I was here? In this crazy effed up jungle, because my dad wanted a few more quid when he was already rich?

I tried to keep the anger inside; I tried not to let it leak out onto my face. Carlos saw it easily. But misread it.

"You're concerned for your young mutant friend…"

"Don't call her that…"

"I'll call her whatever I want. Escobar get her hand. Bring it here."

Escobar twisted Kik-Kik's good arm. She gasped, hitting out ineffectually with her flipper. Stumbling down onto her knees she was dragged forward. Escobar had her tight around the wrist. He peeled her little finger from the fist and held it towards his father. For all Escobar's apprehension about the situation, I could see that he was a chip off the old block. He was enjoying the idea of Kik-Kik suffering.

I wished I could fall out of a tree onto him right now.

"So Samuel, where are the papers, the very important papers, and the merchandise. Why don't you give the mutant a break?"

He smiled his big huge froggy smile. "Before I have to."

Combat Indian held up his hand and shushed Carlos.

Carlos looked at Combat Indian like he'd just taken a leak on his corn flakes. "How many times do I…"

"I said shut up," Combat Indian hissed. "There's something…"

"They're dealing with it! Now shut up yourself, I have bones to break."

"Stop. Please. Let her go," I said.

Carlos's smile was as wide as a piano keyboard. He reached towards Kik-Kik's outstretched finger, like someone reaching for a chicken leg at a picnic.

I threw myself forward and began to drag myself towards Carlos, Escobar, and Kik-Kik. I didn't care what Combat was doing, all I wanted was to get between Kik-Kik and Carlos, somehow take his pain from her and have it transferred to me.

Behind Carlos, the remaining guard said "Ouch," and slapped his hand to his neck.

Ouch sounded such a dainty word in the situation, sounded out of place. Escobar looked at the guard. Carlos hadn't noticed, he was enjoying seeing me crawl.

"What are you going to do, boy? Nibble my ankles to death?" Carlos was warming to the task of torture and humiliation.

Ouch Guard went down on one knee, still clutching at his neck. His eyes bulged.

Combat Indian was backing away to the other side of the clearing.

Clat-Clat-Clatter! *Clat-Clat*-Clatter!

From outside the clearing the machine guns went off. They were close. Bullets whizzed through the clearing, bark exploded, leaves hissed.

I was by Kik-Kik.

I reached up.

"Kik-Kik," I said, and grabbed hold of her left arm. The flipper that didn't work, the arm that was her greatest sadness. I pulled it down, Escobar tried to pull her away from me, and there was a momentary battle. We were back in the arm wrestle. We were back, eyes locked, pushing then, pulling now. Escobar's eyes bulged, his mouth grimaced, I pulled against his leverage, I pulled against his weight, I pulled against the way his legs, those legs that worked and kicked and ran, the way those legs dug into the soft earth.

I pulled.

And I won.

I kissed Kik-Kik's gnarled hand and watched as Tree Face jumped right out from the bark of his tree.

FORTY-FOUR

In mid-air, Tree Face, all branches and screaming mouth, became Fat Jaguar Leopard and landed on Carlos's back. Claws ripping through his shirt and tearing into flesh. Carlos squeezed the trigger on his machine pistol. A jagged line of bullets splashed through the mud and the mulch; crossed my useless legs, blasting four bullet holes across my shins; carried on across the clearing, where two of them thumped hard into Combat Indian's chest.

Combat Indian and Carlos both fell backward at the same time as if they had both been members of opposing tug of war teams and someone had cut the rope in the middle as they heaved.

Released by my hand, Kik-Kik swung forward and head-butted Escobar. He went down in a daze. She fell on him, picked up a handy stone, and beat him unconscious with it.

Carlos was screaming underneath the loopy Jaguar. It was attacking him with claw and jaw. As Kik-Kik got up off Escobar and came to me, Carlos stopped screaming. The Jaguar was biting into his throat.

Kik-Kik got me under the arm again and pulled me from the clearing. As we burst through the brush, in the distance the machine gunfire stopped.

Kik-Kik pulled and I bled.

I looked down at my legs as the leaves and branches of the jungle whipped past us on either side. I could no longer feel anything in my back if it crashed into anything; a warm numbness was spreading from the base of my spine up through my torso. For the first time since the accident, I was glad that I had no feeling in my legs and that I was a paraplegic. I could imagine that getting shot in the shins for an able-bodied person must be very painful. For me, it wasn't. It was a swimmy warmth that brought a weird calm with it.

My dark joggers were wet and shiny with blood. It seeped up and out of the bullet holes on the surface, but under the material it must be flowing freely too. Behind us, as Kik-Kik yanked me along, I could see shimmers of red floating in the tops of puddles like oil, smearing the mud beneath our progress.

Kik-Kik's breath was ragged and her feet slapped on and on mechanically.

"Where are we going?" I asked dreamily.

"Away from the Jaguar," Kik-Kik said in a voice that sounded like it'd been scrubbed clean of the jungle and its origins. She continued. "If I don't get you away, the blood will bring the cat to you next. They can't resist fresh blood."

I nodded. Sounds legit. Leave the Jaguar there to get on with its meal, and get us away. Sensible girl this Kik-Kik. I like her a lot. Can't wait to introduce her to Mum and Dad.

Anyway, Kik-Kik wasn't pulling me now, she was behind me as I skidded along. She was smiling that electric smile, and the Chelsea shirt was intact and she was using a big broom to push the blood, trailing from my legs out to the sides of the track to disguise our progress. I wondered how Kik-Kik could be there with the broom and be pulling me at the same time.

My head lolled back and I had a stupid grin on my lips like that time I'd tried some of Dad's whiskey when he was out and got off my face and had gone around bumping into things and feeling no pain and how Dad had been angry not because I was drunk but because I'd opened a bottle of whisky that was twice as old as I was and had cost him something like six hundred quid. Oh well, anyway my stupid grin was just as stupid

The clouds overhead were darkening, the rainforest was getting ready to drench itself again, and as I moved over the earth, like a dead fish being sent down a slide made of ice, I could see it was Tree Face 2.0 who was pulling me now. His wooden skin rippled and creaked with the effort, his tree root feet dug into the earth. I heard them curling and slipping. The leaves and dreads in his hair trembled in the wind. His head was down; he was pulling as hard as his branchy body would take him.

I liked it when the rain started. I was, truth be told, getting too hot with the dreamy warmth seeping up from my legs.

"Can't we stop for a bit?" I asked. "I'm proper tired and I could totally do with a nap."

"No," said Kik-Kik who was pulling me again. The Chelsea shirt had changed now to the pink P-Star one. Perhaps that's why she'd let Tree Face pull for a bit, so she could get changed. "We're almost there."

"Oh good," I said. But I had no idea at all where "there" was.

Tree Face 2.0 was back on the trail now, he'd stopped and seemed to be drawing branches and saplings down across the path, tying them into huge knots and blocking the track. He did this a few times. Jogging back towards us as we went.

When he'd finished and swapped places with Kik-Kik again to give her a rest, there was no way you'd think there was a track we'd just come down. He'd made it look like the jungle had been growing there forever and was impassable.

"Nice work," I said, and with almost an audible WHUMP the grey sky became light and bright sunlight burst down on us. We were no longer in the jungle. We'd crashed out of the tree line back onto the riverbank.

I looked around, half-expecting to see the platform of gnarled bush and branch that had brought me here, but it seemed to be a different stretch of the river.

Kik-Kik laid me down on the mud, and I heard Tree Face 2.0 behind me, splashing into the water. Kik-Kik took her homemade ruckkie and put the opening of it to her teeth, bit in and pulled. A long strand of vine came away and she ripped out about three feet of it.

She snapped the one length into two, and with her feet and good hand, tied tourniquets around both my legs above the bullet holes in the joggers.

She pulled the vines as tight as she could without the extra hand. I thought about putting my finger on the knot to help but when I lifted my hand, I only had enough coordination to slap myself in the face with it.

"Ouch," I said. But not like the bloke who'd been hit by the poison blowpipe dart.

Kik-Kik came behind me, lifted my body under the armpit, and used all her desperate strength to flop me over the side of the white hull onto a hot, flat, wooden deck.

Tree Face 2.0 was at the other end of the small motor launch, half in the water, half out. He swung the boat around, and he and Kik-Kik pushed me out into the centre of the fast-flowing river.

I could feel the swell and the rush of the water. I could feel the boat lifting and settling. I could see the fronds of the overhanging trees.

"Kik-Kik," I said. But the voice didn't sound like my own, it sounded like it came from a different mouth than mine. I was thinking the words, but it was Tree Face 2.0 who was speaking them out of my mouth,

I grabbed the side of the boat, using my hand to pull myself up. I had to speak to Kik-Kik. I couldn't leave her behind. She had to come with me.

When I looked back at the riverbank, Tree Face 2.0 and Kik-Kik had gone.

The sky was blue, and the Cherokee kept pace with the boat as I was washed downstream on my back in the boat. I knew Dad was flying the Cherokee. The aeroplane had swooped down about three months ago and I'd seen him in the cockpit window, cans on his ears, aviators in place. He'd waved and taken the plane through a series of tight manoeuvres and spins before settling in to follow the progress of the boat.

I think I've been on the boat my whole life really. I think I've been washed along by events on a tide not of my own making. I think the boat was telling me that. I was warm in the sun. Sometimes I prayed for rain, but it never rained.

Sometimes I heard the Cherokee, sometimes I heard another mechanical noise that I couldn't place.

It wasn't the *thub-thub-thub* of an engine.

It wasn't the *clat-clat-clat* of machine guns.

It wasn't Kik-Kik's dance.

I missed Kik-Kik.

I had a little cry.

Clang.

Crunch.

About a year ago on the boat, I'd heard something different from the sounds of the river. It was a…

Clang.

Crunch.

I'd heard this sound before. It reminded me of Escobar and Carlos. I sort of remembered them.

Sort of.

And then, that sound again. I thought I could hear my heart beating. I thought my heart was trying to get out of my chest. The clang. The crunch. What was that? Why was I hearing it on the boat? The boat where I'd lived out my entire life, where Dad, who was dead, flew above, very alive.

Where was I drifting?

Were there alligators?

Tree Face, the first Tree Face, the one who hated me, rose and blotted out the sun. I blinked. He was dark and silhouetted against the brightness. The Cherokee started to leave a contrail of black smoke and its flight became faltering.

Tree Face was all worms and beetles. Tree Face was dripping mud and water onto me. Tree Face was cracking his wooden knees as he knelt over me. His branchy hair was full of dead leaves. They were splashed with blood. His mouth was a broken "O," the teeth jagged behind the red, red lips.

Heroincoke burned in his guts next to my Rolex. I guess the drugs had made him even angrier, given him more strength. Sent him insane.

Tree Face's twiggy hands were around my throat.

He was screaming.

It didn't sound like Tree Face's whispery voice, it sounded more… human.

I kind of recognised it, and although I couldn't breathe now, I sort of liked the feeling. The river pulling me along, the warmth of the sun…

The Cherokee begun to spin in the sky and I realised that the smoke wasn't smoke from the engine; it was smoke from a skywriter. A machine that spews out smoke so light aircraft can be used to write things in the sky.

The Cherokee began to write.

Tree Face pressed harder on my throat. But that was ok. I didn't mind.

The Cherokee finished and signed off with an outside loop around the word.

"You killed my father!"

E...S...C...O...B...A...R was written in the sky. And Escobar was kneeling on my arms and was throttling me.

Panic ripped through me like a razor.

It was Escobar, one eye closed and black from where Kik-Kik had brained him with the rock. Blood and snot bubbled around his nostrils; the one eye that could see eye was wide and crazy. His face sheened with sweat and hot anger. His arms stiff with the strangling.

"You killed my father," he screamed.

Clang.

Crunch.

And then, at last, I saw it and I understood.

It wasn't a mechanic on the other side of the Cherokee before we'd left Carlos's place in the mountains. It was Escobar. That's why he hadn't been there to see us off. He'd been on the other side of the plane, on the orders of his father to plant the engine-disabling bomb beneath the canopy.

Clang.

Crunch.

"You killed my father!" screamed Escobar.

The words exploded inside me.

"And you killed mine!" I screamed back as Tree Face 2.0 came out of the wood of the deck, lifted both my legs, my dead useless legs, and kicked them up into Escobar's face. He spun away as Tree Face 2.0 kicked at him with my legs again.

Tree Face 2.0 rolled me over and I kicked Escobar more. I kick-kicked him. I kick-kicked him again and again until he stopped moving.

I lay back for about a month, hoping Kik-Kik would come back with Tree Face 2.0, but she did not.

I pulled myself up to look over the side of the boat. The last I saw of Kik-Kik was her taking Tree Face 2.0's hand and walking quickly into the jungle. She looked back once; just as the Special Forces helicopter swung over the boat and begun its rescue hover, her face like a shield, her smile like the sun.

And then she was gone.

A nyway, how do you end a story?

The Special Forces were for Dad.

Dad wasn't a gangster.

He was working undercover for MI6 and Halliday was his controller.

He'd been trying to get proof that Carlos was the head of an international drug-smuggling cartel.

Turns out Dad was a hero.

I wasn't supposed to have gone on the trip, but Carlos had insisted I come.

Carlos had discovered who Dad really worked for and wanted us both dead.

He liked it tidy like that.

Anyway, there was a funeral for Dad and lots of important people turned up. People from the government and that.

Seems the papers in my ruckkie had blown Carlos's network wide open.

Anyway, I hadn't killed Escobar. He was in pretty bad shape from the kicking I'd given him.

Yeah. The doctors couldn't explain that either. And neither could I. Someone said something about haematomas on my nerves or something, but my legs never moved again. I'd had some crazy dream about Tree Face and Tree Face 2.0, but I was out of my head with the blood loss from the bullet wounds.

The tribe Kik-Kik had come from was a protected and uncontacted people. Apparently there are laws preventing people going onto their lands and that.

I asked for word about Kik-Kik but the authorities or

Halliday could tell me nothing, and because of the protected status of the tribe, no one would be going in there to find out.

I missed Kik-Kik.

Guess I kind of loved her and that.

Anyway.

Anyway, Mum was holding court in the house on the day of the funeral with the mourners. I wheeled myself out to the garden with my knife and started work on the tree. When I'd finished, I opened a small tin of red paint, and filled in around the lips and eyes, and drew in the hair, because gardens in this part of London were not known for dreadlock vines.

When I finished it looked pretty good. The mouth was around the hollow of a lopped branch.

I peeled a couple of mangos, and put them at the foot of the tree.

Tree Face 3.0 put his hand on my shoulder.

When I looked up, it was Halliday. He put the medal they'd given Dad into my hand.

"He'd have wanted you to have this," he said.

"Thanks."

I could tell Halliday was weighing up whether or not to ask me what he asked me next, it was like the words were sticking in his throat. In the end, his job won over his compassion. "Everyone except the boy, Escobar, died, so we couldn't recover the drugs. They weren't in the wreckage of the... er, Cherokee. I don't suppose you..."

"No," I lied, dredging up as much finality in the tone of my voice as I could create. "I don't."

Halliday had an awkward and defeated look on his face. "I'll... er... leave you to it."

"Thanks."

Halliday went back to the house.

The sky was blue and cold. Clouds were few and far between, just a bit of high cirrus, bright and crystalline, way above a Cherokee's operational ceiling.

Jet planes moved through that high emptiness though, leaving contrails.

The sun was a yellow-white winter ball.

I looked down through the leaves and the branches into the dark between the trees.

Kik-Kik was taking Tree Face 3.0's hand and walking quickly away with him into the jungle.

She looked back just the once, her face like a shield, her smile like the sun.

ABOUT THE AUTHOR

Paul Ebbs is a screenwriter and novelist. Under his own name he has written drama for television, comedy and SF for radio. He has written nearly thirty books writing under other names. He's written many fewer books as himself but is not sure what this really says about him. Possibly more than he would want to let on.

Curious about other Crossroad Press books?
Stop by our site:
http://store.crossroadpress.com
We offer quality writing
in digital, audio, and print formats.

.